FIRST
TIGER

FIRST

TIGER

*To Peter,
a long-time fellow
Jenkintown friend.
Best wishes,
George 12/99*

George Harrar

THE PERMANENT PRESS
SAG HARBOR NY 11963

Library of Congress Cataloging-in-Publication Data

Harrar, George
    First Tiger / by George Harrar
      p. cm.
    ISBN 1-57962-051-5
    I. Title.
    PS3558.A624924 F57   1999
    813'.54--dc21   98-34203
                                   CIP

THE PERMANENT PRESS
4170 Noyac Road
Sag Harbor, NY 11963

"Let me tell you, you need not fear; he has only the appearance of a tiger, but he is not one—inside he is no different from you and me."

A Tiger for Malgudi
R.K. Narayan

One

"IMAGINE BEING DECAPITATED," MY FATHER SAID TO ME ONCE as we were sharpening the kitchen knives in the basement. Flakes of steel floated into the air each time he pressed the tip of the blade to the grindstone. My job was to hand him the next dull knife when he was ready for it. I was only ten at the time, and I didn't know what "decapitated" meant. Dad always assumed I knew more than I did. "Your head falls to the ground," he said as he ran his finger over the edge of the meat cleaver, "and you expect to be dead. But your brain still has a few seconds' worth of oxygen left. You look up and there's the rest of your body still draped over the chopping block. That, my boy, is the most intense moment of existence I can imagine."

Dad could be a pretty depressing guy to live with. Whenever I wished for anything when I was little, he'd say, "Expect death, Jake, and you won't ever be disappointed." That was his philosophy of life: Expect the worst. The worst did happen to him—Mom dying in the car accident ten years ago. It happened to me, too. I mean, I was in the car. I saw her die. But I was only six at the time, and I believed Dad when he said she'd gone off to a better place.

On my sixteenth birthday I decided it was time for me to find somewhere better to live. I had no name for this place and no picture in my mind of what it would look like. I guess I was so used to Dad imagining different worlds for me that I couldn't imagine a new one for myself.

I didn't run because of him or even Jenny, who moved in about a year after the accident. I called her my "mother figure" because she hated me calling her that. She had thick legs and skinny ankles and smelled like beer from serving drinks at The Logan Inn all day. She found something to yell at me about every time she saw me, but she was mostly harmless. The real reason I ran away was because the teachers, cops, and shrinks in town were starting to talk to each other, which meant they might actually do something about me. They said I was troubled. They said I lacked direction. They said I should be analyzed. Jenny told me all of this as we sat around the kitchen table the night after the "Shocking Canal Attack," as the *Gazette* put it in a giant headline. She sipped her whiskey coffee and stared at me with her lips tight, as if about to spit it on me. Dad drank his A&W root beer and picked at the yellow flowers pressed onto the Formica tabletop. My little sister, Krissy, came wandering into the kitchen singing some kid's rhyme, pretending not to be listening. I pulled Mars up on my lap and rubbed the old cat's ears to show I had feelings. Jenny liked to tell doctors that I didn't seem to feel anything. It was her favorite thing to say about me.

We were trying to understand how I had gotten into trouble again. I explained how unavoidable this mess was, like all of the others—the fire in Bantry's tractor barn, for instance, or Gerenser's dog drowning. I showed them how easy it was to get into these situations, at least for me. Jenny didn't like hearing that. She wanted me to be terrifically sorry and promise not to do anything wrong ever again. She wanted Dad to go beyond a simple punishment and on to some long-range plan of handling me. But not being my real mother, Jenny lacked jurisdiction, which made her furious. She pounded the table and grabbed the closest hard object—this time it was the ceramic Santa Claus that never got put away—and she swung it over our heads to make sure we listened to her. She said I had to start taking control of myself, or someone else would. She said I had to change.

That's when Dad's face went blank, and I knew something crazy was going through his mind. He said, "Imagine if ice didn't float."

Normally, Jenny let such statements pass by like some weird sound you hear in the night and don't really want to know about. But this time she shook him by the shoulders and yelled in his face, "What does ice have to do with this?"

Dad lifted his glass and rattled the ice cubes. "Water is the strangest thing on earth. When water freezes, it gets lighter. Nothing else in the world does that. Ice floats. If it didn't, lakes would freeze from the bottom up."

"So?" Jenny demanded.

"If lakes were to freeze bottom up," he said slowly, "life would die out in the first big cold spell. Life began in the ocean, so it wouldn't exist . . . if ice didn't float."

Jenny shook her head and turned away, then remembered something. "But ice does float," she spit out at him.

Dad nodded that she had finally gotten his point. When he left the kitchen, I followed closely behind him, before Jenny could get her hands on me.

•

I was thinking about my father as the train slowed into 14th Street. The doors pulled apart, and a woman stumbled on. She looked older than me, maybe 21. Her eyes were cloudy, like old marbles, and her face was a chalky white. There were plenty of empty seats, but she slumped down next to me as if I was something to lean on. I pulled away, but she slid close again. Her fat legs were busting through her slacks. The knees were worn away, like kids' jeans get from crawling.

She sat quietly for a minute, gripping a red straw handbag the way women do when they're afraid you might grab it. Suddenly she reached inside the bag and pulled out a penny. She bit it and then flicked the coin onto the train floor. "How old your mother?" she shouted into the air. Nobody riding the subway at midnight was going to answer a question like that. Not far down the aisle, two big black women sat side by side knitting, taking up four seats between them. At the end of the car an old guy was reading a newspaper. There was no one else except me.

The woman's head jerked up and down. "How old your mother?" she yelled at me. I didn't know exactly. When somebody dies, you stop counting birthdays. "How old?" the woman shouted again as she pulled a fistful of pennies from her bag and threw them over her head. They rattled on the plastic seats and rolled down the floor. Then her head fell to her knees, and she looked like she was coiling up to explode.

"Thirty-eight," I said, which was how old my mother was when she died. I figured she might as well stay that age forever.

"Alright," the woman laughed and stuck her hand between her legs. Then she started chewing pennies. Every

9

few seconds she spit one out. When the train jumped forward she fell away from me and banged into the railing. She shook her head quickly, like a cat does after you rub it.

In a few minutes we reached Grand Central, and two kids got on. I knew they were trouble. The bigger one had scraped his head with a razorblade that left long red marks. A thick purple scar circled his left ear, like someone had tried to slice it off. This skinhead was flying on something and went right for the crazy woman. He dug into her pocketbook and pulled out a comb, a nametag, a knit hat. He held each thing up, and his buddy laughed like this was very funny. Then the kid jammed the bag down over the woman's head. A few pennies fell on her and bits of paper and crumbs of food. The black women were muttering to each other and looking to either end of the car for help. The old guy folded his paper and left.

The crazy woman jumped to her feet and the kids grabbed her arms and spun her around. Whichever way she moved to get away, one of their hands pulled her back. Each time they touched her she made a strange noise, like the ping of a video game. Then the skinhead lifted her arm and pinched the sagging flesh between his fingers. She squealed and he shoved his hand inside the top of her shirt.

"Let the child be," one of the black women called out.

The skinhead turned on her with doped-up eyes. He said, "You talking to me?" He stepped closer, rubbing his stomach, and the long bulge of a knife showed beneath his black T-shirt. The women looked away, as if he were a German shepherd you wouldn't stare at straight in the eyes.

"Leave her alone."

My voice cut through the screech of the train wheels. The skinhead laughed, and then his buddy did. I stood up and we faced each other, figuring how much we felt like risking on this fucking hot Saturday night in May, somewhere under New York City, over one mental bag lady. She yanked herself free from them and sat in her seat with her hands folded in her lap, like she was in a church. She seemed to forget the bag still squashed on top of her head. The skinhead flicked his thumb at her. "You want to bleed for that?" he said in such a thick accent I could barely understand him. I shrugged—I didn't need a reason to fight.

The train kept speeding on to the next station, rocking us in the aisle. As the lights blinked, the kid reached under his shirt for the knife. I attacked him with a quick side kick, but he stepped backward in time. He grinned at me and flashed the shining blade through the air. I could see he was the kind who needed a weapon to feel safe. That was a good sign. I turned my back on him, then whirled with a round-house kick to his chest. I caught him with his hands down. There was a cracking sound, maybe a rib breaking. He coughed like he had something stuck in his throat and dropped to his knees. "If they can't breathe, they can't fight," was the first lesson I learned years ago at Rocky's School of Self-Protection. The skinhead gasped for air, and I jammed my elbow down between his shoulder blades to finish him off. The kid collapsed to the floor like his bones had turned to water.

I stepped over him to take care of his buddy. "Don't fuck with me," he said, trying to sound tough. But you can't be scared and tough at the same time, and he looked scared to me. I faked with my left hand and followed with a short right jab to his nose. He cursed in some language I never heard before and held his face. Bright blood squeezed out between his fingers.

"That's right, hurt him," one of the black women called out from behind me. I waved my fist across the kid's eyes again to keep his brain occupied and then kicked his balls in with one sharp thrust of my knee. The fight ended as fast as Rocky promised when you get the first punch in to some-one's face. He made a lot of money teaching that skill, and I learned fast.

"Hurt him!" the crazy woman yelled, like she was root-ing at a hockey game.

I jabbed my fist into the kid's chin a few times more than strictly necessary because it always felt good hitting someone who deserved it. He dropped to the floor and rolled down the aisle as the train slipped into the station. Flashes of blue passed by the window, telling me there were policemen waiting. For the first time in my 10 months as a runaway, I didn't run away from them.

Two

"YOU'RE A HERO," CORPORAL MICHAEL ROURKE SAID TO ME on a dark Monday afternoon as he picked up a *Daily News* from Lenny's Smoke Shop. The big cop held out a dollar. Inside his little stand, surrounded by magazines hanging from clips, Lenny sucked on a thick carrot and waved the money away. Rourke tipped his cap and pointed to the head-line at the bottom: "Runaway Busts Thugs, Rescues Bag Lady—Story, Page 4."

"I made page 28 once," he said as he walked me down the street, his heavy hand on my shoulder, "for saving a 200-pound pig from a fire." Rourke shook his head to let me know it wasn't a pretty story. "This huge porker was tied to the kitchen table in a little apartment on Eighth Avenue. When I got there the flames were already turning his tail into ham. The family had left him to burn—didn't even have the decency to cut the rope." He grunted like he had never seen such cruelty, which surprised me. "Vietnamese," he said, as if that explained things. Out in the street, two cabbies were leaning through their windows yelling at each other. One guy got out of his cab and kicked at the door of the other, but Rourke didn't seem interested in their argu-ment. "I had to carry this hysterical pig down four flights," he said, circling his arms to show how big the animal was. "Almost gave me a heart attack. Next day I'm in the paper, the headline says, 'Vegetarian Cop Saves Pig from Frying.'" He poked my shoulder to get my attention. "That night, what do you think? The family celebrates surviving by roasting the pig on the sidewalk for the whole neighbor-hood. Un-fucking believable, huh?"

Rourke, my official police escort, led me to the bus ter-minal, then steered me by the arm to Gate 17, Central New Jersey and Points West. "That's you," he said, nodding at the sign, "Points West." He lit a cigarette for himself, then gave me one. "You know," he said, looking around the wait-ing area the way cops do, "if you wanted to stay lost, you made a big mistake saving that bag lady." I nodded that it was a stupid thing to do and inhaled the good smoke of the Camel. "Of course," he said out of the side of his mouth, "soon as your bus crosses the river, you're no concern of NYPD. You could get off anywhere you want before New Hope, get lost again."

"Thanks for the suggestion."

"No," he shook his head, "it's just a possibility."

The bus driver walked past pointing to the sign on the terminal door saying "No Smoking." Rourke tapped his badge and we kept on puffing. The other passengers started loading, but I stayed there with the cop, smoking and listening to him tell about Brooklyn, where he grew up. People passing by glanced at him and then at me, checking for handcuffs or some other sign that I was dangerous. I liked feeling dangerous.

An announcement over the loud speaker came out half words, half static. We both heard "Pennsylvania" and moved through the gate. The driver, a black guy wearing a white shirt and blue bow tie, leaned out of the bus. "Get on if you're getting on."

"He's coming," Rourke said, jabbing me in the chest. I stamped out my cigarette and picked up my duffel bag. "Hold on a minute," he said as he checked his watch, "she should have been here by now." He ducked into the terminal, and I could see him through the glass door looking around. I didn't know who he was looking for, but I waited there like he said because for a cop, Rourke was pretty cool. He even smoked the same cigarettes as me. In a minute he came back pulling a woman behind him. She wore a black silk jacket and a purple scarf. Her skin reminded me of sunburnt grass. Her eyes were deep green-blue, the color of the Delaware River in winter. I couldn't imagine why a woman like that would hang around a cop.

"This is a friend of mine," he said.

She put out her hand for me to shake. Her fingers felt very cold for such a hot day. "I'm a writer," she said, "and I'd like to write your story."

So she was just another stupid reporter like the ones who had hounded me the day before about what was going through my head at every moment I was saving the bag lady, as if you had loads of time to think in the middle of a fight. "I'm leaving," I said, "that's my bus." The driver was drumming his fingers on the door. He spit on the pavement.

"I don't mean now. I'll come see you in a few days at your home." She smiled when she said this, and I noticed something strange—her top teeth were as jagged as mine. "Is that alright with you?"

I pointed at Rourke's *Daily News*. "I've already been written about, see?"

She dismissed the paper with a flick of her hand. "That's trash, and anyway, it just covers Saturday night. I want to write about your whole time on the streets as a runaway, and what happens when you go home."

"You expecting something to happen?"

"I don't know, what do you think?"

"Not much," I said, "about that kind of stuff. Anyway, I don't need some reporter following me around."

"Not many people get a big feature written about their life," she said, "especially when they're fifteen years old. And I've got a publisher friend of mine interested in a book. You could be famous."

"I'm sixteen," I said as I hoisted my heavy duffel bag to my shoulder. "The paper got it wrong. And besides, why would I want to be famous?"

She looked to Rourke for help with the question. He winked at her and lit another cigarette for himself. "Don't decide now," she said. "We'll talk about it when I come visit you, okay? I'll be in New Hope in a few days." She said this as if she were used to people doing what she wanted. Then she reached out and touched my arm. "Don't talk to anyone else—that's important, okay?"

I nodded that I wouldn't talk to anyone, and Rourke hurried me to the bus door. "You can trust her," he said in my ear. "She covers midtown for the AP. She'll write your story just like it is, no faking it."

He handed over my ticket to the driver and I climbed on board. The bus was half empty, but I headed to the back where nobody ever sat except kids like me. As the bus pulled out, I looked through the window, and there was Rourke and the writer smiling and waving at me, as if we were old friends.

•

I was going home to the Delaware, if anything.

I spent more time on the river than anywhere else. When the summer nights got too hot to sleep, I'd sneak out of the house to the riverbank to hunt. I carried a flashlight and Uncle Toby's World War II knife. Caught rabbits mostly, some small coons, and woodchucks.

Jenny used to yell at me for staying out all night until the morning she saw me skinning a rabbit on the back steps. My sneakers were smeared with blood and my hands were dripping red. I happened to be holding the knife blade up when I told her to get off my back. Usually it took a lot to shut her up, but not that time. Not being my real mother kept her wondering, I guess, what I might do next.

I always left the rabbit meat in the basement sink for Dad to deal with. He'd be stumbling around down there looking through Grandpa's boxes of old *Lifes* and *National Geographics*, the ones the mice hadn't eaten away yet. Then he'd smell the dead meat and find the rabbit. He'd come after me in my room as if I'd killed something human. I'd fake sleeping as he shook my body, telling me to wake up and listen to him. He wouldn't leave until I opened my eyes and he could explain to me again about forever, which is where I sent a lot of little creatures. "Forever is the worst thing that can happen to you," he'd say. "You slip into it one day and never get out, just like your rabbit." Then he'd go downstairs and make stew out of the meat, mixing in celery, peppers, and raisins. Dad hated seeing an animal die for no reason, and food was a reason he could understand, even if he was a vegetarian. He'd put it on the table that night for dinner saying that his father had eaten rabbit during the Depression when they were a lot poorer than us. Jenny said he should stop carrying the past along with him so much, and eating rabbit when you didn't have to was a perfect example. She never touched the rabbit. She said we'd probably die from eating a wild animal. Dad and I never had more than a few bites. The meat always tasted too gamey.

The long bus ride home gave me time to remember a lot of things, such as moleing. I earned good money from the New Yorkers who bought the big stone houses north of New

Hope to have a place to breathe during the summer. You could see them all the time standing in their yards or sitting on the front steps doing nothing except sucking air and looking happy about it. I biked up River Road in May just as they were planting tomatoes. I'd hop off my bike and explain to them how much moles loved eating tomato roots. I told them that if you planted a garden along the Delaware, you had to hire a kid to keep the moles away. City people went out of their way to believe me. I wore a blue bandanna around my neck and a red T-shirt that said "No Hope High" on the front. They always asked about that. After I made up an interesting life story about the T-shirt, they usually agreed to pay me ten dollars for the season, which seemed reasonable to them and a fortune to me for doing nothing. Some of the guys wanted to take me inside for ice cream and stuff, but I just smiled and said I was too busy right then, which made them think that maybe sometime I wouldn't be too busy if they just kept giving me money.

I did catch a few moles each summer, mostly in Jenny's rhubarb garden. I'd drive the fireplace shovel through the mole's tunnel just ahead of him and spike the heel of my boot down behind him. I stood over the shaking mound of earth, watching the little animal turn around and around going crazy being trapped. If his mind could have made the leap vertical, then it was freedom, a new dimension for moles everywhere. But none I saw ever escaped being what they were—dirt-loving moles. I sent them off to Animal Heaven with the back end of my shovel. I figured they were better off there.

The best time living near the Delware was in August when the rains broke from the clouds as if they had been bombed open. You could feel the storm coming all morning. Then the sky would go black, doors would blow shut— that's when I'd run for the river. I'd crawl out onto the wing dam and let the rains and rapids pour over me. The river tried to sweep me into it. The water was thick as air. I used to lie out there feeling like a fish.

Dad told me that sometimes after a violent storm you could see God in the clouds. So I hung onto the wing dam in the middle of the river through terrible winds and rain, even a hurricane. I waited for God to suddenly step out of the sky and look around and not see anybody else brave enough to be outside. I wasn't going to ask Him to send Mom back—I just wanted to know how she was doing in Heaven.

He never came, and I learned later that the story was a lie. God doesn't show up in storms or any other time.

There aren't many good terrors left when you get older, not like waiting for God in the middle of a hurricane when you're eight years old.

•

During the spring runoff from the mountains, the river turned into "The Deadly Delaware," as the *Gazette* called it. The rapids below New Hope Bridge always surprised the weekend canoeists who were expecting just a little heavy water. I used to ride into town for a snowcone at Gerenser's and then sit out on the dam. They floated by and waved and some of the guys threw cans of beer to me. I waved back and laughed like they had nothing to worry about.

Then the rapids sucked them in. Most of them tried to back paddle, which was just the opposite of what they should have done. A few of them got lucky by doing nothing. But some panicked and rocked the boat so much they ended up drinking the Delaware. At first they'd laugh at each other like it was a real great adventure. But then they'd realize that they couldn't stand up and their canoe was floating away and the water was too strong for them to swim to shore. The current just kept dragging them down river toward Scudders Falls. I'd yell to them, "Watch out for the falls!" and point south, in case they didn't know about them.

Sometimes I went for help if there was a hot-looking woman in the boat and I was done with my beer. I'd call the cops from the phone inside Flannery's Pottery Shed and they'd come racing out of town with their sirens blaring to a spot just above Scudders where the river narrowed. They got pretty good at throwing in their ropes to save people from going over the falls. They got pretty angry, too, after the second or third rescue on a weekend.

I never actually saw death on the river, but I read plenty of stories in the *Gazette* every summer. "Manhattan Banker Feared Drowned below New Hope," the headline would say, or "Brooklyn Couple Lost at Scudders Falls." A week or so later the paper would report the missing body found in Trenton or some other place down river. Old man Metzgar used to shake his head and say, "The river rats have to eat, too, and they might as well feed on New Yorkers."

In the summer I spent every weekend on the water. I'd hitch a ride up River Road with my raft, which I made out of old floorboards from Flannery's. Most people from town would drive right past me, but there were plenty of tourists who stopped and seemed to like figuring out how to tie my raft onto their car top. I let them take care of it.

I put in eight miles upriver at Point Pleasant. In some places the water was so low I could pole off the bottom. I dunked lots of times just to cool off. I got knocked around on the rocks sometimes, but no other trouble came to me even though I never learned the proper way to swim. It always seemed to me that the closer to danger I put myself, the safer I ended up. Jenny used to say that daring trouble like that caught up with you eventually.

•

I got to remembering so much about home that I missed my bus stop. I hurried down the aisle dragging my duffel bag behind me and tapped the driver's shoulder. "That was my stop back there," I said, "at the bridge."

The man took his eyes from the road for a long time without slowing down, looking at me and hating me an awful lot, I thought, just for asking him to stop an extra time. He pulled the bus over at the train station and opened the door. I stopped on the steps for a second, like I wasn't sure I wanted to get out there after all. "Fucking kid" he muttered, which I guess was the worst thing he could think to call me. I jumped to the curb as the doors whipped shut on my heels.

I swung the satchel over my shoulder and headed back to Main Street. The town was swimming in tourists, just as I had left it 10 months ago. It was Memorial Day, the first big weekend of the year for New Hope. I was wearing my usual clothes—cutoff jeans, a blue T-shirt that said "Nuke

18

New York" across the front, and a yellow bicycle cap pulled down over my eyes to keep out the low evening sun.

The sidewalk was so crowded with people that I moved out into the street to walk alongside the slow line of cars. At Playhouse Bridge I stopped to watch the water drop over the little falls, and from there I could see between the buildings to the river. A motorboat was docking at the pier. The people getting out were dressed up, as if they were coming to the play that night by boat. That was odd, a motorboat so far down river. It made me wonder if they'd gotten rid of the rapids somehow. Whenever someone drowned, Jenny would always say, "They ought to do something about those rapids."

Night was falling fast. Lights were coming on inside the shops, and New Hope looked like a movie set, a place where something interesting might happen. I kept walking, past The Logan where Jenny worked, past Class Act, which was my favorite place to lift clothes, and on to Sam's Indian Reservation. Some old people were touching the hands on the eight-foot tall wooden Indian that guarded Sam's front door. A woman dressed in black with a white pearl necklace was just going in the store. Sam wouldn't like her. He always said that rich people were the cheapest he ever met.

From Sam's I took the shortcut down the alley past the Mule Barge Shop and headed across the marsh, which was already pretty dry even though it wasn't even June yet. I used to kick around this meadow in summer looking for snakes, especially at midday when they hid deep and still in the grass keeping cool. I'd coax the little black ones to curl around a stick and then fling them into the river for one last wild ride. I always wondered what they thought was happening to them.

I took the river path home so I could see for myself about the rapids. They were still there—I could hear them even before I reached the water's edge. I slid down the riverbank on my heels and there was the Delaware bubbling up white foam in the early moonlight. It made me feel good seeing the rapids and knowing there was still fast water close by my house.

Three

I KNOCKED ON THE FRONT DOOR OF A HOUSE THAT DIDN'T FEEL like mine anymore. But it still looked the same. Weeds were growing up through the porch deck like before, and the gray paint was shedding off the shingles in long strips. I reached for the bell but then pulled my hand away. Sometimes the buzzer stuck, and Jenny couldn't stand that sound. Next to the door there was a light rectangular spot where a wooden sign saying "Paine" used to hang. Grandpa made it in the cellar his last winter, when he was still trying to be useful. Dad nailed the sign up even though the final "e" was almost squeezed off the edge. Jenny took it down the day after Grandpa died.

I knocked again, harder, and the living room suddenly went dark. I could see the outline of Jenny's face pressed to the porch window trying to see who it was. I flattened myself against the house, hiding from her. I felt like a stranger, even though the squeaking of the porch and the rustling of the maple trees and everything else seemed so familiar.

The front door opened slowly, and Jenny stood inside the screen squinting at me. "You came back," she said after her eyes had adjusted to the dusk. "It's you, Jake?"

"It's me."

"You grew some."

"Yeah, I did."

She looked heavier to me, and older, more like pictures of Jenny's mother than Jenny herself. Her hair was cut short, showing the pink birthmark on her neck. Her face looked fatter to me, like an old football inflated a little too much. Still, she was kind of pretty for a woman in her forties, pretty enough to get propositioned by lots of guys she served at The Logan, at least the ones interested in women.

She flicked away a mosquito that had gotten in through the rips in the screen. "The police called from New York. They said they were putting you on the bus, but they thought you would get off before New Hope."

"I could have run again," I said.

"I figured someday you'd show up like this. Still, it's surprising now that you have."

I didn't know what to say to that, so I made some sort of expression, kind of twisting up my mouth to let her know I heard her.

"You planning on staying?"

I couldn't tell from her voice which answer she was hoping for, but she still hadn't opened the screen, which meant something. "Maybe for a little while."

"Nobody chased you away," she said.

"I know," I said, even though I really didn't. When the choices were to run away or get sent to some mental ward, there was a certain feeling of being chased.

Jenny's hand still held the knob so she could slam the inside door if she wanted to. She used to slam doors a lot. "Just as long as you know we didn't chase you," she said.

"I know, okay? You don't have to keep telling me."

She pulled back from the screen because of how loud I'd gotten, and I squeezed myself and the duffel bag inside. She looked a little scared now that I was on the same side of the door as her. Suddenly I felt a power over her that I never had before, simply by being so much bigger. I hadn't even realized that I'd grown so much until then, standing over someone who hadn't grown at all.

"Who is it?" Dad called from the living room. I could hear his rocker squeaking louder than ever.

"See for yourself," Jenny answered him.

I nodded into the living room. "How's he doing?" She shrugged, which meant that the answer would be obvious soon enough. "Worse than before?"

"Once you're over the edge, it doesn't really matter how far over you are, does it?"

Dad came out of the dim light carrying his reading glasses in one hand and a book in the other.

"It's me," I said.

"Jake," he said flatly, like naming some inanimate object for the first time. He set his glasses and book on the hall stand and rubbed his eyes hard. When he pulled his hands away, he stared at me like an animal that sees something in the distance but doesn't know what to make of it. "You look different," he said.

"You, too," I said. He had gained some weight, which meant he was eating normally and not getting weird about all of the poisons in food that could kill a person. His hair was longer than I had ever seen it, curling over his ears and down to his shirt collar in back, as long as he had worn it in college. He kept one picture of himself from the late sixties, a photo that ran in the *Philadelphia Bulletin*. Dad was lying on the steps of Independence Hall during a war protest, waiting for the cops to drag him off. The camera caught him looking scared when he realized he was the next one going into the police van. Three months later, just a week out of Temple University, he was down at the induction office getting processed for Vietnam with all of the other kids too poor to buy their way out.

"Jake," he said my name again, but as if he were saying a different word now, one that could make him smile a little and reach out to touch me on the shoulder, a word he knew real well. "This house hasn't been the same without you," he said.

"Sorry it wasn't, Dad."

He threw his arm over my shoulder as if we were war buddies greeting each other at some reunion. He was wearing his loafers instead of sneakers, which was a good sign, because it meant he wasn't planning on walking up the canal later. Dad had this habit of wandering around New Hope late at night to settle his nerves. "I hope you never experience your nerves going bad," he'd say. "It feels like your skin's going to shake off." Getting outside air was the only thing that quieted him down. Sometimes he was gone for hours, leaving Jenny and me at home wondering if this was the time he wasn't coming back. There always seemed like lots of reasons he might not. My sister Kris slept through most of those nights. We never told her that her father was out in the dark somewhere, trying to keep his skin from shaking off.

Sometimes people living in the canal houses caught him staring in their windows, which bothered them more than seemed necessary to me. They'd call 911, and the cops would catch up with Dad somewhere along the canal, sitting on the restraining wall and dropping stones into the water. He never denied looking in the houses. But he said looking wasn't against the law since he always stood on public property and people left their shades up. The cops said that he was invading privacy and causing a disturbance, which were against the law. They brought him home dozens of times. One rainy night they shoved him out of the squad car into our front yard and hit the horn. He was lying on the grass when we reached him, holding his stomach, curled up like a dead possum on the road.

Dad drew me close to him now. I didn't fit under his chin anymore, but he still felt big to me, bigger than six feet. He was breathing fast. His body started to shiver. "You just ran off," he said, and there wasn't much I could say because that's what I did—ran from home to keep from being sent away to a hospital full of crazy people. It seemed the reasonable thing to do at the time. Dad held me away at arm's length and looked me over from my cap to my sneakers. "I missed seeing you grow up," he said.

"You probably saw enough."

Then Jenny's hands came between us, and we pulled apart like she wanted us to. She gave me a quick hug and stepped up on her toes to kiss me on the forehead. "You got his size," she said. That's all she said, but we both knew she was wondering what else my father had passed on to me.

•

Upstairs in my room I switched on the old desk lamp and the fluorescent bulb flicked on. That reminded me of something Dad had told me—that even when the light seemed on, it was flickering sixty times a second, too fast for people to notice. But flies could see it, so for them the room was always going back and forth between light and dark. From then on I always wondered, what other things might be happening around me that I didn't know about?

The night's darkness had already sealed off my bedroom window so I couldn't see out. The room seemed very small, like a little kid's room. The desk chair creaked as I sat down on it. The desk calendar showed my escape with the days crossed off with big red Xs, the countdown to running away on my birthday, July 18th. I pulled out the top drawer and saw my journal. Uncle Toby sent it to me for no reason I could figure except to give me something. On the inside cover he wrote, "Someday you'll want to know what you were thinking all those years." I fell asleep many nights writing in that book, smelling the covers. I imagined that's how Uncle Toby smelled, like good rich leather.

My room was stacked with books from all over the world, mostly from U.T., as he always signed them. He sent me thick paperbacks on astronomy and chemical reactions and magic and big cats. He sent me novels about pirates and mountain climbers and Vikings and African bushmen. I read the novels the day they arrived, sitting down by the riverbank, cooling my feet in the water. Then I'd stack them in the fireplace, which hadn't worked for as long as I could remember. Dad said the damper got stuck closed just about when I was born. He often kept time by when things broke.

Uncle Toby traveled everywhere because he retired early and didn't need any more money than he'd already made selling hardware for thirty years. He wrote to me the day he sold his business in Laramie, Wyoming, saying it was a relief not dealing with practical things and practical people every hour of the day. He sent me lots of other things besides books, like shells and stamps and rocks and knives, even though I never met him. He wouldn't come East because he didn't like anywhere people outnumbered "real animals." He said there were lots of ways for people to know each other and we had one way—through the mail. He said that the Toby I imagined was probably a lot cooler than the actual one, anyway. I wrote back that I didn't care if he was cool or not, but he still wouldn't come to Pennsylvania.

My favorite book from him was *A Tiger for Malgudi* because it was written in "first tiger," as U.T. put it. In the beginning, the tiger roams the jungle killing animals and people, mostly because that's what he thinks a big cat should do. He was "living up to expectations," as my uncle wrote inside the cover. Expectations, he added, can get you into trouble. Halfway through the story, the tiger tells about being hunted down and put in a circus and made to do trained cat tricks, like jumping through a burning hoop. The trainer's special trick was to bring a goat in the cage and have the two of them drink milk from the same bowl. One day the tiger's instinct overwhelms him and he bites off the head of the goat. It seemed like the right thing to do at the time, the tiger says, and I knew exactly how he felt.

After I read that part, I wrote a letter to Uncle Toby in East Africa somewhere and told him not to bother sending me anything else because I was heading off to see the world for myself.

•

"Boo!"

I sprang off the bed and swung my hand at the sound. When my eyes cleared I saw my little sister lying on the floor. "Kris," I said, reaching down to her, "I didn't know it was you." She crawled backwards and stood up in the doorway, rubbing her chin where I had grazed her. "I was daydreaming," I said. "I didn't hear you."

"Nobody hears me," she said as she came back in my room, "unless I make a lot of noise. I do that sometimes." She scratched her arm for awhile, looking at me. "When I get civilized," she said, "I can go to camp in Yellowstone and ride horses all day."

"Who told you that?"

"Mom did. She promised."

"Where would Jenny get the money to send you to Yellowstone?" Kris shrugged as if she didn't worry about that. "She'll get it like she always does."

"You seem civilized to me already," I said.

"I am right now but sometimes I'm not. She said I have to be always, which is pretty hard."

"What do you do when you're not civilized?"

Kris pushed my door almost shut behind her and grabbed my sleeve to get me standing. I bent over so she could whisper in my ear. "I yell like this—'HELLLPP!'" She turned her head up, listening for a few seconds and then yelled again, louder— "'HELLLLLLPPPP!' I like yelling that 'cause people always come running."

"Nobody's coming now."

"Mom probably can't hear me 'cause Dad has the radio on. If I yelled out in the hall, I bet she'd come."

She started toward the door, but I caught her arm. "You better not yell anymore."

"I wasn't going to really," Kris said, "'cause I'm trying to be good." She stood under me, her head reaching just above my waist, staring at my stomach. "I could climb on you," she said after a while, "if you want."

"Okay."

She dug her fingers inside my belt and pulled down hard, at the same time trying to balance her foot on my leg. She slid back to the floor a couple of times till I hoisted under her backside and settled her on my hips. She slipped her fingers around my neck, and then her eyes crossed and she shook her head so that her hair flew across my face. "You're bigger than I remember," she said, "which is okay for some things, I guess. But we can't play much anymore."

"Why not?"

As she thought why for a minute, her tongue curled up to touch the tip of her nose. "I'm good at that, and I learned how to thumb wrestle pretty good, and I can spit five feet through my teeth. But you'd win everything else. You're too old and big now. Do they always go together?"

"Not always," I said right away. I figured that when a seven-year-old asks, "Do they always?" the answer has to be "Not always."

"I did get bigger and older, you're right," I told her, "but you did, too."

She bit her bottom lip and then pulled it out for me to see the groove she had made. She blew plaster off my shoulder, and I looked over my head to see the ceiling cracked and peeling away. "It's falling everywhere," she said. "It fell in my tomato soup last night and Dad said don't eat it and Mom said to just take it out with my spoon and then Dad yelled 'DON'T EAT IT!' so I didn't because he scared me."

She stopped talking, and I realized that it was my turn.

I tried to think of something exciting about myself. "Did I ever tell you about when I ate worms in the backyard?"

"No," she said, "I would have remembered that."

I was only going to eat one worm that day, just to feel it on my tongue. Then I saw the second one inching along, going somewhere, I guess—I grabbed it and swallowed fast. I could have stopped after two, but I dug up a third little worm by Dad's old cement birdbath and chewed on that one. Eating three worms seemed to mean something to me then that eating just two worms didn't. I learned very young that I could do even the worst-sounding things. Inside the kitchen that afternoon, Jenny was drying dishes, pretending not to see me.

"Why did you eat worms for?" Kris asked.

"Well, I was reading a book about Appalachia—"

Kris scrunched up her nose at the strange-sounding word. "What's that?"

"Appalachia is a very poor part of the country, kind of down south—"

"Poorer than us?"

"Way poorer. The kids there get so hungry sometimes that they have to eat worms for food. You never did that, did you?"

She shook her head. "I don't think I like eating worms."

"If you eat too many they get caught in your throat and choke you."

She pulled down hard on my left ear and then frowned at me. "That means turn, horse. When I pull like this," she yanked my left ear again, "you turn left, except I'm backwards so maybe you turn the other way."

"Which way do you want to go?"

She pointed all over the room, so I ran with her around my bed to the fireplace and then the doorway. When I galloped back to the middle of the room, I spun her faster and faster until we collapsed onto my bed. She stared up at me with her red cheeks and curly hair, and I imagined this was how Jenny looked as a kid.

"Mom told me you were never coming back. She said to forget I ever had a brother."

That didn't surprise me. I figured Jenny would try to erase me from the family. "So, did you forget me?"

Kris shook her head and reached over to poke me in the stomach. "I didn't forget. You used to give me piggyback rides and take me into town for an ice cream and squirt me with the hose. We could do that on Saturday, if you want."

"Okay."

"Except I have to ask Elise first."

"Who's that?"

"She's my best friend. She's nine years old, but she lets me play with her every Saturday because I act nine even though I'm not really. That's why she's my best friend. They have a coal bin in their cellar and nobody else does, and there's still some coal. Sometimes we write on her driveway. One time she wrote, 'Krissy doesn't really have a brother.' She writes things like that to make me mad. But she lets me borrow her old bike, so I don't mind. I need my own bike so I don't have to borrow her little one, and then I can keep up with her. I could go anywhere I want in New Hope, if sidewalks go there."

"You should have a big bike," I agreed as I lay down next to her on the bed.

She stuck her thumb in her mouth and made it pop. "How come Elise wrote that?"

"I don't know—maybe it's because I'm really your half brother."

"How can you be half a brother?" Kris asked.

"Because Jenny's your mother, but she isn't mine." It surprised me that she didn't know this, and I wondered if there was some reason I shouldn't be telling her.

"Where's *your* mother?" she asked.

I shrugged as if I couldn't remember, because I didn't think she needed to know that mothers could be alive one minute and dying in front of your eyes the next. I stretched out her yellow sweatshirt and read what it said—"Buy Me a Horse!" Underneath there was a drawing of a little girl on top of a great white stallion. "You really expect somebody to buy you a horse?"

"Yep," she said firmly, "if you want something like a horse and think about it and let people know, then it will come true, if you just wait long enough."

28

"That's crazy," I told her. "How long have you been wearing this shirt?"

"Since Christmas—'Lise had it made for me in town. But I don't wear it every day. Mom makes me change sometimes." Kris yawned wide and held her mouth open longer than she needed to, showing me all her teeth. Then she rolled over on her stomach and buried her face in my pillow. "After you left I wished for another brother," she said, her voice just a whisper, "but a lot smaller than you. I wanted a brother I could beat up sometimes, if I felt like it."

"That would be nice," I said.

Her arm was sticking out from her sleeve, very thin and white. I pushed up her shirt and walked my fingers on her skin. She twisted around and watched my hand go higher and higher. "That tickles," she said.

"It's supposed to."

She squeezed her eyes shut, trying to block out the feeling, and when she couldn't she yanked her arm away. Then she jumped off the bed and grabbed my duffel bag. I liked that—she wasn't afraid to touch something that wasn't hers. "What's in here?" she demanded.

"Just things I picked up while I was away."

She felt the bulges in the canvas, wanting something inside there especially for her, a gift brought back from wherever I'd been. So I pulled the bag away from her and parted the drawstring. "Maybe there *is* something for you," I said, reaching deep inside. I felt through my clothes and found a piece of granite that I had saved from New Hampshire. I held it in front of her like a rare diamond.

"A pet rock!" she yelled. "'Lise's mom has one and—" but I shook my head. She guessed again—"It's to hold down paper, like homework." I said no again. "A club," she said, picking it up in the middle and trying to hold it over her head, but it was too heavy for her little hand. She thought some more, looking at me and then my gift to her. "Maybe it's just a big rock!" she said and laughed as I nodded that she had finally guessed right. She sat it on her lap, thinking hard, smiling once up at me. Then she stuffed the rock under her shirt, tucking it in tightly.

"You better go now," I told her, "I have to change."

She sat back on the bed and propped her head up with a pillow. "I see Daddy plenty of times," she said. "He doesn't care."

So I pulled my shirt over my head and tossed it across the room onto my desk. I loosened the laces to my old black Cons and kicked them off. I unbuckled my jeans and sat back on the bed to pull off the legs. Kris leaned over me and pointed at the rough skin just above the elastic band of my shorts. "What's that?" she said.

"It's a scar."

She pushed my shoulder back to let the light from my desk lamp shine on it. "I never saw a scar like that before. What did that?"

"A knife."

"Can I touch it?" She didn't wait for me to answer. She traced along my stomach with her index finger and pricked at the raised skin with her nail to see if it would hurt. She held her hand away for a moment, then let her fingers run across my stomach. I brushed her off with one arm and raised up over her to attack. She screamed, not knowing what I would do next and liking that. I formed my fingers into claws and let my eyes go wild . . . .

"Jake!" It was Jenny, her voice piercing through the air ahead of her. "For God's sake, get off my daughter!" She came running in the room and pulled with both of her hands on my arm. They had no strength over me, but I sat back on the bed anyway.

Kris drew herself away to the headboard, feeling something horrible in the room now but not knowing if it came from her mother or me or herself. The rock sagged strangely inside her shirt. Jenny looked from Kris' shirt to my undershorts, which were rubbed down a little in the tickling.

"You watch it, Jake," she said. "You're old enough to know how to behave in this house." She turned to Kris, who was sitting with her knees pulled to her chin. "You're not to see Jake alone until I say so. Do you understand me?"

My sister tightened the pillows about her ears, but the fear still got in her, the fear of me.

Four

I FLIPPED OFF MY BEDLIGHT AND SANK INTO THE SOFTEST mattress in the world. I hugged my pillow and smelled—Jenny always used laundry soap with perfume in it. On the road I used to think about my bed a lot, especially when I was sleeping under bridges and over heating grates and inside cardboard boxes. Now I closed my eyes and remembered the other things I missed about home—a shower more than anything, food in the refrigerator, and a room of my own where I could close the door and be left alone. What I didn't miss was Jenny in her slippers shuffling down the hallway. Her footsteps stopped outside my room, then the door squeaked open. She stood there, a shadow in the light from the hall. "You asleep yet?"

"Sort of."

She came in, leaving the door wide open behind her. "I didn't mean to yell at you with Kris," she said, slurping the words. "There was nothing to it, I suppose." She popped an ice cube from her mouth and rubbed it on her forehead, then sucked on it again. "This heat kills me," she said, "and it's just Memorial Day." Being from Maine originally, Jenny never could get used to the steamy nights along the Delaware.

"I guess it looked strange," I said, "with Kris, I mean."

She sat down on the bed and I could feel her leg through the thin sheet. Her white summer nightgown was very short. "It's been a long time since I came in to talk to you like this," she said as she leaned back on the bed to get more comfortable. It was always hard for Jenny to sit up straight after a day lugging drinks. "You remember what we talked about?"

"Nothing much," I said, "except maybe about the river."

"You talked about the river, I didn't. We could be living next to a nuclear plant for all I care about the river." Her wet hand pinched my leg through the sheet. "We talked about you—and your father. Don't you remember anything?"

"You said *don't* a lot—I remember that."

"Don't get smart with me," she said and then laughed

31

that she had used her favorite word again. "I should have said it more often." She stared at the sheet for awhile, as if she could look through it. "You never did wear shorts or anything to bed," she said, "even as a boy."

"Nope."

"I don't know how you stand that, especially in the winter."

"It feels good being cold."

"Feels better being warm." She sat there next to me, not touching me, but close enough that I could feel her anyway. She sucked on the ice cube, and the noise almost made me sick. "I guess you got a lot of experience out there with girls," she said.

"Not that much."

"You didn't get into that other stuff, with boys—"

"Not really."

"That won't get you anywhere but dead. You can see plenty of that in this town."

"I know."

"I'm telling you another thing, too, if you want to stay in this house." She scratched my thigh through the sheet with her short, sharp fingernails. "You listening to me?"

"I'm listening."

She made a fist with her free left hand and shook it in front of my face. "Stay away from that Indian." Her right hand was kind of teasing me now, crawling up my leg. Sometimes you never knew which Jenny to listen to—the one that was shaking a fist or the one that was tickling. "I never could understand why he let you hang around his store," she said, "unless he—you know."

"He never touched me."

"Then I don't understand it. What else could it be?"

I shrugged that I didn't know. "Sam didn't cause any of the problems," I said.

"He didn't help. He just twists things up until you need lawyers to straighten them out."

"I said he didn't cause anything."

"I heard you. Just stay away from him." She sat there for awhile, thinking hard about something. "Your father," she finally said, "he's been selling some books these last few

months, and made a little money. That's important for us."
I nodded that money was important. "I don't want you
upsetting him," she added, but as I remembered it, Dad got
himself all worked up about things. He didn't need any help
from me. "I could have done better," she said, which
sounded to me like the beginning of a long, boring speech.
"I know I could have, but you didn't want another mother."
She was sure right about that. One mother is enough for a
lifetime, and I had had mine. Mothers shouldn't be replace-
able. You get one, and if you lose her, that should be it. "I
had three sisters and a mother," Jenny said. "So when I
moved in with your father, I didn't know what to do with a
boy like you all of a sudden."

"I didn't know what to do with you either, Jenny."

She leaned forward and took my head in her hands. I
could smell the old familiar coffee on her lips, with the
fresh scent of whiskey mixed in. Jenny always needed a
drink before she could come up and talk to me like this. "I
did want things to work out with us," she said, "no matter
how it seemed."

"Thanks," I said. I really believed her at that moment,
even with so many memories telling me otherwise.

•

Some time later my bedroom door rattled open again
and I woke up fast. I'd learned from sleeping in parks and
runaway houses that you had to wake up at the first sound
or you could lose your money, and some of your skin, too.
I saw that happen to a kid named Shawn from Louisiana.
Some black guys took an iron to his arm and burned off his
tattoo, a Confederate flag.

Remembering I was home calmed me down quickly. It
felt good waking up in the middle of the night someplace
safe. A big familiar hand wrapped around the door. "That
you, Dad?"

"It's me."

"What's up?"

"Couldn't sleep," he said. I leaned off the bed to see him
better. "So I got up—to make sure you really came home."

"I did," I said and rapped myself on the chest a few times to show I was real. "So you can go back to bed now."

He didn't move. "I'll go," he said but didn't.

"You want to talk for a minute?"

He came in and sat down on the edge of my bed just about where Jenny had been a couple of hours before. "I was dreaming," he said in a dramatic voice.

"You always dream."

"I dream a lot, that's true. This time I was walking into a department store, a very fancy New York store, and one of those women handing out makeup grabbed my arm. I told her I didn't want any, but she kept rubbing lipstick on my face and shaking powder on my cheeks and spraying my hair." He breathed out hard to let me know that was all he could remember. "What do you think it means?"

"I doubt it means anything, Dad. You're not the kind of guy who wears makeup."

"That's what makes it strange," he said. "But it does mean something. Dreams always mean something. Dreams are life." Dreams seemed like just dreams to me, but I didn't feel like arguing. Dad whistled a few weird notes, something he was making up. Then he whispered, "La vida es un sueño."

He often forgot that we couldn't understand when he spoke Spanish. He'd picked it up working nights at a Puerto Rican grocery in Philadelphia to get himself through college. He started studying Spanish again after Mom died because he said he could feel his mind slowing down, and that scared him. There was nothing like learning a language, he said, to exercise your brain.

"La vida es un sueño," he repeated in a louder voice.

"What's that mean?" I asked him. He always wanted you to ask him what stuff meant.

"Life is a dream."

He seemed to be talking in circles to me. "So let me get this straight," I said. "Dreams are life, and life is a dream. That about it?"

The bed springs creaked as Dad shifted his weight. "That's only part of it. If life is a dream, then whose dream? The bushmen in Africa say the dream is dreaming us." That was too deep for me. "I have to admit," Dad said, "I don't know what they mean by that. The bushmen are magical people. They see things in the world that we don't. All I know is that if life is a dream, then none of this really exists."

I followed the sweep of his hand around the room, but I couldn't see much in the dark. "If this doesn't exist, Dad, somebody went to a lot of trouble fooling everyone, don't you think?"

"You're right," he said, in a strong voice again. He patted me on the arm. "You know better than your old man." He sat quietly for a minute. "What do you dream about, Jake?"

"Nothing."

"Sure you do."

"No, I really don't dream, at least that I can remember."

I could see the outline of his face staring at me, perfectly still. Then he said, "In this light, you look like her." He had never said anything like this to me before. I had Mom's blue eyes, and maybe her chin, but everything else about my face was more Dad's than hers. I had his wild brown hair, his pale skin, his long eyelashes. Everybody said that. He touched my shoulder. "You've grown up to look so much like her—it's amazing." I held still and let him see Mom in me, if he wanted to. He brushed the back of his hand across one of my cheeks, then the other, and that scared me. Dad had never touched me like this before. His fingers felt stiff and cold. "I'm sorry that I let them chase you away," he said. "I should have stopped them. She would have stopped them."

"There wasn't much you could do," I said, which was true. Dad wasn't the kind of man who changed the course of things. "Anyway," I said, "I wanted to leave."

He shook his head as if he knew better. "A leaf blows off a tree and floats to the ground," he said. "Where it falls it thinks to itself—this is exactly where I wanted to land."

"Leaves don't think, Dad."

We listened as the wind outside rattled something loose on the house—the gutter maybe, or a rainspout. "It's the illusion of free will," he said. "Nobody can predict how things will turn out, so they say, 'That proves it, anything can happen'. But anything can't happen. We can't see where life's heading, but that doesn't mean it can go anywhere." He started tapping his thigh with his hand, which meant his mind was really humming now. "Do you know Nietzsche, Jake?"

"Never met him," I said, and Dad laughed at my joke.

"He was a philosopher, and he said that if you could stop the world and see how everything was for that exact moment, then you could predict life forever. It's just a matter of understanding all the variables." I fell back on my bed and closed my eyes, but Dad didn't get the hint that it was the middle of the night, not the best time for him to talk to me about this stuff. I had trouble keeping up with him during normal waking hours. "Nietzsche," Dad said, "understood chaos long before people made a theory out of it. A butterfly flaps its wings in Brazil," he said and snapped his fingers a few times to sound like flapping, "a few months later there's a hurricane in Florida. From a little cause can grow a large effect. You just have to know all of the little causes."

That sounded unlikely to me—the part about butterflies causing hurricanes—but I didn't want to get any deeper into chaos at two o'clock in the morning. "This is fascinating and all," I said, trying to coax him to the end of his thought, "but what do hurricanes and butterflies have to do with me running away?"

"Did you really choose to leave?"

I wanted to get out of New Hope to see the world for myself, not just read about it in Uncle Toby's books, so yeah, I chose to run. But it was their choice, too, because they were going to send me to a mental hospital and pump me with drugs so they could train me like some caged tiger. "Sort of," I said.

"It's always 'sort of'—all reasons and no reason." Dad stood up. "I like your room. It's a good place to think." I nodded that it was okay. "I slept here sometimes," he said, "while you were gone." He stood there as if forgetting what he was going to do next. His mind had led him into my room, into telling me about leaves blowing in the wind and butterflies flapping in Brazil, and then it had stopped, suspended, unable to go one thought further. The doctors said that wasn't unusual for someone who had undergone the trauma he had, watching Mom die. They figured those few minutes' worth of shock had wiped quite a few blank spaces into Dad's brain.

"I'll leave you alone," he said finally. But he stayed there, next to my bed. "You know, it's so dark in here you almost can't see your own hand." The door had swung shut behind him, blocking out the hall light. "I slept here with the door open," he said.

"I like the dark."

"That's good," he said as he opened the door wide now to let in the hall light. "You know, Jake, in my dreams, you never left."

Five

LOUD VOICES WOKE ME, JUST LIKE OLD TIMES. THE WHITE curtains blowing in from the wind off the Delaware reminded me where I was. I kicked away the top sheet and let the air chill my skin awake. A voice filtered up through the floorboards—it was Jenny trying to be convincing. I grabbed my jeans from the headpost and knelt behind the banister so I could see downstairs. There was Kris pulling Dad by his belt toward the door, as if getting him out of the house was the answer. I could have told her it never was before.

"I can't do it today," he said. "The world doesn't need another salesman." His hands were turning a black umbrella around and around.

"Stop talking like that," Jenny said. "You're selling books, and they're good for people who have the time to read them. Besides, somebody has to sell them. And you don't need that," she said, snatching the umbrella from him. "People don't trust a man carrying an umbrella in a little drizzle."

"I shouldn't go today," he said. "Jake's been away so long."

"It's Tuesday. You just had a long weekend with Memorial Day. You have to go back to work."

Dad took a deep breath. "You don't understand. It's killing me."

"A lot of people sell things everyday, and it doesn't kill them," she said. "Just talk easy to people. Get them on your side. You're a natural at it. You can sell anything."

She was outright lying now, and Dad knew it. He told me once that he hated even the idea of selling, that he felt like a thief with his hands in other people's pockets. It was Jenny who convinced him to try sales when she came to New Hope. He had been out of work since Mom's death and needed someone to tell him what to do.

Jenny met him once in town and moved right in. She took the bills that he'd been stuffing in the kitchen drawer for months and spread them out on the table to make him see he had to earn money doing something. She got him a job selling clocks in a shop in Peddler's Village, but time wasn't the best thing to surround Dad with. He lasted a week. Then he found a position at a Pontiac dealership, but it went out of business after three months, before he could move even one car off the lot. He sold encyclopedias from a booth in the mall for a while and then time-sharing condos by phone from home. He finally settled on the thing he enjoyed most in life, books—the classics. Still, he found it hard to take money from people. He always wanted them to own the books even if they couldn't afford them, so he made lots of sales at cost. The Great Books Co. didn't mind because he was only cutting out his own commission.

"It's the worst thing," he said to Jenny now, "having to sell yourself everyday." Mars, Dad's cat for as long as I had lived, jumped down from the front window ledge and fell over on the rug, begging for a rub. Dad got down on his knees to stretch Mars out by her paws and then blew into her white belly like he did to Kris when she was a baby. Mars never reacted, but Dad was sure she loved it.

"I know it's tough," Jenny said, which was an angle I hadn't heard her use before—sympathy. "I wouldn't ask you to go out today if we didn't need the money so much."

Dad lifted his face from Mars' fur. "People don't sit home waiting for me to come sell them these overpriced, gilt-edged books." He stood up and brushed the lint from his knees. "Most of them don't even know what *gilt-edged* means, so how are they going to understand what's inside?"

"That's not for you to worry about," Jenny said. "If they want the books, just sell them."

"They never want them," he said. "I have to persuade them, and I can't do that today." Kris stood underneath Dad now, holding onto his belt, waiting for something to happen. She looked like a calf in a herd of cows, just trying not to get stepped on. "I have to think about this," he said as he dragged her with him toward the chair at the bottom of the stairs. Jenny rushed behind him, afraid of him seated worst of all, beyond her strength to move him. He sat on her.

"Get off!" she said so loud that Kris covered her ears.

He jumped up and she did, too—she caught him leaning toward the door. She kept pushing as Kris opened the screen. They shoved Dad out of the house like an unwanted animal. Mars ran out, too, the banging screen just missing her tail. Jenny closed the front door and locked it. Then she pulled Kris to her, wrapping her arms around my sister's head. "He's a good man," Jenny said. "Your father just gets a little overwhelmed sometimes. It happens."

•

Hours later, I was just getting up when I heard a car pull into the driveway. I hurried into Kris' bedroom for a better view and saw a small foreign car parking under the maple. A woman got out. She wore a thin yellow dress. I couldn't see her face from that distance, but I figured it was the writer from New York. She stretched her arms over her head and then shut the car door. Mars ran out to investigate but got scared when the woman came closer and ran off. I hurried out to the hallway and crouched at the top of the steps.

Jenny was already at the front door when the woman got there. "Is this the Paine house?"

"Might be," Jenny said, unfriendly from the start. She didn't like unexpected things happening to her. She used to say that you couldn't imagine the trouble strangers can bring to your door, and usually did.

"My name is Larkin Daley," the woman said.

Jenny hated weird names like that and didn't give her own. "What do you want?" she snapped.

"May I come in?"

"If you're selling something, I'm sure I can't afford to buy it."

"No," the woman said, "I'm not selling anything. I'm a writer from New York, and I'd like to talk to you about your son."

"You mean Jake? What's he done?"

"Nothing wrong, if that's what you're asking," the woman said.

"Of course that's what I'm asking."

"Maybe he did something right."

Jenny laughed at that. "We're talking about Jake here?"

"It isn't possible that he did something good?"

"Everything's possible," Jenny said, "just don't bet the car on it." She opened the front screen enough to let Mars in. "What's anything he did have to do with you, anyway?"

"Nothing yet," the woman said. "I just read about him in the paper last week."

"There wasn't anything about him in the *Gazette*."

The woman smiled like Jenny had said something funny. "It was in the *News*, the *New York Daily News*—how he had run away for almost a year and now the police were sending him home."

"Lots of kids run away and come back when the thrill goes out of it."

"But Jake's case is a little different."

"Why's that?"

"Saving that homeless woman was quite a story in New York. It made people feel good about kids for a change."

"Who saved the woman?"

"Jake . . . you didn't know?"

"I wouldn't ask if I did," Jenny said.

"Then why don't I come in and tell you?"

The screen door scraped open, and I couldn't hear any more because Jenny led the woman to the kitchen and there was no way of listening to them without showing myself, which I didn't feel like doing at that moment.

•

"I suppose you heard everything," Jenny said to me when I came downstairs a half hour later. I stepped up next to her at the front window, watching the woman back up the driveway in her light blue Volvo.

"Not really," I said.

Jenny let the curtains fall back across our eyes. "You're a hero—that's what this lady says. They must be pretty desperate in New York to turn you into a hero."

I didn't much like Jenny talking about me like that, and I would have told her off, except she had a point. I hadn't saved the woman for her own sake anyway, even though

41

that's what everyone thought. I'd just been heading uptown to the park to sleep out, ready for a fight but not going out of my way to find one, which was the way you had to be in New York on a Saturday night. Most of the guys riding the trains around midnight were looking for action of some kind or another. The fight just happened to find me.

"She said she spoke to you."

"Not much, just for a minute at the bus station."

Jenny walked into the kitchen, knowing I would follow her. "She says she's got a publisher interested." Jenny picked out a tangerine from the shopping bag on top of the refrigerator and tossed it to me, then took one for herself. She hunted through the bag until she found a contest card and scraped away the gray circles with a spoon. "$10,000 Winner!" came up under the first spot and "$10,000 winner!" under the second, but "Free JOY" showed under the third. Jenny crumpled up the card and threw it back in the brown bag. "Just what I need," she said, "detergent. Once in my life I'd like to be an instant winner—I don't think that's too much to ask."

"What would you do if you won?" I said to get her thinking about something other than me.

"I'd buy food—raspberries, strawberries, steaks, lobster, real butter, real cream. We'd eat like everybody else in this country."

I could have told her I'd seen plenty of people eating worse than us. But Jenny liked to think we were as bad off as anybody. We leaned over the kitchen sink together, peeling the bruised skins off our tangerines. "They want her to write the story fast," Jenny said, getting back to the woman, "while people in New York still remember you."

"Write it where?"

"In a book."

"Who wants to read about me saving some penny-eating street lady?"

Jenny shrugged that she didn't understand it either. "I don't suppose you'd mind your story being told like that, for anybody to read." She spread open her tangerine and sucked some slices of it into her mouth.

"I don't care, I guess."

"She's willing to pay $2,000 if you talk to her."

"Pay me $2,000?"

"Pay us."

"I don't have anything to tell her worth that much."

"She seems to think you do. I'd say she knows exactly what she's doing."

"So you think I should talk to her?"

"If it was me, I'd head the other direction from a woman like that. But you, maybe it makes no difference."

I didn't say anything because I didn't know if it did make a difference to me or not.

"You know," Jenny said, "I almost didn't get your father out to work today."

"You mean because I'm back?"

"That's right," she nodded. Jenny always said straight out what she was thinking, even if it made you feel rotten.

•

By dinnertime, Dad hadn't come home. Jenny held off putting food on the table and kept looking out the front window every time a car went by. I was in the living room playing with Dad's short wave, trying to get Radio Argentina, his favorite Spanish station.

"You know why he isn't home, don't you?" Jenny said to me at eight o'clock when she finally put the cold meat loaf and stewed tomatoes on the table. I nodded that I knew. Dad had an old doctor friend from college who could get him into Doylestown Medical any time he needed some shots of lithium. They'd been in Vietnam together, and he owed Dad, although we never knew exactly why. Dad would only say that he had an open account when it came to lithium. He'd just phone in to his friend, and a few hours later they'd pump him with the drug, trying to knock his brain out of depression or whatever rut it happened to be in.

"He hasn't gone for a treatment in nearly a year," Jenny said. "The new medicine he's on has been helping him." It wasn't hard to figure out her meaning. I turned the knob on the short wave just slightly so the sound was all static. Jenny hated static. She took it as long as she could and then disappeared from the doorway.

By the next night, we still hadn't heard from him. Jenny didn't bother to call anyone because she knew that, by the old pattern, he would be home by dinner. She made lamb, her favorite. She always treated herself when she was angry. She put out Grandma Paine's handmade tablecloth and the few pieces of real silver left from her old wedding set. She opened some red wine, a bottle that had lost its label. She poured for herself, then for me and Kris. She'd given us sips of wine before, but this time she filled our glasses.

"A toast to our family," she said, holding out her glass, "such as it is." Kris and I started to drink, but Jenny yelled "No!" so loud that her hand shook and spilled wine onto the tablecloth. She rubbed the red spot slowly with her finger as if she was trying to rub it in rather than out. "You have to clink your glasses first," she said, holding hers out again, "or else the toast won't come true." I touched mine to hers and Kris did the same. "Now you may drink," Jenny said.

We drank and ate for an hour. The lamb was over-cooked, like all Jenny's meats. But there were two loaves of day-old French bread and plenty of butter that Jenny brought home from The Logan when she finished work each day. Kris smeared the hard bread with butter, then poured packets of sugar on it and crunched away. It was her favorite dinner.

By eight o'clock, Jenny's head was so swimming in wine that she couldn't hold it up any longer. She laid her head down on the table, next to her plate, and began to sleep.

•

A taxi brought Dad home.

He came through the front door and said "hello" very low as if he didn't want to disturb whatever we were doing without him. He walked around the table to kiss Kris on her forehead and his Phillies cap fell onto her plate. Dad picked it up and put it on again. He was blinking fast, waiting for us to do something. He looked back and forth at Kris and me, trying to get a reaction. We didn't have any to give him. "I had an errand to do," he said, as if that could explain why he was a day late for dinner. "Lamb?" he said, trying to figure out what the occasion was.

Jenny lifted herself up with the importance of a great animal rising from the grass. The color came back to her face. Her eyes widened. Her mouth opened. "You gave in again," she said slowly, her mind running faster than her tongue could form the words, "didn't you?"

He nodded and picked up a chunk of lamb that had fallen on the tablecloth. He threw the piece toward the meat plate and wiped his hands on Kris' napkin. Then he strung out my sister's hair in his hands. "Your daddy's home now," he said softly to her. "Everything's okay. You go upstairs to bed."

Kris ran off as Jenny rose to her feet. "We waited for you," she said, "waited for what?" She moved within a foot of him and grabbed the lapels of his jacket to hold herself up. "We waited for nothing."

He didn't have any excuse for her. He backed away from the table and saw me. He drew the armchair, his chair, up close to me and sat down. "Jake," he whispered, "you understand, don't you?" Jenny banged her elbow down onto the table, rattling the plates, reminding him that she was watching as she sank back into her seat. He inched nearer to me, closing off her view of our faces. The sharp bones of his knees pressed against my legs. "Your old man's a failure," he confessed to me, as if I didn't already know that. "Failure is like a broken record, Jake—around and around you go," he said as if it were a lullaby, "always in the same groove, until something knocks you out of it."

My father was explaining the failure of his life over a dinner table full of things half-eaten. I'd heard this speech before as a kid sitting on his lap—no fairy tales of bears or fucking princes, just drugs and shock treatments and broken records. "I need the lithium," he said loud enough for her to hear, "it's better than a shock treatment. Afterward, I don't . . . think so hard on things." He was sweating from the forehead. Tears fell down his cheeks. The skin of his neck rolled

45

over his shirt collar. I looked at these things so as not to have to look in his eyes again.

He always made me look at him. He would search for me all over the house or chase me down at the river or tackle me in the backyard as if we were playing football like other dads did with their kids. Then he'd hold me at arm's length and say, "I'm not much of a father, I know that. Your old man's a failure." Even when he was young, before he actually became a failure, he said he could feel it swelling up inside of him ready to take over his life.

Then it did, on a blindingly sunny afternoon on a part of road he had driven a thousand times before. He said he was thinking of some lines from a Ginsberg poem: "A nice day in the Universe . . . sun shines today as it never shone before and never will again." He was admiring the Universe, he told me later, and didn't see it until too late—a red squirrel dashing from the brush into the road, then freezing there, just a dark spot on the asphalt ahead. Dad swerved, the Buick skidded sideways, and Mom's side took the direct hit against a telephone pole. Sitting in the backseat, all I could wonder was, why had Dad swerved like that?

He sat back in his chair now as I punched his shoulder a little to show that he was an okay father. He looked at Jenny, slumped on the table. She was breathing hard. "I really do it for her," he said quietly, so as not to rouse her, "I try to be what she wants." He pushed up the sleeves of his white shirt and then locked his hands behind his head, holding it up. "I gave up cigarettes," he said, "and I started jogging up the road just before you came back. I've tried to get better." I shrugged, which was wrong for him, so I nodded a little encouragement and sort of smiled. "I take the pill she wants. Everyday she asks me, 'Did you take your Prozac'?" Dad's voice went high, the voice Jenny used with Kris. "I've taken it, but I don't feel better," he said. "Sometimes I feel worse, as if I'm going through life without really knowing I'm living. That drug makes her feel better, not me." He stared at me with watery eyes. "If I didn't take lithium," he said, "I know they'd put me through the shock treatment again, and I couldn't stand that." He starting blinking fast, remembering those times when Jenny took him to the hospital. "They say it only takes a minute and it's painless, but then why was I screaming? I know I was screaming," he said, shaping it like a sphere with his hands, as if a scream were solid and round and could be held. "But you can't hear yourself, and you think you must be dead. You wonder if maybe this is death. How could you know? And do they know? Can they see you're still alive, or do you seem dead to them, too?" He was leaning so close to me that I was breathing in the same air that he was breathing out. His breath smelled like peppermint. He was suddenly very loud, losing control of his story. "Don't ever let them do that to you, Jake. Don't let them!" He stood up and closed around me, his elbows on my shoulders, the voice almost gone from him, just faint words at my ears. "You know, Jake, you're my only son, and you're just like me."

I threw his arms off me. "Don't say that. I'm not like you." I shook his shoulders and his head bounced up and back, an involuntary yes. "Don't ever say that again." Jenny's eyes widened as my voice got loud.

The lines on Dad's cheeks tightened, making him look older than I'd ever seen him. "You are like me," he whispered.

"No," I shouted and shoved him back into his chair so hard that it fell backwards and rolled him head over heels onto the rug. He crouched there shielding his face with his arms, as if expecting me to hit him. That scared me all of a sudden, seeing my father scared of me.

•

Someone ran past my door and into the bathroom at the end of the hall. There was a choking sound, coughing, silence for a minute, then crying. I got out of bed and saw that it was 1:25 on the alarm clock. I grabbed my shorts off the wall hook and pulled them on as I stepped into the hall. My parents' door was closed as usual. Kris' door was wide open.

In the bathroom I found my little sister crouched on the floor, her hands circling the rim of the dark red toilet bowl.

She looked up at me, her face wet from tears and cold sweat. "I feel terrible inside," she said, "worse than I ever did."

"It's the wine. Your stomach isn't used to it. You'll feel better after you throw up."

"But I get scared throwing up," she said, "because I won't stop and my insides will come out and then I'll die."

"Nobody ever died from throwing up. You have to get the sickness out of you, and throwing up is the way to do it. I've thrown up hundreds of times," I said, "so I should know." Actually, I'd almost never thrown up in my life—even after eating the worms—so I didn't know anything about it except by watching other people do it. In the shelters, there were lots of guys gagging up their insides. None of them ever died that I saw, although they looked like they wished they would.

Kris gripped the bowl, ready to give it a try. I pulled her back a little by the shoulders. "Relax and take a deep breath, it's easier that way."

She did, took a few deep breaths. "That feels better," she said. "Maybe I don't have to throw up really."

She started to get up but I pulled her back to the toilet. "Yes you do. Put your finger on the tip of your tongue and slide it back."

She stuck two fingers in, slid them back, and a second later the sickness rattled up through her body. I held her bending over the bowl and pulled her hair away from her face as the vomit poured out of her. She leaned back on her heels after a minute, then got up to go. I stopped her at the sink and turned on the cold water for her to wash her face and mouth. She toweled off fast and smiled up at me. Then she reached up with her hands to pull my face down to her. She kissed my cheek, and that made me feel like a big brother again.

Six

SCRATCHING WOKE ME. MY EYES OPENED TO SEE MARS LUNGING at me from the floor. I turned my head fast enough that her claws landed in my hair instead of my face. I tried to shake the stupid cat off, but she held on until I gave up and relaxed. Then she retracted her claws and began to purr. When I rolled over she licked my cheeks. Her breath smelled of fresh tuna. Dad always made sure Mars ate well.

"You got me again," I said as I lifted the fifteen-pound calico off me to the floor. She left my room with her tail sticking high in the air.

I jumped out of bed and the house felt empty to me, like a place where no one lived. I didn't bother pulling shorts on and walked down to the bathroom. Dad's razor was lying out on the sink next to a can of shaving cream. Jenny had obviously gotten him up and out somewhere. After a treatment Dad would always do what she told him, as long as he didn't have to go to work. She knew he needed stimulation after taking lithium or else he might sink into the living room couch for weeks, which he'd done before.

I turned on the radio sitting on the bathroom windowsill and switched stations until I found some techno music to wake my brain. I sprayed the shaving cream into my hands and lathered up. The sharp blade of Dad's razor felt good on my skin even though I didn't have much of anything to scrape off. I slapped some water on my face and turned—there was my sister standing in the doorway. "Kris," I said as I grabbed a towel around my waist, "what are you doing?"

"Just looking," she said.

"Well you shouldn't be looking."

"Daddy says it's a free country, so I can watch you shave, if I want to."

I gave her a fierce look, which didn't seem to scare her, and left the bathroom. She followed me to my room and squeezed in before I could shut the door. "Jenny will kill me if she finds you here like this," I said. "You're not even supposed to talk to me, remember?"

Kris picked up a book from the fireplace and rubbed the cover, a raised picture of a lion, against her cheek. "Mom took it back about being alone with you. And she's not here anyway. Nobody is. You're supposed to watch me."

"Who told you that?"

"She did. She said, 'If he ever wakes up, tell him he's babysitting you.' Then she took Daddy to get the car where he left it, and after that they're picking up her check at The Logan and going for food."

I stepped behind my closet door and pulled on a white tank shirt and shorts. "Why can't you watch yourself?"

"'Cause I'm seven."

"That's old enough," I said. "You should be taking care of yourself and not sneaking up on people. And anyway, this is Friday—how come you're not in school?"

"Mom says I'm sick 'cause I threw up last night."

"How'd she know that?"

"I told her."

"Well, you're not sick."

Kris shrugged that it didn't make any difference to her and went to the window. "There's a man out there."

"What man?"

She shrugged again. "He's been there since Mom and Dad left. I've been watching him the whole time you were sleeping to make sure he doesn't do anything."

"Like what?" I said. She squeezed her lips tight, which she always did when she was thinking hard, but couldn't come up with anything. I looked out the window. The sun was high and hot already, the kind of day when I used to ditch school and explore along the Delaware. There was no man. "You're seeing things," I told Kris.

She grabbed my arm. "Come look from my room." She led me down the hall and made me sneak into her room along the wall. She peeked through the curtain, then told me to. There in the middle of the driveway was some old guy leaning against our maple tree. He had a pad in his hand, like maybe he was drawing the house. He didn't look scary to me.

"Forget him," I said and headed downstairs.

The kitchen smelled of something burnt. In the sink

were a couple of black pieces of toast soaking in a bowl of water.

"I drowned them," Kris said, creeping up at my elbow, "so Mom wouldn't make me eat them later."

I looked around for something fast for breakfast, but there weren't any bananas or raisins or even cereal. The strawberry jam jar sat open on the counter with a spoon in it, so I scooped out some and ate it. "That's what I did, too," Kris said.

"Didn't Jenny feed you this morning?"

"She was in a hurry, and Daddy wasn't moving very fast."

The doorbell rang, and we looked at each other because that didn't happen very often in this house. "It's him," Kris said, "let's hide."

"You don't hide from people in your own house. Come on."

We walked down the hallway, and Kris slipped her hand in mine. Her fingers felt warm and small. I opened the door, and on the other side of the screen was an odd-looking man with black-rimmed glasses. He smiled—or at least that's what I think he was doing. "I'm Bill Kinnert," he said, "from the *Gazette*."

Kris poked him in the stomach. "We could arrest you for watching our house."

The man looked down on her as if surprised that she could talk. He probably didn't have kids of his own. "I was making some notes before coming in," he explained to me. "I'd like to speak with you for a few minutes."

"What for?"

"How about if I come in and tell you?"

I let him inside and shook the hairy hand he held out. He bent over to shake Kris' hand, too, and the top of his head was bald, like he was wearing a little round cap of skin. Kris put her hands behind her back, and Kinnert stood up.

"We can go in the living room," I said. "It's the coolest place in the morning."

"Do you have air conditioning?" Kris asked as the three of us sat down on the sofa. "We don't."

"Yes, I do." Kinnert was breathing heavily, his cheeks puffed out like a blowfish sucking air.

"You're sweating," Kris said, pointing to his white shirt and wrinkling her nose. He loosened his collar.

"Go upstairs now," I told her, "and I'll do something with you in a few minutes."

"Okay," she said, "'cause talking's boring."

Kinnert waited until we could hear her reach the second floor, and then he said, "I guess you know why I'm here."

"Not really."

"You left New Hope pretty suddenly, right after the incident . . . at the canal, I mean."

"So?"

"That was a big story in New Hope, and you were part of it. People would be interested in knowing where you've been, what you've been doing, and what you're planning to do."

"I'm not planning to attack anybody, if that's what they're worried about."

"I didn't say anyone was worried."

"That's what you meant."

Kinnert pushed his glasses down his nose and wrote something on his pad. "Why did you run away?"

Suddenly I remembered him, the reporter with the weird voice that went up and down like he was practicing notes for a song. I remembered his little black mustache, too, which looked like it was penciled in for some bit part at The Playhouse in town. Kinnert was the first to get to me outside school the day after the attack, and I answered him without even knowing who he was. Then he was waiting outside the police station when I was taken in for questioning, and he snapped my picture like I was some big-time criminal being locked away forever. But since I was only fifteen at the time, the *Gazette* could only use a shadowy side picture that didn't show my face. That seemed stupid to me, since everyone in town knew it was me.

Now Kinnert was inside my house asking me what horrible crime I was going to commit next. He was such a little guy that I could have picked him up and thrown him through the front window. But that would be giving him what he wanted—a great story about "Crazy Violent Teen Menace Jake Paine."

"You wrote all about me before, didn't you?" I said, standing up so that he could see I was big enough to kick his ass, if I wanted to. "You knew what was happening around here. You knew why I had to leave." Suddenly I thought of Dad's leaf, floating wherever the wind would take it. But I didn't feel like a leaf. I felt more like a toy missile bouncing off the walls and ceiling and floor at all crazy angles until it lost its energy. You couldn't know where it was going to hit next, but you knew it was going to hit somewhere.

"You weren't charged," Kinnert said, rubbing under his lip. "You were never brought to trial, never proven guilty, so what were you afraid of?"

"I didn't say I was afraid."

"Then why did you run away?"

He hadn't changed. He would always come back to a question he had asked before, the one you didn't want to answer. "Lots of people still thought I did the stuff at the canal," I said. "They blamed me and wanted me out of town."

"Why do you think that is?" he asked me in his stupid voice, as if he really didn't know.

"Because they need somebody to blame for everything. That makes them feel better, like nothing is their fault."

"But why was it you so often? Why did people blame you in particular?"

"I'm different. It's easy to blame somebody like me."

Kinnert clicked his pen point in and out, in and out until I was ready to grab it from him and smash it under my foot. "Your father," he said, "how are things going for him?"

"Same as they ever were."

"You mean as bad as they ever were?"

"There's nothing wrong with him."

Kinnert laughed a little. "I'd say that's a matter of opinion in this town."

"I'm telling you my father's fine."

He checked some notes on his pad. "You know that he kept protesting at the construction site for months after everyone gave up, don't you? Some people say he started the fire."

"That place should have burned down," I said, "but he didn't do it," I added quickly, in case Kinnert thought I was admitting something. "My dad sticks to things he believes in."

"Do you know that he still gets picked up by the police for looking in people's windows along the canal, and—"

"I'm not talking about him anymore."

"And he follows women around town if they're wearing fur. He tries to scare them out of New Hope."

That was a new trick for Dad. I could just picture him stalking the rich women walking down Main Street, their mink coats flapping in the wind. Suddenly they'd feel someone a little too close to them. They'd glance around and see his wild eyes, his blank stare. He'd mutter something too low for them to hear. They'd ask him what he said. He'd mutter again. They'd try to walk away from him, but he'd walk faster. Finally they'd run to their car and drive themselves away from New Hope forever. Dad could do that to a person.

Kinnert reached over to the end table by the sofa to grab a picture. He blew dust off the glass and held the frame in front of my eyes. It was a picture of me, age twelve, just back from the river. My hair was wet. My eyes were wide, as if looking for something. My mouth was grinning. "What about this kid," he said. "What happened to him?"

It was a trick question. I was supposed to answer fast and say something strange that he could put in his story. "That's just one second of how I was four years ago," I told him. "That's not me now or even then."

Kinnert kept the picture staring at me. "Are you afraid of being happy again?"

That question surprised me. Being happy wasn't anything I normally thought about. Sometimes I liked feeling good, but that meant getting pounded on vodka and beer, or maybe some weed. "Being happy," I told Kinnert, "isn't my goal in life."

"What is your goal?"

I thought of a bumper sticker I saw once that made a lot of sense to me. It said: "Whatever."

"Whatever?" Kinnert repeated. "That's not a very specific goal, is it?" I shrugged—he could see it that way if he wanted to. He put my picture back on the end table. "You realize you scare people, don't you?"

"Like you?"

He looked in my eyes for as long as he could. "No, not me. But some people in New Hope—they don't know what you'll do next. That scares them."

"Maybe I don't know either."

He nodded at that possibility and wrote it down.

•

Jenny was the first to see the story.

She burst through the front door Monday afternoon, shaking the newspaper in her hand. Mars ran for cover behind the sofa, and Kris followed after her. Dad tried to get Jenny to stop yelling so that we could figure out what was wrong.

I could tell she was stirred up about me again, and I headed for the stairs, but she grabbed my arm at the landing. "Look at this!" she said, opening the *Gazette* for Dad and me to see. "I was walking past the stack of newspapers outside The Logan, and there it is on page one—our house!" She held the paper in front of my face. Our house was spread across half of the page, with a small picture of me cut into the roof, as if that's where I'd been hiding out. It was the same photo the *Gazette* had run before—the one Kinnert took outside the police station—but this time my face wasn't blacked out. The flash had surprised my eyes wide open, and I looked like a moron laughing. The headline read: "Runaway Boy Returns Home After 10 Months." Underneath the photo, the caption said, "Jake Paine tells New Hope: 'I don't know what I'll do next.'"

"You were supposed to keep quiet for awhile," Jenny said as her hands twisted the paper into shreds. "You were supposed to blend in, maybe get a job." That was news to me. I would have run off again before working in New Hope—but it didn't seem like the time to say that. "But no," Jenny continued, "you go and talk to a reporter. How can you be so stupid?"

55

"He just came around and asked a few questions," I said. "I didn't know he was going to make a big story of it."

Jenny hurled the paper across the room. The *Gazette* hit the wall and fell behind the sofa. "What did you think, that he just stopped by to talk?"

She had a point there. "Guess not," I said.

"I could strangle you," she said, and that must have sounded like a good idea to her when she heard it because her hands flew at my neck. Her fingernails drew blood before Dad could pull her off me. "You should do something," she yelled at him. "I shouldn't have to." Dad let go of her, and I covered my neck in case she attacked again. "You should start acting like his father," she said. Dad looked at her and I did, too. "Look at *him*," she said, still shaking.

He looked at me as if he didn't think I'd turned out so bad, considering. He put his hands in his pockets. "Strangling him isn't going to teach him to behave," Dad said, like I was some dog they were trying to train. "Jake did what he felt was right at the time. You can't change someone from doing that." That sounded better—Dad speaking up for me.

Jenny didn't want to hear it. "Something's got to change him," she said. "We can't live like before. I can't take it, I really can't." She stopped ranting for a moment, and it shocked me—Jenny's eyes had tears in them. I knew I should feel sorry for upsetting her, but it made me feel sort of good that I could hurt her that much. Dad just kept staring at her. When Jenny saw she wasn't getting the reaction she wanted from us, she blinked a couple of times, and suddenly her eyes were dry. "Maybe you two don't care," she said, "but I work in town, I know people. What am I supposed to say—'I'm not really Jake's mother, you know. He's not my mistake.'"

Her words hung out there between us for a moment like some heavy puff of smoke that has no place to disappear to because the air is already so thick. Dad grabbed her by both arms and held her still. "Don't talk about her," he said in a low rumbling voice that I'd never heard from him before, kind of like Mars' growl when you hold her up in the air for too long. "Don't ever talk about her!"

Jenny nodded that she understood, seeing the red of his eyes and feeling the strength of his hands on her arms.

•

Next morning, Dad retrieved the *Gazette* from behind the sofa and insisted I sit next to him in the living room to read the Police Blotter. It was his favorite section. He had this idea that the local police notes revealed all you needed to know about a place.

He wasn't wearing a shirt this morning, just a pair of gray shorts and the moccasins Sam gave him one Christmas. Dad obviously wasn't planning to go out to sell the classics today. The lithium was still lingering in his mind.

He held together the torn strips of paper. "May 29," he read, "3 pm: An Aquetong Road resident reported a skunk in her driveway with its head stuck in a bottle. Police were unable to get close enough to save the skunk, so they shot it."

I nodded that the story was pretty odd, humoring Dad so that he wouldn't start lecturing me about Jenny. "You don't understand the point, do you?" he said, letting the paper fall to his lap. He hadn't shaved yet. Sometimes when he didn't go to work he wouldn't shave until right before dinner, and only then because Jenny wouldn't put food on the table until he did. He looked kind of wild even with just a day's beard.

"Sure I understand," I said. "They shot the skunk to save it from suffocating."

"That's stupid," Kris said, popping up from behind Jenny's big yellow chair where neither of us had seen her. She was wearing a paper headband with a little bird's feather stuck in the back. "I'm practicing sneaking like an Indian," she said. Jenny called from the kitchen for her to come eat her breakfast so she could drive her to school, but my sister didn't move.

"Is it stupid?" Dad asked me. He wanted me to say yes. He always wanted me to agree with him that things were stupid, or crazy, or unbelievable.

"Yeah," I said. "The skunk was stupid for sticking his

57

head in a bottle, and he would have sprayed the cops if they'd tried to yank him out."

"The point," Dad said, "is that people are so afraid of how a skunk smells that they'd rather shoot him than try to save him, and then they pretend that's the humane thing to do. Sometimes," he said, "I wish I weren't human." That seemed to me a pretty strong thing to say over one stupid skunk getting snuffed out, but that was my father. He always took the animal's view of the situation.

"Dad," I said, shaking the paper to get his attention. "I've been looking around the house. Everything's broken or rotting. There are holes in the porch, and Kris' window doesn't open, which is a fire trap, isn't it? And the ceiling in my room looks like it's going to cave in on me some night."

"Things fall apart," he said. "That shouldn't surprise you. You've seen the world—it's disintegrating, isn't it?"

"We're not talking about the world, just this fucking house."

He waved his hand at me. "Your sister is in the room," he whispered. I pointed to the ceiling above him, and he looked at the long cracks in the paint as if seeing them for the first time. "Grandpa didn't set the beams well," Dad said, "he was a bus driver, not a builder. You could paint that ceiling a dozen times and it would still crack like that."

"What about the windows that won't open, and the fireplace that doesn't work, and the wallpaper that doesn't stay on the wall?" The yellowed columns of purple corsage boxes were peeling behind Jenny's chair. Kris took a piece about two feet long and pressed it back into position. When she let go, it flapped down again. Wherever I looked, there was something else in the room that needed repairing. In the corner, pieces of wood were piled up, what used to be a chair. The back support was broken off from the seat and it leaned upside down against the TV. I went over and picked up a few pieces, holding them out so he had to see them.

"I let things fix themselves around here," Dad said. That was news to me, or maybe I had just never noticed before that things stayed broken in our house forever. "Like the TV," he said. "We could get a picture but no sound for a month until Jenny kicked it just right. We didn't pay a cent.

If it wants to work around here, it will. Or we'll do without it."

"Some things need a little help," I said, "like this chair." I pointed to the pieces of old mahogany. "You expect this wood to fix itself?"

"I never expect anything good to happen," Dad said, "and you shouldn't either."

Seven

A WEEK AFTER HIS LITHIUM TREATMENT, DAD WAS BACK TO reading some of his Great Books, which meant that he was getting interested in life again, at least the made-up side of it. "Listen to this," he called to us from his lounge chair on the back patio. Jenny was yanking weeds, loosening the slabs of slate as she did it, then stamping them back down with her canvas shoes. Every once in awhile she took them off and shook the dirt out, staring at Dad as she did. She wanted him to help but wouldn't ask him to, because that way she could be angry at him. Kris was playing jacks on the only piece of slate that wasn't cracked yet. I was just back from the mailbox, holding the one letter sent to us that day. My name and address were written on the envelope in red crayon. "'A sturdy Cossack,'" Dad read, "'nicknamed Lushnia, knocked Prokoffey's head against the wall and exhorted him: Don't make a sound, not a sound, you're all right. We shan't touch you, but we're going to trample your wife into the ground.'"

Dad closed his book and set it in the grass. "Interesting, isn't it?" he said. "The Cossack tells Prokoffey not to worry, they aren't going to hurt him. All they're going to do is trample his wife to death."

"Yeah, Dad," I said, "that is interesting about the wife getting stomped on."

Jenny tore out a weed and threw the clump of dirt over her shoulder. "William," she said, "why don't you go get us Chinese food for dinner?"

Dad wanted to read more to us about the absurdity of life, but it wasn't often Jenny said we could afford Chinese. So he took the $20 bill she was holding out and left through the backyard gate.

"That letter for you?" she said as soon as he was gone.

"Yeah, it is."

"Kind of odd," she said, "you getting mail after just coming back. You didn't get any letters while you were gone."

I opened the envelope in front of her to show I wasn't worried about what might be inside. "It's a welcome back letter," I told her, which was sort of true. In crayon again, it said: "Welcome home, Scum. When you least expect it . . . "

Jenny sat back on her heels, rubbing the sweat from her face with her apron. "Who's it from?"

"Just somebody in town," I said. I didn't have to say any more, because we both knew the letter meant trouble, either sooner or later.

•

Dad took a long while getting the food. Jenny had time to finish weeding, wash up and put the colored plates out on the kitchen table. She poured milk for him, saying as she always did that it turned her stomach to watch him drink it with eggrolls. Kris sat in her chair with her knife in one hand and fork in the other. She was ready to eat.

Dad came in after an hour and a half, holding two paper bags to his chest. They were soaked through with sauce on the bottom, and his blue shirt was stained brown. Jenny rushed to meet him at the front door and took the food to the sink. He took off his shirt and tossed it toward the back hallway where the clothes hamper was squeezed in.

Jenny tasted a forkful. "It's stone cold," she said and turned on the stove. "Where have you been all this time?"

"Chang's was crowded," Dad said.

"At this time of day?" Jenny asked. She knew there had to be more to the story.

Dad shrugged. After a minute he added, "I met someone on the way, someone Jake knows."

"Who's that?" Jenny asked when I didn't.

"The policeman—Alvin Decker."

Jenny shuddered at the name and I did, too. Decker was one guy who could make your skin crawl just thinking about him. The day after the canal attack he picked me up as I was coming out of Now and Then Records. Luckily, I'd paid for the CD in my hand. He told his partner to take a walk, and then he slapped his fat arm over my face until I couldn't breathe. Later, when they couldn't make the charge against me stick, Decker looked bad. The *Gazette* called it a clear case of sloppy investigating.

Jenny loaded up a tray with the cardboard boxes of food. "That'll burn," Dad said.

"No it won't," she answered him in just as sure a voice.

"You can't put paper in the oven."

"Watch me," she said and did.

Kris banged her fork on the table. "I'm starving," she said. Dad found the fortune cookies soaked inside a bag and handed us each one. Kris bit into her cookie and pulled the slip of paper from her mouth. "'Every Long Journey,' she read, with Dad helping on the word *journey*, "'Begins with a Single Step.' What's that mean?" she asked.

"It means you won't go anywhere if you don't try," Jenny said, looking at Dad. He didn't seem to notice her meaning, being intent now on his own particular fortune. Jenny shook her head at her message and tossed it into the sink.

Kris tapped my arm. "Read yours."

I yanked the paper from my cookie and read: "'There Is Never Enough Time for Someone Who Keeps Checking His Watch.'" Since I never wore a watch, I figured that must mean I had all the time in the world.

"Listen to this," Dad said: "'You Will Feel an Arrow Through Your Heart.'"

Jenny took the paper from him and turned it over to see if the real message was on the other side. It wasn't. "'You Will Feel an Arrow Through Your Heart,'" she read again.

"Whose heart?" Kris asked him.

"Mine, I guess," Dad said as he rubbed his bare chest.

"Somebody's going to shoot an arrow at you?" Kris asked.

"No," Dad laughed, "don't worry, I'm sure it's just a bad translation, probably left over from Valentine's Day. These fortunes don't really come true anyway. They're just for fun."

•

It was still early after eating, not even five o'clock, as Kris pulled me by the arm to her room to play Truth, a game she had learned at school. I stomped with her up the stairs as if we were marching, and the pounding of our heels on the wood echoed through the house. She shoved her stuffed rabbits and plastic building blocks under her bed to give us room under the window. We had to sit cross-legged, she said, facing each other. Then we had to say something important about ourselves and hold our hands out, palms pressed together.

"Then what do we do?" I said.

Kris looked at me as if that were obvious. "You guess whether it's truth or not."

"You mean whether you're telling the truth or not?"

"Yeah, like if I say, 'I hate horses,' you say false, but that's too easy."

"Okay," I said, "you go first."

She thought for a second, laughed a little, and then put her hands out for me to touch. "Two boys kissed me on the playground last week."

"Truth," I said.

She shook her head. "It was three boys, so I won."

"Okay, so that's how you want to play."

"Now it's your turn. Go ahead."

I looked around the room for something to jog my thinking, but there wasn't much to see, just bare white walls. There weren't any posters, even of horses. "You don't have anything on your walls, Kris, no pictures at all."

"That's too easy," she said, "truth."

"I wasn't playing the game, I was just talking about your room."

She put her hands out to touch mine. "Come on and play."

"Okay, let's see—I wish I had a million dollars."

"Truth," she yelled, and I shook my head. "You can't lie about it," she said. "You have to tell the truth if it is."

"It isn't," I said.

"But everyone wants a million dollars."

"Not me. If you have a million bucks you just have a million things to worry about. I only want enough money to buy a car so I can drive anywhere I want to."

"My turn," my sister said. She bit on her fist. "I know where a gun is."

"Truth," I said right away, because I'd found the gun, too, exploring the house at her age. It was wrapped in a ragged red towel, sitting on the top shelf of Dad's closet.

"Yeah," Kris said, disappointed that she hadn't fooled me. "Your turn."

"Wait a second. About the gun—you didn't take it down, did you?"

"Not all the way," she said. "I just unwrapped it to take a look, and I pointed it once at me in the mirror, like it wasn't me, but somebody who wanted to shoot me. Then I put it back."

"Krissy, listen to me. Don't touch the gun again. You understand?" I pinched her shoulders to make her remember what I was saying.

"That hurts," she said and wiggled out of my grasp.

"It's supposed to, so you won't forget." It was a lesson I learned in school once, about some people long ago who didn't have a written language. The elders beat the children as they watched a great event so they would always remember it. That was the only history they had, and it seemed to me that was all anybody would ever need. "I mean it," I told Kris, pinching her arm again. "Don't touch the gun."

"I won't," she promised. "It's no fun just holding it, anyway. I can shoot it, I bet."

"I said don't touch it."

"Okay, it's your turn."

"I'm going to run away again," I said, and I didn't know why because I wasn't thinking about it, unless I was thinking about it without knowing it.

Kris pulled her hands away from mine and rolled over onto my legs, staring up at me backwards. "If you ran away," she said, "I won't have a brother again, right?" I nodded that that was sort of true. At least she wouldn't feel like she had a brother. "Then you can't," she said. "That's false."

"Okay," I said, though I wasn't so sure, "you're right."

"My turn." She stuck her tongue out and sucked on it a minute. Then she blurted out, "Mom kissed a man that wasn't Daddy."

"Truth," I said, figuring Kris wouldn't say it if it weren't. She nodded and looked at me like she'd said something very bad and wanted to tell me more. "What man?" I asked her.

She got to her feet and ran to close the door. "I walked into town one time to give Mom a message. Daddy wanted her to bring home a book from the library—he wrote the name down so I wouldn't forget it. I went in The Logan from the back where the kitchen is—nobody heard me 'cause I was sneaking like I shouldn't be there. Then I saw Mom, she was kissing him."

"Kissing who?"

"The man, he works there cooking and gives me money for ice cream to get rid of me."

"How were they kissing?"

Kris stood next to me, not much taller than me sitting down. She threw her arms around my neck and sunk her lips into my face, biting a little. "That's how," she said.

"You didn't say anything, did you?" She shook her head. "Don't play truth about it anymore," I said. "And especially don't tell Dad."

"Okay," she said, feeling special that she knew something that she couldn't tell anyone else in the world.

Eight

THE PHONE RANG, AND AS USUAL, NOBODY WENT TO ANSWER IT. Kris was on the front porch juggling crab apples. Dad was lying on the floor in the living room with his earphones on and eyes closed, listening to his Spanish tapes. Jenny hated when he fell into one of his Spanish periods because he could go hours without speaking English in the house. Sometimes he wouldn't answer us until we tried talking in the little Spanish we had picked up from him. I was sitting on the staircase packing rope, a flashlight, gloves, a canteen, and other supplies into the old Army knapsack that Uncle Toby had sent me.

After the fourth or fifth ring, Jenny leaned over the railing upstairs and yelled, "Somebody get that!" So I did, even though the last few times I'd answered there was just breathing on the line.

"Jake?" the voice said after I said hello.

"Yep."

"This is Frank."

Frankie—I'd figured he'd be the first one to call me, maybe the only one. He'd want to know why I had run off without telling him or taking him. He'd want to know what I'd been doing and how everything felt and what I was going to do next. He used to ask me questions like that all the time.

The first time I ever spoke to Frankie I was hanging from the cross support under the New Hope Bridge, feeling the vibrations in my arms as the cars rumbled overhead. I almost lost my grip when I saw him leaning out over the railing looking down at me. He didn't say anything, just waved. Frankie turned up a lot like that in the beginning. I'd be rummaging through the gym lockers for some extra money or hiding out behind the cafeteria catching a smoke and suddenly I'd feel watched. I'd look around, and he'd wave.

Frankie was a grade younger than me at school, but I still knew who he was. Everybody knew everybody at No

Hope High since the whole school only had two hundred kids. He lived off River Road in a converted inn called The 1776 House. According to Frankie's father, George Washington ate there before crossing the Delaware below New Hope. One year he told his story to the *Gazette* for its Christmas issue and got to ride in the giant rowboat for the reenactment of Washington Crossing the Delaware. Frankie and I hid along the riverbank and threw stones at the boat, but we didn't hit anything but water.

Frankie's father was the chief heart surgeon at University Hospital in Philadelphia. He was kind of rich and sort of famous, Frankie said, but more rich than famous. He opened people up three times a day, six days a week, to fix their hearts. Some nights he worked so late he didn't bother coming home. Frankie's mom usually stayed out late, too, with friends, leaving Frankie home with their housekeeper, Leda from Czechoslovakia. Their rooms were next to each other on the third floor, and he said he could hear her bed creak as she rolled around in it. Once he thought he heard her calling to him, but he didn't go to see. He said he couldn't imagine touching a women who was almost forty.

Frankie was only two months younger than me, but he seemed like a kid brother you can't get rid of. He tried to pay me to let him hang around. I told him he'd have to give me something he didn't have much of, not something he had too much of, like money. So one day when I was testing one of my rafts at the edge of the Delaware, he came down to the water holding out a baseball wrapped in plastic, autographed by Mike Schmidt. I asked him who that was and he said, "One of the best Phillies players ever."

That didn't really impress me, and I told him I probably wouldn't keep it.

"That's okay," he said, "do what you want."

What I wanted was to throw the ball into the river. I held it up for him to take one last look, then hurled it as far as I could into the Delaware. His face froze, as if I had just thrown away his Rolex watch. But then he shrugged and jumped on the raft with me, and we were off.

Frankie liked to get into trouble—at least he liked the

idea that he was doing something that could get him into trouble if he were caught, which was close enough for me. The actual getting caught part really scared him, though, so he needed me to say that the crazy thing I had in mind would turn out all right. Even when it didn't end up as I'd promised, he still believed me next time. Frankie wanted me to be right.

"Jake?" he said on the phone now.

"I'm still here."

"I read in the *Gazette* that you were back."

"Yeah, I got home a couple of weeks ago." I cradled the phone in my neck as I stuffed everything into the knapsack.

"You going to stay?"

"I don't know. I'm just seeing how things go."

"Some guys were talking about you," he said.

"Yeah, what were they saying?"

"It was Kelly's brother, Pat, he graduated last year and pumps gas at the Shell. He's telling everybody you're home and shouldn't be allowed to come back like nothing happened."

"I can live here if I want. It's not like I was convicted of something."

Frankie didn't say anything. Maybe he was remembering his part in my defense. I never asked him for help. I just told him what happened—how I ran into these guys from Lambertville under the Mechanic Street bridge and got to drinking with them, and how this girl looked over the railing and saw us. Then she came clicking down the stone steps in her thick heels knowing we were drunk and waiting for her. She asked for a cigarette, and one of the guys stuck his tongue out and told her to suck on that instead. Then they grabbed her and she seemed to fight a little but not enough that you would stop. One guy ripped her blouse open and she yelled. A dog started barking and I took off because I was already in enough trouble explaining how Bantry's silo caught fire when I was in the neighborhood. I never saw what else the kids from Jersey did to her. I hitched up River Road to Frankie's, and we sat in his bed watching movies with the sound turned off, drinking his father's vodka by the capful. We fell asleep as the hot June sun was coming up and the crows were hollering in his backyard. The last thing I remembered was Frankie whispering in my ear, "Don't worry, I'll lie for you." I guess even he didn't believe me.

"So, you want to get pounded?" he asked me now. That was our way of saying getting high when somebody might hear.

"It's kind of early for that," I said, looking at the kitchen clock. It was a strange piece of pottery that I'd never seen before, with a deep blue background and dots instead of numbers. The hands were just half the regular size and colored blue, too. This was the kind of clock I could see Dad buying—one trying hard not to tell time. As near as I could figure, it was about two o'clock. Normally we didn't get high until dark.

"We could just ride around town," he said, "if you want."

"I got something to do," I said.

"I don't." Frankie never had anything to do. "There's no fucking excitement around here," he used to say. At school he hung with the straight kids, did his homework, and got elected to the Student Council, just like his parents expected. He was naturally smart and polite, which meant that people never believed he caused any of the trouble we got into, and most of the time he didn't. But he followed me into trouble awful closely. I was Frankie's fucking excitement.

"You can come over," I said, "but you have to be here in a half hour, and wear your worst clothes, because you'll have to throw them away after today."

•

Jenny came up from the cellar carrying wet clothes. "We might as well dry these outside," she said, handing me the basket. "They smell better that way and saves the dryer."

"I'm heading out with Frankie," I said, pushing the basket back at her, but she wouldn't take it.

"You're hanging up the clothes first. And get your father to help you. He needs to do things."

I found Dad upstairs on his bed, lying the wrong way, with his sneakers on the pillows. I told him he was supposed to help me, but he waved me to be quiet. "'We are no other than a moving row of magic shadow-shapes,'" he read, "'that come and go round with sun-illumin'd lantern held in midnight by the master of the show.'" He held the thin book over his head. "Do you remember this—*The Rubaiyat of Omar Khayyam*?"

"Maybe a little," I said, "but listen, Jenny wants us to hang up the wash."

"Your mother used to read these verses to you at bedtime," he said. "'The moving finger writes . . .'"

"' . . . and moves on,'" I said automatically, from some part of my mind where those words had sat for years.

"'' . . . and, having writ, moves on,'" Dad corrected me, "'nor all your piety nor wit shall lure it back to cancel half a line, nor all your tears wash out a word of it.'"

I held up the basket of clothes, and he nodded that Jenny's wishes could not be ignored. We went downstairs, Dad a step behind me, repeating the verses that he had just memorized. Outside the air was fresh, blowing off the Delaware. "Do you remember when we hung the clothes out," I said, "and we forgot to bring them in after dinner? Jenny came home and yelled at us 'cause it was raining like the devil. And another time that fat old raccoon was swinging on her nightgown." Dad smiled a little but didn't say anything as we strung out the towels and socks and shirts on the clothesline. He began staring at the sky. I looked up, too, but there wasn't much to see, just a few small clouds floating in the vastness of the blue sky.

"Sometimes I feel like disappearing," he said.

I tapped him on the shoulder and handed him the edge of a white sheet. "Where would you go?"

He pinned his end to the line and I pinned mine. "Nowhere. I'd just be gone. Not here."

"Like being dead?"

"Not exactly. I'd rather not go through dying to get to disappearing. Sometimes I'd like to just evaporate out of living."

"That's not the way it works, Dad."

"I know, but it should. You shouldn't have to stay in life if you don't want to."

"You don't have to stay," I said before I could stop myself.

"Sure, I know what you mean." He reached out and put his hands behind my neck to pull me closer. "I'm too scared to do it, Jake," he whispered. "Isn't that funny? Jenny says I'm too scared to live, but I know I'm really just too scared to die."

I ducked out from under his hands. I always hated when he talked like this. I didn't think a father should tell his son that he's scared. "Everybody dies, Dad—you can do it."

"I guess I'll have to," he said. "It's just . . . I don't want to feel myself slipping into not being. You know what I mean?"

"Not really."

"Sometimes when I'm in bed," he said, "I close my eyes, but my brain's still awake, and I can feel the darkness closing in. I feel dying." He looked at me as if I should understand now, but I didn't. "It's not explainable," he said. "If you don't feel how bad death is, then that's good. But for me, I can't get it out of my mind."

I knew that already. Dad talked about dying as if it was something he had to face tomorrow, or even today, not years from now. You couldn't really say that Mom's accident had made him this way. Her death just seemed to confirm something inside him that was scared already.

A gust of wind rifled the clothes hanging from the line, and Dad tightened the clothespins. "I'll be out in the yard like this," he said as he finished the row, "and something will happen—maybe a cloud moves across the sun and it suddenly gets colder and darker. I'll look up, and then the universe seems to open so wide, I feel like I'm going to come unhooked from the ground and float up into it, like in that painting with the cow—by Chagall, I think." I looked up at the sky overhead to try to see what he was seeing. The sun and clouds were drifting into each other now, but nothing else was happening. "You know what forever is?" he said.

Of course I did. It was one of his favorite lectures. "Yeah, Dad, I think maybe you've mentioned it one or two hundred times before."

That didn't stop him from explaining it again. "Forever is a religious word meaning you don't have to die anymore. It's everything staying the same for the rest of time. But what's on the other side of forever? There has to be something." Dad often went off on binges of thinking like this. He'd been a philosophy major in college because he thought that was the subject that could help him understand what he should do in life. But then he got sucked into Vietnam, and he came out two years later more afraid of life and death than ever. "Think, Jake, think of time," he said to me, "it's just things happening one after another. But forever is the same thing happening over and over. Forever is the opposite of time." He hung up Kris' white socks very carefully, one clothespin per sock. "I couldn't stand being caught in forever," he said, "with nothing after it."

I picked up some of my sister's little T-shirts and pinned them to the line after her socks. "I don't see why you think about this stuff so much," I said.

"Because there are only a few possibilities, and you have to be ready for one of them: Death and nothing, death and reincarnation, death and hell, death and heaven. That's about it."

"I'll take death and reincarnation," I said, "and come back as a butterfly. Then I can spend all day flapping my wings causing hurricanes."

He looked up at me with his hands full of Kris' wet play shorts, and I could see he wasn't going to let me joke him into forgetting about death today. "It's dying into forever that I don't like," he said. "How can God fill up forever? There has to be something outside of it, but what's that—another state of being? Another God? Then what's outside that state and that God? It just goes on and on. I can't imagine what the end of it all might be. My mind runs up against the idea like I'm ramming my head into a wall. I never break through, and I never stop ramming." The wind gusted up and the sheets flapped like loose sails. "That's a nice sound," he said, "like you're on a ship going somewhere."

.

Frankie arrived a half hour later, driving an old Mustang that looked like it had been saved after a few minutes in a compactor. The front wheels tilted inward. The hood was wired to the grill. The outside mirror was taped onto the aerial. The back driver's side window was cracked in fine pieces, but not broken. "My new car," he said and patted the roof. "Paid for it myself." He was wearing black galoshes, fisherman's pants with straps that went over his shoulders, and no shirt. "All rubber," he said, pinching the pants, "and nothing underneath." He held the waistband out to prove it, but I took his word. "You look good," he said, "for being gone so long, I mean. You don't look different, just bigger."

"You got bigger, too," I said.

"Yeah, I ate everything in sight last winter to get my strength up for wrestling. But I still lost every time. Except once the guy twisted his neck throwing me and had to forfeit. Coach says I need to get an attitude to wrestle."

Frankie looked like a kid waiting to get beaten up. You could tell from the softness in his face that he couldn't take a punch. He could even make cops feel sorry for him. He got himself out of a lot of trouble by looking like he'd hang himself by his belt if he wasn't let off. Sometimes all he had to do was promise not to hang out with bad elements, meaning me, which he always agreed to after I told him it was the smart thing to say. It didn't hurt that he had an important father.

Frankie kicked shut the door of his old Mustang. "So where are we going?" he asked.

"Some place dark, cold, wet, and very dirty. You might lose that fancy jewelry there," I said, pointing to the chain around his neck.

"Oh yeah, almost forgot." He unhooked the chain from the back and held it out for me to see. "Liquid silver," he said, "pretty cool, huh?"

"Where'd you get it?"

"It was a gift," he said, "from a friend," he added.

"New haircut, too," I said.

He fingered the few spikes of hair sticking out from the

back of his head. "My father threatened to cut them off while I'm sleeping," he said. "I told him if he does, I'm going to cut off something of his a lot shorter."

"Seems fair," I said, though I doubted Frankie would ever talk like that to his father.

He tossed the chain into his car. "So what are we doing?"

"We're going underground."

"Underground where?"

"Near Metzgar's house, in the open land behind his pasture. There's a way down into a cave that nobody knows about except me."

"How come you never took me before?"

I hoisted the knapsack over my shoulder. "You get claustrophobic, remember?"

"Yeah," he said, sounding surprised that I knew that.

I set off toward the river before Frankie could think about what he was getting into. We zigzagged up and down the bank, talking about the Delaware, how cold the water was this year, even in June, and the town, how filled it was with people we didn't know. He told me there were fights all the time now with gangs from Philadelphia who came in to buy drugs or beat up the gays.

"I used to like New Hope," Frankie said as we broke from the scrub of the riverbank and hit the meadow.

"I never did," I said.

He told me that the Jersey kids who got me in trouble at the canal came back to New Hope a few times and bragged how they had gotten away with attacking Kelly. But then one night while they were drinking behind the Playhouse, her brother and his buddies jumped them and pushed their car in the river. "Nobody's seen them in New Hope since," Frankie said.

I shrugged that it didn't make any difference to me what happened to the Jersey kids. I only knew them well enough to get into trouble with them, and that was almost a year ago. We stood there at the edge of Metzgar's land for a minute, and the sun burned through a cloud and heated up our faces. As far as we could see there was green grazing

74

grass in front of us. In the distance we could hear the clanging bells of a few cows or sheep wandering the fields.

We hopped the fence onto Metzgar's land. I paced off ten steps toward the big beech tree and got down on my knees to dig away the scrub grass. In a few minutes I felt the plywood cover, and Frankie helped me rip it out of the earth.

"It really is a cave," he said as he leaned into the hole.

"It's great," I said. "There are rooms big enough to stand up in."

He pulled his head out and sat back on his heels. "The thing is, I really am claustrophobic, like you said."

"You'll be all right with me," I said as I tied the clothesline around the beech and threw the other end into the hole. "You want to go first?" Frankie shook his head and backed away from the hole, as if I might shove him in. I handed him the knapsack and grabbed onto the rope. Then I crawled over the edge of the hole and lowered myself down about eight feet till I hit bottom. Frankie tossed the knapsack in after me and stood there looking down. "You coming or not?" I asked him.

"Maybe just to there." Once he said that, I knew I could get him in all the way. Frankie always had to try on an adventure one foot at a time before jumping into it. He closed his eyes and slid himself over the side of the hole, kicking dirt down on my head. "Sorry," he said, as I shook it out of my hair.

I knelt down to clear away the entrance to the main tunnel as Frankie talked about how his parents were never home anymore and when they were home they barely said a word to each other. He didn't seem to care that I wasn't listening. Frankie's mom and dad were pretty boring, even as parents go. I shoved the flashlight into the tunnel, then my head, then pulled myself through with one arm. I turned the light back through the crawl space and yelled for Frankie to come ahead. He didn't answer. He didn't come through, either. I pulled the light back and sat there looking around the cave, which was long and narrow, like the inside of a bus.

"Jake?" he finally called in to me. I didn't say anything,

and in a minute his hands popped through the hole, and then his head.

"Don't touch the walls," I said as I pulled him all the way in. "You'll spook the bats."

Frankie swung his flashlight around the room. "I don't see any bats."

"It's all bats, the whole wall. Listen." There was no sound, and then after a few seconds, there was just a quick fluttering of wings. "Hear it? They fall one by one and then fly back to stick in the mud. That's what they do all day long, except there's no day in here, or night."

"You didn't mention the bats," he said.

"They leave you alone, if you don't spook them."

"If I don't spook *them*?"

The room was so low it grazed our heads as we stood there, hunched over. I counted six tunnels shooting off in all directions. The first tunnel on the right from where we crawled in, that one, I remembered, led to the big room.

"Let's go," I said and dropped to my knees.

Frankie shot his light on me fast. "Go where?"

"To the big room. It's just a short crawl."

"I can't go any farther, Jake."

"Okay, you stay here."

"Wait," Frankie said, grabbing the waist of my jeans.

"What?"

"This is starting to get to me, like the whole thing might fall on us."

"This cave's been here for about a million years. It's not going to fall in today just because you're here."

Frankie was a sucker for logic. He thought about that for a moment, then closed his eyes. "Okay, just a little farther."

"We have to slide," I said and took his arm to push us off. We fell sideways over each other to the bottom of the cave.

"Shit," Frankie said, spitting out dirt. "All the mud in the world must have drained into this cave."

I crawled over to the mouth of the tunnel and widened the entrance with my hands. "I'll go first," I said. "It's only about 15 feet. You can hold my legs if you want."

The hole was tighter than I remembered it. Probably no

one had crawled in here for months, maybe years, not since Dad showed me this place. It took Frankie and me about 10 minutes to dig our way through to the big room.

"That must be the longest 15 feet in the world," Frankie said as we sat by each other, getting our breath. "You sure there's enough oxygen in here?"

"There's plenty," I said. "There was this whole family down south that got lost in a cave for five days, and they didn't run out."

"That's really comforting," Frankie said as he flashed his light slowly around the walls. The room looked to be about fifty feet across, maybe bigger. You could hear water dripping and bats wings and our breathing—that's all. "You still got the guide rope, right?" he said.

"Why," I asked him, "you getting scared?"

"I'm scared out of my fucking little mind," he said.

I liked that about Frankie. He wasn't afraid to tell you what he was feeling. "Think of something else," I said, "like the mud. Take your gloves off and feel it." I grabbed some slime in my hands and held it up for Frankie to see in my light. "This is pure, 100 percent, all-American mud."

"What am I doing here?" he asked all of a sudden.

"You asked to come, remember? You always asked to. Even when the cops told you to stay away from me, you still kept coming around."

"That's not so strange."

"It is to me. Most other kids were heading in the other direction."

His light beam stopped zigzagging, freezing to a spot on the wall. "So, what, I need a reason to be friends with you?"

"Yeah."

He laughed a little. "It's nothing queer, if that's what you're thinking."

"I'm not thinking anything."

"Maybe I just like hanging around with you," he said.

"Because you want to piss off your parents?"

"I didn't say that."

"You like getting in trouble?"

"I didn't say that, either."

"You want to be crazy like me?"

77

"Fuck the questions," he said, almost sounding tough. Frankie liked cursing at me.

"It can be dangerous around me," I said. "You never know what's going to happen next, right, and maybe you like that."

He grunted that that was true. Lots of times Frankie came along when I was sneaking in some place—like into the school during the summer, or breaking into cop cars behind the police station, or climbing into the Playhouse through the roof. Sometimes he even suggested the adventure, saying something like, "You think we could find a way to get inside the Playhouse to see the concert?" "There's a way in everywhere," I told him then. We scaled the three stories in fifteen minutes and found a door open on the roof.

"I could go crazy right here," I told him now, sitting twenty feet underground, "and choke you to death. There's nobody to stop me."

"I'd stop you."

"Oh yeah, big wrestler. You wouldn't have a chance. I could strangle you and no one would ever know. I could drag you so far into these caves only the bats would find you. I wouldn't even have to kill you. I could just lose you in the tunnels. You'd never get out."

"It's too late to scare me," he said. "I hit the limit when I jumped into this cave."

I didn't believe that. I knew he could be scared some more. "Give me your light," I told him, "it's brighter than mine. I want to check out some of the other tunnels."

"We'd better get back," he said, but I grabbed the flashlight from his hand.

"Yeah, soon," I told him and dug my fingers into the wall to pull myself standing. Bats flew away, dozens of them flapping their wings. I stepped back from Frankie during all the noise. Then they went silent again. I closed my eyes and spun around a couple of times, letting both lights flash across the room, spinning together. "You can lose all sense of direction in a cave, even which way is up or down. Like now, I could forget which way we came in. You remember, Frankie?"

"No," he said, "that's why we have the rope."

I shut off the flashlights and the cave became the blackest insides of the earth. "What rope? Where is it?"

"You like thinking you could kill someone, don't you?" he said like something he had thought about for a long time.

"Yeah, sometimes I do."

"That's why you used to hunt all the time, because you actually enjoy killing things."

"I never said that."

"How could you do it—kill little animals?"

"They're out there eating each other anyway. I was just another way they could die."

"And what about Gerenser's dog at Washington Crossing? Were you just another way she could die?"

"You weren't there," I told him. "You don't know what happened. I answered the cops, and Gerenser, everything they asked, so don't talk about that."

We didn't speak for a minute. Nothing moved. Nothing made a sound. Then the silence got to him. "Turn on the light, will you?"

"This is the way it is in a coffin," I whispered out into the cave as I pictured Mom there, lying in the midst of Dad's forever. "Lie flat, Frankie, and think of a coffin, your coffin, all around you. They pack you in pillows so you'll be comfortable forever. Then the lid closes just above your nose . . . "

"Turn on the light!"

"Imagine it," I said, thinking of Mom in her coffin. But I couldn't remember her face, and that scared me. I could remember how she looked in pictures but not how I actually saw her ten years ago.

"Jake?"

"The coffin won't open again, Frankie. It's lights out forever. It's just you and the blackness and the silence."

"Come on, Jake, I'm losing it." The words shook off his tongue. "You're just playing around, I know that, but I've had enough, okay? You've scared me, now let's get out of here." He stood up, but he didn't know which way to go. "Jake?"

I let him stand there feeling alone.

"Why are you doing this?"

His feet moved a little but went nowhere. I could hear his hands swiping the air trying to find me. "I'm sorry I brought up the stupid dog," he said. "I didn't mean it, I know you didn't do anything. Now give me the light," he said like he had the power to order me. "Come on, say something, Jake, you're still there, I know it, I can feel you. I really am claustrophobic. I got to see you or I'm going to flip out." He was breathing hard, more scared than I'd ever seen him before. "Don't do this to me, come on, please, don't leave me here, I mean it," he pleaded. "Say something . . . Jake!"

I stepped forward into his hands and they grabbed me, they held me tighter than anyone ever had. He was shaking and breathing in fits, almost crying. "I got to get out of here," he said, "I can't stop shaking. I'm going to die in here, if you don't get me out . . . I can't breathe."

"It's okay," I said and rubbed his back to get him to relax. He gasped for air at my neck. His voice at my ears begged me to get him out. "It's okay," I said over and over to him, "I won't lose you. We'll go out now." I tried to pull back from him, but he wouldn't let go. "Look," I said, turning on the flashlight, "there's nothing in here to scare you."

"Get me out."

"The rope's around my waist, you can feel it." I took his hand off my arm and put it on the clothesline. "All we have to do is follow it back."

I talked to him as we crawled through the narrow tunnel. He held onto my legs the whole time and then grabbed my arm when we stood up in the entry room. It took about fifteen minutes to make it back to the base of the hole. I boosted him up and then wedged myself up the sides and out into the bright Sunday afternoon. Frankie lay back in the grass, his arms spread, looking at the wide open sky. Mud covered every inch of him.

"You did that on purpose," he said after awhile. His hands were digging out clumps of grass. He was still breathing very fast. "You took me down there just to scare me like that. After all this time, that's what you do to me when you come back. You're a fucked-up jerk, Jake."

I could have kicked his mouth shut for calling me that.

I'd beaten up kids for a lot less of a reason. But this was Frankie. "Don't you think I've done worse?" I asked him.

"And you're proud of it?"

"I'm not proud of anything. You can walk away anytime, you know."

He raised up to his knees. "Right—you don't need anybody. You treat people like they're little animals for you to play around with. And it's okay because you never asked for company anyway, so that makes it right." He got to his feet and started back toward my house.

"You can't leave yet," I said.

"Why not?" he called back over his shoulder.

"I wasn't trying to hurt you down there," I said. "I was just trying to make you feel something you never did before."

"I didn't ask for that."

"You said you were bored, you had nothing to do."

He turned around. "You think that's why I hang around you, to get scared?"

"I don't know—is it?"

"I'm not a little kid anymore, you know, I don't need this stuff."

"You mean you don't need me anymore?"

He thought for a moment. "I don't need that," he said, flipping mud off his hand toward the hole.

"I'm sorry I scared you, okay?" I said. He nodded a little and I followed him to the river where we helped each other rub the mud off our skins.

Nine

SHE WAS SITTING ON THE FRONT PORCH AS FRANKIE AND I CAME slogging up from the river. Her bare feet were stretched out to the railing, next to a coffee mug and Thermos. She looked up from a pad she was writing on and waved.

"Who's that?" Frankie said as he reached through the window of his Mustang to open the door from the inside.

"Some lady I met in New York—a reporter."

"What's she doing on your porch?"

"She wants to write about me running away."

"No shit?"

"Yeah, and she'll pay me a couple thousand dollars for the story. That's what Jenny says."

Frankie kicked the side of his car to knock some mud off his sneakers. "She's hot," he said as we looked over at the woman, sitting deep in Dad's green Adirondack chair, her legs spread open a little. "She's after your body, Jake."

I dug a handful of dirt off my chest and threw it at the ground. "A woman like that can get any guy she wants in New York. She doesn't need some wacko kid covered with mud jumping on her." Still, she knew we were looking at her, and she didn't lower her legs.

"Jake," Frankie said, as I thought of her cold hands rubbing the mud off my chest and stomach. "Jake!" he yelled in my face, "listen to me." I turned away from the woman. "I'll kill you if you try anything like that again," he said. "I swear I will." I imagined looking over my shoulder someday as I walked into town and seeing his busted up Mustang bearing down on my ass. But in my mind, the car veered away from me at the last minute and Frankie jumped out saying he was sorry and asking me not to be mad at him.

He got in the car and gunned the engine, then raced out of the driveway, his tires flicking up stones. I walked toward the house, and she was watching me. She didn't turn away like most people do when you catch them staring. Every few seconds she wrote something in her book without looking down.

I headed around to the back of the house because I knew Jenny would kill me if I tracked mud in the front door. Going past the porch I stripped off my T-shirt in case Frankie was right that she wanted me. At the back door I pried off my sneakers and went in the house through the kitchen. Luckily, Jenny wasn't there to start the inquisition about what I'd been up to. I reached the front stairs just as the woman came through the screen door.

"Hello again," she said.

"Hi," I answered and kept going.

Upstairs Kris came running out of her room with a paper cat's mask on her face. She tilted the eye holes into place and looked me up and down. "What happened to you?"

"I was cave crawling. There's a lot of mud."

She thought for a moment. "You could take me some time if you wanted."

"Yeah, okay."

"When I'm older?"

"Older doesn't have anything to do with it."

"Good," she said, and then held onto the railing to go downstairs.

I went into the bathroom and turned on the shower full blast. I pulled off my shorts and tossed them into the sink. I was already hard. Under the cold water, the brown skin of mud washed down the drain. As I soaped myself clean, I tried to think of exciting stories I could make up for this excellent looking woman from New York.

•

"We were never formally introduced," she said, standing on the front porch with her hand out. "I'm Larkin Daley. Do you remember me?" Did she really think I could forget her? I shook her hand and it seemed small for a woman almost as tall as me. "You were covered in mud," she said, and I couldn't tell if she was asking or telling me.

"Yeah," I said, leaning against the porch post, "it was mud." My hair was slicked back. I was wearing gray shorts and a dark blue pullover, colors Jenny said I looked good in.

The woman settled back in the Adirondack. "How did you get that way?"

Suddenly I felt like a six-year-old explaining how his jeans got dirty. I tried to make it sound like a big adventure. "Frankie and I went spelunking in this cave that's probably a million years old, and it was kind of muddy."

"That's interesting," she said but didn't ask me anything more about it. "So Jake, I hope your mother filled you in on our conversation."

"Jenny? She said you wanted to write a book on me."

"That's right, about your experiences as a runaway."

I shrugged at the subject, but then I figured that was wrong, so I laughed it up like there sure were lots of wild things that happened.

"Have you been thinking about what you could tell me, like I asked you?"

"A little, on the bus home."

"So you'll talk to me?"

"Yeah, but I'm not going to tell you everything," I said, because suddenly, remembering the last ten months felt like reliving them, which I definitely didn't want to do.

"I need to know everything," she said. "That's what my publisher expects for two thousand dollars."

"Two thousand doesn't buy everything."

"How about two and a half thousand," she said, and when I didn't answer, she added, "or three thousand?"

"Nothing buys everything," I said, "but three thousand gets you a lot closer."

•

Dad invited her to stay for dinner. He forgot that Jenny was working the piano shift at The Logan and there weren't any leftovers for him to warm up and serve. He wasn't much of a cook. He went into the kitchen, mashed up a few tomatoes, added spices as he fried them, then toasted some bread and set that on the dining room table. The woman didn't look like she knew what to do with this particular meal, so I grabbed some toast, tore it into pieces on my plate, and poured the fried tomatoes over them. I figured she'd get the picture.

"You're from New York?" Dad said. He had put on a white shirt and shaved without being told to.

"Yes," she said as she broke up her toast, "but not originally. I grew up in Virginia, near Manassas."

Dad grinned because he knew all of the Civil War towns. He used to say that there was a war one person could make a difference in. He poured himself coffee and handed the pitcher to the woman. "Why would you move from Bull Run, Virginia, to New York?"

"It seemed like a good idea at the time," she laughed. Then she saw that Dad was serious, he really wanted to know. "I guess I hoped to be at the center of things in publishing."

Dad reached halfway across the table to pick up the toast plate in one hand and the bowl of squashed tomatoes in the other. He gave Kris two pieces of bread to tear up and then spooned the hot sauce over them. "If that's where the center is," he said, "what are you doing here?"

The woman seemed unsure what he was getting at. Dad could make you nervous like that. He'd ask questions or say things without any feeling to them, so you couldn't tell whether he was being sarcastic or just asking. "You start from the center," she said, "and move out to where the story is."

"And the story is here right now?" Dad asked.

"Yes," she said, forking up her first bite of tomato toast. "I think so."

"Kind of strange, isn't it?" he said.

•

She started interviewing me right after dinner. She told me to call her Larkin, her first name, which was actually her mother's maiden name. I'd been avoiding calling her anything. Even thinking about her, I hadn't been putting a name to her. She was just the woman from New York, the writer. But when we sat down in the living room, her on the couch under the only light that worked, and me stretched out on the floor where the rug was worn to threads, she said, "Please call me Larkin. It sounds so old to be 'Ms. Daley.'"

"Ms. Daley" hadn't even occurred to me, so I said fine,

Larkin it was. Then her questions started. "What was a typical day like on the road?"

She was wearing a dress the color of the sky on a cool summer night just before the sun goes all the way down. "Nothing ever happened the same way twice," I said. "I never knew what was going to happen."

"You must have stayed in the same place for a few weeks at a time," she said, "established some kind of routine."

Her hair was pulled back by a silver barrette. "Not really," I said.

"You didn't fall into a pattern at all, a time to wake up, things to do, a certain number of miles to hitch?"

Her eyes were soft brown, very soft, and suddenly I wanted to lick her eyelids.

"Jake?"

"Yeah?" I tried to remember her question, something about having a routine. "I stayed a few weeks in some places," I said, "maybe even months."

"Where was that?"

"I don't know, just around."

She reached down to the side of the sofa and turned off the tape recorder. She said, "This isn't going to work if you don't think about your answers."

"Maybe you should ask better questions." I could tell from the shock on her face that she wasn't used to being talked back to. It seemed to me we might have a problem here, since I was very used to talking back. She had stopped smiling, which I didn't like much, because her face looked kind of old without a smile on it. So I said, "I lived in New Hampshire last winter until it got so cold I couldn't sleep at night." She clicked the recorder back on. "It was a hunter's cabin," I continued, "so nobody was using it then. It had a woodstove for heat but no running water or electricity."

"You just moved into somebody else's cabin?"

"It's not like it was their personal home. There was just an old sofa that I slept on and a table, a few cans of food and some old dried-out books that fell apart when I opened them. I read pages from lots of different books."

"It didn't bother you that this place wasn't yours?"

"Sure, the owners could have shot me for trespassing—they can do that in New Hampshire—except I figured that deer season was over and nobody would be around until spring."

"Did you get into drugs, prostitution, stealing, things like that?"

"There wasn't a whole lot of that stuff in the woods."

"I mean during your entire time away."

"Just because I ran away doesn't mean I lived like that."

"So you didn't take drugs?"

"I did sometimes."

"What kind?"

"Nothing hard, just weed mostly and a few pills."

"Did you sell drugs?"

"No."

"Hustle?"

"Not really."

"You either did or didn't. There's no in between."

"There's always in between. It's never like you just said, either one way or the other."

"Okay, did you ever sell yourself—sexually, I mean—for money?"

She seemed to be really interested in this question. I started getting hard just hearing her say *sexually* the way she did, like it was the most important word in the sentence.

"Sometimes I went home with them—with guys," I said, "but just to get off the street if it was freezing or pouring. Mostly I let them watch me do stuff if they wanted."

"They didn't try to touch you?"

"They wanted to, but I didn't let them," I said, which was true except for when this guy offered me $100, which was $99 more than I had in my pocket at that moment. I didn't want Larkin to think that maybe I enjoyed fooling around with guys, so I left this particular incident out.

"Did you ever steal from them?" she asked.

"Not really. Sometimes I took a few dollars if I thought they had more than they needed. Most of them did. They were living like the kings of the world. They have giant TVs in their houses and jacuzzis and gyms to work out in and pools and tennis courts outside, and then you go back on the streets and see people crawling in Dumpsters for food, even kids."

"How did that make you feel?"

"Like killing the kings and giving their money away."

Dad came in the living room carrying a book. "Did you know that Aesop was a hunchback?" he asked Larkin.

"No," she said, looking kind of surprised at the question, "I guess I didn't."

"A hunchback," Dad repeated, "and he was very ugly. But the kings kept him around and treated him well. Do you know why?" Larkin shook her head. "Because he was very clever at devising and solving riddles. Aesop," Dad said, "wouldn't be able to find employment today with those job skills."

Larkin laughed like that was a good joke and then she saw that Dad was serious again. He kicked off his moccasins, sat in Jenny's beat-up armchair and put his head back to doze.

She looked at me to see what we should do, and I just shrugged not to worry about him. "What else do you want to know?" I asked her.

"What kind of haircut do you call that?" she said, pointing at my head as if it looked strange.

"Short," I said.

"Not a skinhead haircut?"

"No way."

"You don't like the skinheads?"

"I don't think about them if they don't hassle me."

"Do they hassle you?"

"They hassle everybody, especially outside the clubs. They think they own some places and you have to look like them and think like them."

"What happens when they hassle you?"

"I get in fights."

"You enjoy fighting, don't you?"

She was pretty smart like that, knowing how I felt about things even before I told her. "Yeah, I do, it feels good hitting a guy sometimes."

"Fighting isn't supposed to feel good."

"Maybe not, but it does. Any kid will tell you that, at least if he gets in the first hit."

•

At the end of a half hour, she flipped out the used-up cassette and put in another. She did it so fast I hadn't even finished yawning when she started up again. "Why do you call your mother by her first name, but not your father?"

"He's my real father," I said, looking over at him sleeping in the chair, with his head tilted back and mouth open. He looked dead. Grandma's copy of *Aesop's Fables* had dropped out of his hand. Larkin picked up the book and put it on the table next to him. "I guess you think he's kind of weird," I said, "for talking about Aesop, I mean."

"Not at all," Larkin said. "He was just reading a book and wanted to share something from it with us."

I liked it that she didn't think Dad strange, so I decided to explain what he was talking about. "Back when Aesop was living," I said, "the different countries or states or whatever they were sent riddles to each other to try to stump the other one. They'd have to give up some treasure if they couldn't figure it out. Pretty outrageous, huh?"

"Yes," Larkin said, "outrageous. But you were about to tell me why you call Jenny by her first name."

It seemed to me that Aesop was a lot more interesting than Jenny, but I answered Larkin anyway. "Jenny's not really my mother," I said.

"She's your stepmother?"

"Sort of like that."

Larkin wrote this down even though the recorder was taking everything in, so I figured it must be important. "What happened to your real mother?" she said.

"She died." That's all I wanted to say about it, but I knew already that Larkin would keep asking.

"How did she die, if you don't mind telling me?"

So I told it the way I'd gotten used to, just the quick facts and nothing more. "It was a car accident," I said, and the scene filled up my mind again, "on Red Lion Road, which is about a mile from here. A squirrel ran into the road so Dad swerved and we skidded into a telephone pole. Mom's side got the worst of it. She was pinned inside."

"You mean you were in the car, too?" she said, as if that was the bad part of the story. "And you weren't hurt?"

"Just a scratch on my head right here," I said, rubbing just under the hair on my forehead where I could still feel a little indentation. "And Dad only had a few bruises."

"But your mother . . . ?"

Larkin was sitting with her pen hanging over the paper and the tape going around, both waiting for this terrible story that must be coming. It *was* pretty terrible, which is why I didn't normally talk about it. But Larkin was expecting her three thousand dollars' worth. "Dad pulled me out of the car," I said, "and told me to stand off the road. Then he went back for Mom, but he couldn't get her door open. Her chest was kind of crushed anyway, so she couldn't move. He reached through the window and held her hand, and they talked for a few minutes. Then she died." Larkin's body shook like she'd taken a jolt of electricity. I saw tears in her eyes, and it surprised me that she'd cry over someone she didn't even know.

Standing in the mud at the side of the road that day, I saw Dad let her hand go. I saw Mom's fingers slip back inside the car window. If he could have just held on, I remembered thinking then, she would be alright. But he let go. Then he kneeled there by the car until the police came blaring to the scene, as if they could be any help. They pulled Dad away from the wreck and grabbed me, too, like I was some kid who just happened to be standing there. I tried to run after Mom when they finally got her out of the car, but the cops stuffed me in a squad car and told me it was better I didn't. How could it be better, I wondered, that I couldn't see my own mother?

Dad told me later that I couldn't imagine how it was holding the hand of someone dying and knowing you couldn't do anything about it. He said that he shouldn't have swerved, that he was always swerving out of the way of things and he had to stop it. If he had just run the squirrel over like everybody else would have, Mom would have lived, he said. But I knew Dad would never purposely run over an animal. He would always swerve and take his chances.

"How old were you when this happened?" Larkin asked.

"Six," I said, "and three days."

Larkin flipped through her pad and found a question she had written down before. "When did your father marry Jenny?"

I didn't know they had, that's what I said. Sleeping in the chair, Dad didn't look any more married than when I left.

"They aren't married?" Larkin said.

It surprised me that she was so surprised. I'd have thought she understood that stuff, being from New York. "They weren't married when I ran," I said. "Maybe they did it afterwards, but nobody told me."

"But you said she's your stepmother."

I shook my head no, I hadn't said that. "She just acts like a stepmother."

"How long has she been living here?"

Seemed like forever to me, but I didn't say that. "Maybe nine years, since pretty soon after my mom died."

"So she really raised you, as a mother, I mean?"

The idea that Jenny was more of my mother than Mom was kind of sickening to think about. "She didn't have anything to do with me," I said. "She just lived here."

"Your father raised you?"

"He was always around, that's one thing, since he didn't work much after Mom's death. So you could say he raised me. But mostly I raised myself."

"Did he teach you the normal things a father does?"

"You mean like how to fix a car?"

"In terms of how to act," she said, "how to behave."

"None of the usual stuff, like going to church or studying or when to shut up, if that's what you mean. He didn't hassle me about any of that."

"You never went to church?"

"We used to go sort of regularly, then we stopped all of a sudden. Dad said his idea of God didn't go very well with the regular kind of churches."

"Which one did you attend?"

"It's in the center of town, I forget the name—one where they don't really care what you believe in. That's the only kind Dad would set foot in."

"Unitarian?"

"Maybe."

"Why did you stop going?"

"We were sort of asked to."

"By whom?"

"The priest or minister, whatever he was. He didn't wear black, like he was supposed to, I remember that about him. And he had this great gold watch you could see when he raised his arms during the sermon. When I was little I used to wait the whole service just to see him raise his arms. His sleeve would fall back," I said and raised my arms to show her, "and the light on his watch would shine over everything."

Larkin smiled at my memory. "Why did you stop going?"

"After church one time he asked us to come behind the altar where his office was. I remember the clock on his wall—it looked like it was melting. Then he said some people saw me taking money out of the collection plates instead of putting it in, which was the usual way of doing things. Jenny started apologizing right away for me. She believed him right away."

"Were you taking money from the collection plate?"

"Maybe I did sometimes, but not that much, just a few dollars. They were always talking about giving money away to people who needed it, so . . . we needed it."

"I'm sure the church would have given your family money or food or clothes, if you had asked for help."

"Oh yeah, they want to help you but only by their rules on how to do it." Larkin wasn't understanding much if she thought we'd ask for charity. She sat there looking at me like I was a rotten kid for taking money from church. Nobody dressed in a rich blue dress with a silver necklace and a car in the driveway worth $25,000 could understand that.

"Lots of people are poor," she said, "and they don't steal from their church."

"Lots of people cheat on taxes, don't they? And they sell you stuff that doesn't work and rob you and blow up airplanes . . . "

"Those are rationalizations," she said. "You know what that means?"

"I know exactly what it means—you think you can judge the whole world."

"That's funny," she said as she closed her notebook. "I was thinking that's what you were doing." We seemed to be hitting a stalemate here, and we fell into silence. Larkin broke first. "So the church kicked you out for taking money?"

"Not really," I said. "We showed up the next week, and I let the plate go by without putting my hand in, so everything was fine, except the minister started preaching about how God had put man on earth to dominate everything else. He said that before the big flood people were vegetarians, but after the flood God put man in charge of all the animals and birds and fish. I knew Dad wouldn't like hearing that. He slipped off his shoe and threw it at the minister. Then he got up and led us down the aisle and out of church forever."

•

I got thirsty talking so much, so I went to the kitchen to get a root beer, which Dad always kept stocked in the refrigerator. When I came back to the living room, Larkin was rummaging through her briefcase. Then she pulled out a piece of paper. "When you were twelve," she said, "you were caught putting dead rats in mailboxes, is that right?"

"Yeah, pretty childish, huh?"

"Where did you get the rats?"

I liked that question, and I knew right then—10:35 pm on June 11—that I liked this woman, even if she was rich.

•

She went upstairs to use the bathroom, saying that the coffee was shooting right through her and she shouldn't drink so much caffeine at night. But when she came back down to the living room, she unscrewed the top of her Thermos and poured herself another cup. "Tell me," she said, "what was it like growing up with your father?" She raised the coffee to her red lips and sipped.

I swigged down some A&W. "He read to me all the time

from his books. And he was always asking me crazy questions. Like one time we were driving by this cow in a field and he stopped the car and asked me what I saw. I said 'a cow,' and he asked me what kind. I told him I didn't know what kind, it was just a black and white cow. That's when he snapped his fingers and I knew we'd come to the punch line. 'You know that the side of the cow we can see is black and white,' he said. 'You don't really know anything about the other side, do you?'"

"He was making a point that you can't assume things in life," Larkin explained, as if I hadn't figured that out yet.

Dad groaned in his chair. "It's not opening," he said. "It won't open." He drew his legs up to his chest.

"A dream," she said.

"A nightmare," I corrected her.

Dad's fingers were digging into the arms of the chair, trying to get a hold. "I can't open it," he said, kind of crying the words. "I can't," he said, louder now, "I can't . . ."

I jumped up and shook his shoulders. "It is open," I said. "Mom's alright."

"No, it won't open . . ."

"Look, Dad, you can see the door opening. Mom is getting out. She's okay." His eyes shook under the lids. "She's fine, Dad," I said over and over, until his snoring returned.

"Does that happen often?" Larkin said softly as I sat on the sofa, imagining that door opening and my mother getting out, alive and smiling at us that everything had turned out okay after all.

"Right afterwards he'd dream about the accident every few days," I said, "and then like every month or so. But this is the first time I know of since I've been home."

"What about you, Jake? Do you dream about the accident?"

"I don't dream," I told her, just like I'd told Dad.

•

After his nightmare, Dad started snoring so loudly that Larkin picked up her tape recorder and waved me to follow her into the kitchen. It was getting near midnight, but she

94

didn't seem to want to quit. Jenny would be home soon from waitressing, and I didn't think she'd like seeing Larkin still there. I figured she might make a real scene, especially if she'd been drinking on the way. Then again, Jenny definitely wanted her cut of the money.

Larkin sat across from me at the kitchen table and pulled a pack of cigarettes from her briefcase. "Mind if I smoke?" she said.

"Why would I mind?"

"Some people do," she said as she took out her lighter, "especially in New York." She lit the cigarette and took the first breath of it deep into her lungs. "I've been trying to give it up," she said, kind of waving the cigarette in front of me. "As you can see, I'm not doing a good job of it."

"Can I bum one?"

She thought for a moment. "Your parents—I mean your father and Jenny—they let you smoke?"

That was a stupid question to ask a kid who had just been on his own for almost a year. "They don't have anything to do with it," I said. "If I want to smoke, I do it sometimes."

She tapped the box on the side of her hand until a cigarette popped up. She lit it for me, and I sucked in the smoke. "Pretty weak," I said.

She nodded and crushed hers out in the ashtray, which was odd since she had just lit it. "Do you like your house?" she asked suddenly.

It seemed to me she was getting pretty desperate with her questions to ask that. "There's not much to like about it," I said. "It's falling apart, but it's okay."

"Why did you break into other people's houses?"

"It was fun seeing how they lived," I said. "And I like being off"—then it occurred to me that I hadn't mentioned anything about housebreaking, which was a blood secret between Frankie and me. "How did you find out about that?"

"I've done some asking around town in the last couple of days, at the school and police station. I know a lot about you." She smiled when she said this, as if it were a game to find out as much as she could.

"They never caught me breaking in anywhere. The police couldn't have known about it."

"They didn't *know*," she said, "but they suspected. And now I know it's true."

That didn't bother me, because the cops couldn't arrest me without any evidence, especially after a year, and I sure wasn't going to admit anything to them. What got me worried, though, was that Larkin had been able to trick me. I would definitely have to be more careful around her. "So what else do you know about me?" I asked.

"I know you were suspended from school twice, and you had trouble making friends—"

"I had friends, as many as I needed."

"Like Frank Collins—he was your friend, right?"

"Frankie, yeah, he still is."

"Your only friend?"

I got up and went to the back door, as if there was something I needed to look at in the backyard. In the yellow light from the kitchen, I could see the old groundhog's main hole right in the middle of the grass, where it had been for years. Jenny always wanted to plug it up or set off an ammonia bomb to kill the "good-for-nothing creature," as she called him. But Dad wouldn't let her. I turned back to Larkin, "How do you know about Frankie?"

"It's my job to find out things about people I'm interviewing," she said. "How did you come to have him as your best friend, a boy who was a grade behind you?"

I finished my root beer and tossed the bottle past Larkin's head into the trash basket. "I don't know," I said and took a puff of the cigarette. "Maybe I was maladjusted."

"Is that what you think?" She was staring at me with such a beautiful face, such great eyes and asking me stupid questions about why I had only one friend in the world, like having friends was a rule. If you didn't have them, something had to be wrong with you.

"One friend is enough for me," I said.

"Why did you break into houses?" she said, getting back to her original question.

She seemed to want some deeper reason than just that it was fun, so I thought up something for her: "I like trying on different lives," I said. "People are always wishing they're someone else, you know, like a baseball player, or president or some famous actor. So that's sort of what I was doing. Breaking into people's houses was like being on the inside of somebody else's life looking out."

"How did you get in?" she asked.

"People always left windows open or hidden keys. I never broke into the big houses because they have alarms all over the place. I broke into places where the people would never think anyone would bother breaking in."

"And how did you know when they were away?"

"Frankie was a paperboy," I said before I could stop myself from mentioning him.

"He told you?" Larkin seemed surprised, as if she knew him personally and he wasn't the type to do that.

"Sure, he came with me, too," I said, figuring that it didn't make any difference now to talk about it. "We drank so much of this guy's Coors one night we collapsed on his bed and didn't wake up till next morning when the family came home. We hid in the closet, and the woman sort of knew something was wrong but she didn't know what. She kept walking around all of the rooms. The guy kept telling her to shut up and start breakfast because he was dead tired from driving all night."

"How did you get out?"

"We ran out the back door while they were unloading the car."

"Did you take anything from these houses?" she asked.

"We ate some food, that's all. Most of the people never knew we were there."

"How do you know that?"

"Anybody who calls the cops gets their name in the Police Blotter in the *Gazette*. A few times people reported food missing, like jars of peanut butter and six packs, or cookies. You'd think they'd feel pretty stupid calling the cops about that. Then there was a big story once about how strange it was food was missing from so many houses in the same month, but nobody figured out why."

Larkin turned off the tape recorder and stuffed it into her brown leather briefcase. "I've been asking all the questions tonight. Do you have anything you want to ask me?"

"Yeah," I said, "you married?"

"No."

"How come? Don't you want to be?"

"Some time I do, just not yet. I want to see the world through my own eyes for awhile longer before I take on someone else's viewpoint, too."

That seemed like an odd description of what happens in marriage, but I figured she was closer to it than me and must know what she was talking about. "So how old are you?"

"Twenty-seven."

That was older than I thought, but at least she wasn't thirty yet. "Do you do this all the time," I said, "go find people and write about them?"

"Not really. Most of the time I invent people and put them together on paper and see what they do. It's called *fiction*," she said, as if I'd never heard of it.

"But you can make the people do what you want. You're the writer."

She shook her head. "That's not the way it works, at least for me. If you create real characters, you just start them off with a personality, a description of where they live, plus the beginning of the plot—something happening. Then the characters start acting like real people and you don't know what they're going to do or say. I just follow along behind them and write down what I see and hear."

It seemed to me she was having trouble separating real life from her made-up stories, but I didn't say that. "Sounds cool," I said.

She smiled at a thought. "One time I created a woman in a story called 'The Woman Always Wore Red.' In every scene, she wears red, I never had a reason why. It didn't really make a difference to the story, but I liked the title so I put the woman in red all of the time. I figured by the end of the story she would do something that made sense for a lady in red. Anyway, this woman has a fight with her father, and even though he's dying, she won't visit him one last time."

"So what happens?"

She shook her head as if disgusted. "Unfortunately, nothing else happened. I couldn't finish the story. Sandra wouldn't let me."

"Who's that?"

"Sandra—the woman in red. She wouldn't go home to see her dying father, and that's where the story was. I gave up trying to make her."

"You could have just killed her off, though, right?"

"Well, I guess so," she said, thinking of the possibility. "But that wouldn't have worked because I already had the father dying. You can't have too many people dying in the same story."

"Shakespeare massacred all of his characters, didn't he?"

She looked surprised, like I shouldn't know that kind of stuff. "Yes, sometimes he did, but since I'm not Shakespeare, I have to be more careful."

"You ever kill characters because you don't like them?"

"There have been a few that got me so angry I wanted to club them with a bat or push them off a cliff." She laughed a little when she said this, as if she were confessing a secret criminal urge.

"That'd be radical," I said, "having the power to do that."

She looked at me funny, like I meant the real thing.

Ten

NEXT MORNING, I WOKE UP HARD. IN THE SHELTERS I NEVER HAD A room to myself where I could lay back on my bed, kick the covers off and let my hands go wild like this. But just as I was getting going there was a knock on my door.

"It's me," Dad said, "can I come in?"

"I'm asleep. Go away."

He didn't say anything for a minute, but I didn't hear him go away, so I pulled the sheet over me in case he decided to burst in.

"Jake," he finally said, "I want to read you something."

"Not now, Dad."

"Why not? You aren't sleeping."

"I'm jerking off."

"You can do that later," he said as he pushed the door in. Dad and I had always been pretty open about this sort of thing after he caught me the first time in my treehouse outside their bedroom. I must have been making some kind of odd noise, because he came to the window with his flashlight and caught me pulling up my shorts. Later that night he talked to me for awhile about sex, particularly sex outdoors, and up a tree, which he admitted could be exciting, especially at my age at the time, which was fourteen. But I shouldn't do it regularly, he said, particularly outside the window where Jenny might see me. I should use my bed like other kids did. That was fine with me, I told him, except in our house Jenny treated a closed door as if it must have blown shut accidentally.

"Dad, how come you're not working?" I said to him as he stood over my bed. "Today's Monday, right, like a workday?"

"Well Jake, how come you're not in school?" Dad had a point, and I decided to drop my question if he would drop his. "You don't really need school," he continued. "You're a bright boy—you could educate yourself if you read more."

"Sure, Dad."

"You always liked good books," he said, "even when you were a baby." I didn't know that about myself and wondered how I let him know that before I could even talk. He started to sit on my bed but then looked at the sheets, which were kind of sweaty. So he backed away and sat on the edge of the window sill. The morning sun was flooding the room with so much light that I could barely keep my eyes open. "Listen to this," he said, waving his book in the air too fast for me to see the title. "'Notice your neighbors,'" he read, "'if perchance a death takes place in the building. They were asleep in their little routine and suddenly, for example, the concierge dies. At once they awake, bestir themselves, get the details, commiserate. A newly dead man and the show begins at last.'"

I nodded as I always did when Dad read me some passage from one of his Great Books. "A newly dead man," I repeated, "and the show begins at last."

"You have a good mind for words, Jake, you remember them. I forget and have to go back and read a part over and over."

It was true that I remembered. Even years afterward on the road, some passage he had read to me would slip back into my consciousness from wherever it had been hiding. A lot of kids thought I was pretty weird for knowing so much from books, especially since they knew so little. But now wasn't really the time I felt like hearing about death. "Come on, Dad, you bust in on good sex to read me about some guy dying?"

He looked over his book at me, and it seemed like he wanted to laugh but had gotten out of the habit. "I wouldn't call that good sex," he said, "not when you're alone."

"What is it then, perversion?" Dad liked it when I talked about things kids didn't normally mention to their parents. I pulled the sheet down some on my chest like I might yank it all the way off and really shock him. "You think your kid's perverted, Dad?"

"The world's perverted, Jake. You're as normal as me."

"Great company," I said as his eyes disappeared behind the book, which I could see was *The Fall*. He began to read again: "'Moreover, is it mere chance that I should speak of a concierge? I had one, really ill favored, malice incarnate, a monster of insignificance and rancor, who would have discouraged a Franciscan. I had even given up speaking to him, but by his mere existence he compromised my customary contentedness. He died and I went to his funeral. Can you tell me why?'"

I nodded to the last question. "I can tell you," I said.

"Why?"

"Because when you go to someone else's funeral, it's like going to your own."

"Yes," Dad said, "I think that's almost it. We're practicing for our own."

We didn't practice with my mother. Dad paid the funeral home to take care of her quickly with no viewing, no church service—just a short ceremony at the cemetery for the family. The last thing he wanted was for people to awake, stir themselves, get the details, and commiserate with him.

"Dad?" I said.

"What?"

"This discussion has been interesting and all, but I'm kind of losing the urge to jerk off."

He shut the book and stood up. "I guess I'll go whack at the wasp nests now. Jenny's been after me all week to do it." For as long as I could remember, the wasps had been breeding under the eaves around the house and squeezing in through cracks in the shingles. He hated killing them as all living things, even the large black and white spiders that lived in our kitchen. He'd lay his hand down on the tile so that they'd walk onto it, then carry them outside. He could hardly bring himself to put them out on a cold day in the fall, worrying that they would freeze to death. "Kris got bitten on the ear last night," he said to explain the mass murder that he was about to commit, "so now the wasps must go."

•

"You almost ready?" Jenny called upstairs to me in a voice as clear as if she were standing in the hallway. She had studied acting in college, so she knew how to project.

"Hold on a minute," I shouted, "I'm jerking off."

"Don't talk like that. And get down here or I'll go alone."

I was jerking off again, or still—at least trying to get hard again. I'd fallen asleep after Dad's visit and not woken up until after noon when I heard him climbing on the roof over me to get at the wasp hives under the back gutters. With a cool breeze coming in the side room, it seemed like a nice afternoon for fucking. I had been lying there thinking of girls I'd met on the road, which didn't help me get hard at all, so I started imagining girls I'd like to meet. But a woman came to mind—the writer, with the blue dress sticking to her skin.

"Right now!" Jenny shouted for the last time. You could tell it was because she let the screen bang shut as she went out the front door. Once she slammed the screen so hard it popped a hinge and hung cockeyed all summer.

I jumped up, stuffed myself into my shorts and then grabbed through the duffel bag to find my blue pullover with "Alcatraz" written on the front. It was a shirt I'd won on a dare that I couldn't steal the hubcaps off a squad car with the cops sleeping in it. Gary, the kid who bet me, bombed the cruiser with stones as I was prying off the front left hubcap, the most dangerous one. It banged onto the sidewalk and made a terrific racket. I scooped it up and ran for the bushes full of poison ivy and stickers. The old cops came wobbling out of their car, shining their lights into the woods and shouting what they'd do if they caught me. But how could they catch me if they wouldn't come in the woods? They pretended to return to their car, but I could hear them doubling back and crouching at the edge of the trees, waiting for me to be stupid and raise my head. I stayed low, breathing in the cool damp pine needles pressing against my face. The wet earth reminded me of sleeping out on the riverbank.

It took me only a few hours that night to track down Gary on the streets of Concord, New Hampshire, which wasn't a very easy place to hide in for a kid without a home. He was drinking beer outside Taps with some local guys and feeling loose. He didn't see me come up behind him and smash him over the head with the hubcap. He fell like one of those pro wrestlers who staggers for awhile before hitting the mat. It was tough getting the Alcatraz shirt off Gary since he was unconscious, but I did.

I hurried now to the bathroom, threw some water on my face and ran downstairs. Jenny wasn't kidding about leaving without me, and I didn't feel like walking the mile to town. She didn't really want me to go anyway, even though it had been a week since the *Gazette* article made it sound like Public Enemy Number One had returned to New Hope. She said I shouldn't underestimate how some in town felt about me, and I knew from the anonymous phone calls that she was right. A lot of people seemed to take the canal assault personally even though they didn't even know Kelly Siever. Dad said they were looking for someone to blame for all the violence in society, and as the only New Hope kid in the pack, I was a good target. Jenny said that most people had probably forgotten the whole thing until the *Gazette* stirred them up. She said that what I had to do was act like a model kid. She tried to be serious when she said this, but we both started laughing a little.

When I got outside, she was standing by the old Buick looking in. Dad was sitting inside with the windows up tight and his fingers gripping the wheel like he was driving around a racetrack. She rapped the window with her knuckle. He looked over and kind of grinned.

"Did you finish with the wasps?"

He shook his head and opened the door to talk to us. "Not quite," he said, which for Dad meant pretty much not at all.

"Are you going somewhere?" Jenny asked.

He shrugged as if he hadn't quite decided yet. "I was going to," he said.

"And?"

"It occurred to me that if I went somewhere, in an hour or so I'd just be here in the car again as if I'd never left."

"That's the way things work," she said as she took his arm and coaxed him out of the car.

"The world should be more interesting than that," he said. "Sometimes you should come back to a different place, one you've never seen before."

"Well," Jenny said, "if we aren't home in an hour, you'll know that's what happened to us."

•

We took the back way into New Hope—down New Street to Mechanic, then over Stockton—to avoid the long line-up of cars on South Main. Jenny drove the old green Buick like a tank that expected everything to get out of its way. When a car held its ground or some tourist didn't run across the street fast enough, she hammered the horn with her fist and speeded up to show she wasn't kidding. She never drove real fast, just steady. She hated having to stop because starting up again was so hard. The Buick never did run on all cylinders. It clattered along like somebody had left a wrench inside the engine.

She dropped me at the corner of Main and Bridge streets, "The Crossroads of New Hope," as the sign on Steve's All or Nothing antique shop said. Steve used to live in Brussels where a sign like that meant something. She did-n't bother to pull over to let me out, and no one could get around the Buick while she hunted in her pocketbook for some money. She handed me ten dollars, hoping, I guess, that I wouldn't steal what I could pay for. Jenny didn't have a very good memory. "Watch what you do now," she said to me as I waved her to get going. As I crossed Bridge Street she yelled "Think!" which made a few people turn their heads. Even for New Hope that was a strange thing to call down the street.

I waited till she turned up North Main and couldn't see in her rear view mirror that I was heading for Now and Then Records. I wasn't supposed to go in there, which wasn't a law of Jenny's or anybody else's as much as a condition for the owner, Mr. Schneider, not to press charges a few years ago. As Jenny would say, "It was understood."

Now and Then was divided in half—the Then side filled with records by Janis Joplin, Jim Morrison and Jimi Hendrix, people who went out of this world pretty fast but seemed to have a good time going. The Now side where Frankie and I spent our time had the latest CDs from

Cracked Skulls and Vino Vomitus. The problem started when Schneider decided we were hanging around too much and spending too little and scaring some of the Then people from coming in. First he told us to get away from the front of the shop where we used to kick around the hackysack, and then he said we could come in only before five pm, and then not at all on weekends, so we told him to fuck it and messed up the store a little the next night. There was only a girl wearing a yellow stretch top working the cash register, and she ran to the storeroom and locked herself in as soon as I kicked over the rack of Country Top 40. She told the police I threatened her, which was sort of true because I said I'd like to kiss her.

When I got to Now and Then I stopped to look in the window. The big picture of Morrison's face was still sitting there in the middle of an American flag. Underneath it said, "I am a guide to the Labyrinth," which I never did understand. Another poster announced a celebration at Washington Crossing State Park on the anniversary of Abbie Hoffman's death. "Bring your own picnic," it said. City Garden in Trenton was advertising bands I never heard of—the Have Nots, False Virgins, and Chicken Scratch. Frankie and I used to walk over the bridge to Lambertville and hitch down to Trenton. Sometimes Patton the bouncer let us stand in the back for the early show if Frankie gave him $20.

I opened the door and jangled the bells that were put in as a first line of defense against Frankie and me. The guy at the counter looked up. He was wearing a headset and tapping a pencil. Since I didn't know him—which meant he didn't know me—and Schneider didn't seem to be around, I figured I didn't have to worry about getting hassled. The guy smiled at me like he was gay and I smiled back like maybe I was, maybe I wasn't. It was useful to know how to do that in New Hope.

Dad couldn't fake it. His hair was too wild and he wore flannel shirts even in summer, usually gray and purple. He was too sloppy and dull-looking to be gay. He should have been able to get a job selling something in town, but nobody would give him a chance after he got fired from Class Act.

They said he made customers nervous. He sure didn't put people in the mood to buy things they didn't need, which is mostly what New Hope sold.

"Can I show you anything?" the guy at the counter said. He stood up to show himself off. He was pretty thin, like all the gay guys in town, and he wore a yellow shirt unbuttoned halfway down his chest.

"I could really use some *hot* music," I said, "but I'm out of cash, you know?"

His eyes got wide. He came around the counter to check me out. The "Alcatraz" stitched on my shirt didn't seem to scare him away. "How much money do you need?" he said.

"Not much at all, just enough for a CD."

"I could buy something for you," he said, "if you'd pay me back somehow."

I thumbed through the CDs until I saw one with a burning cross on it. "You'd really buy this for me?" I said and reached under my T-shirt and rubbed a little.

The guy was starting to look a little nervous, like maybe I was dangerous. "You live around here?" he asked.

"Yeah, I do, right in New Hope—but not too close," I added, in case that was a problem.

The door opened and the bells rang. A couple of small kids flew in with a woman hurrying behind them. The gay guy looked from them to me.

"You buying this for me or not?" I said.

"Okay," he said and went behind the counter. He pulled out a bag and slipped the CD in. "Come back at seven o'clock. That's when I get off."

I took the package, making sure not to touch him. I never liked touching a guy's hands when they wanted to touch me. "I don't think so," I said. "I'm not into that stuff."

"You don't have to do anything," he said, whispering now. "I'd just like to talk to you."

I didn't believe that—who would want to talk to me?

The little kids ran up to the counter, showing him the ice cream cones they were licking. I left, shaking the door a little to rattle the bells.

Eleven

"SAM," I CALLED OUT AS HE LIFTED THE AX OVER HIS HEAD. HE flexed his knees and swung the ax head down through the log, splitting the pieces out sideways. He set the next log on the block and then squinted over at me before swinging again. The ax caught deep in the wood, and he struggled to pull the head out. At 250 pounds, Sam looked a lot stronger than he really was, which I knew because we used to arm wrestle, and I beat him even when I was fourteen. "Jake," he said, finally remembering my face. He gave up trying to free the ax and called over to me, "What are you doing back?"

I shrugged that I didn't know, that as usual, things just happened. He grabbed his red work shirt off the hammock hook on the outside of his cabin. He took his time pulling it on and buttoning it up, looking at the ax stuck in the wood and then at me. "Let's go in and talk," he said, as he tucked the shirt into his khakis. We both knew that as always, he'd be doing most of the talking.

The cabin looked like an old shack from the back where we went in. Sam said he spent most of his time inside looking out, so why should he care about the outside? He let the shop side on Main Street run down, too. He figured his customers should get the real Indian experience, not some slicked up version like they'd see in Santa Fe. He covered the broken front window with tar paper and let the paint peel off the door. He was creating an authentic reservation-style store, and it cost him nothing to do it.

The town tried to make Sam shape up. The other shop owners said his "Indian Reservation" offended the tourists who came to New Hope to spend good money and deserved something better to look at when they turned onto Main Street from the south. Sam said that if they were coming from Philadelphia or Trenton, they sure wouldn't be bothered by how his place looked. He said that the other store owners were just prejudiced against a hard-working red man.

Sam also stirred up people with the cigar store Indian he dragged out on the sidewalk each day. He put a black cowboy hat on the wooden head, stuck a cigarette between the Indian's lips, and wedged an empty Johnny Walker's bottle between his body and arm. Sam liked to make a statement at the same time he was trying to lure people into his shop like any good businessman. That painted wooden Indian sure got me to come inside. I was about eleven and always on the lookout for something different the year Sam moved to town. Inside the old oak door was a roomful of everything he could lay his hands on from the Southwest. Some of it was handmade Indian, but a lot of it was fake stuff he could buy very low and sell very high. He said it felt good to sell the fakes even though he was making enough money in real Indian pottery and jewelry that he didn't really have to anymore. He couldn't explain why, but there was just more pleasure in cheating white people, he said.

Sam pushed open the sliding screen, and I followed him inside. "I'll get us some beer," he said as he headed for his supply room. The cabin was just as I had left it last summer when I stopped to say goodbye to him. He didn't try to talk me out of running except to say that if I was expecting freedom to feel wonderful, I'd be disappointed. He said that I would just find new problems to substitute for the old familiar ones I was leaving behind. I told him that was fine with me. Then he handed me $100 so that I wouldn't have to steal right away.

Sitting back in Sam's cabin again, I felt like I had never left, as if the ten months had just slipped away from me in a chunk. Everything in the room seemed just as before, and it made me feel right at home. The place was jammed with furniture and tools and books everywhere. His bible was *The Importance of Living*, by a Chinese philosopher named Lin Yu Tang. Sam always kept it within arm's reach. He said he needed a lot of reminding why living was important. He also read and reread *Raintree County*, the only book he said he wished he had written himself. He memorized short descriptions of places from it and repeated them later as if they were his own words, his own life. Places were important to Sam, even though he said he didn't feel like any one place was his anymore. Dad gave Sam some classics about Indians, but he wasn't interested. He said the goal of his life was to feel human, not Indian—and maybe not even human, just alive.

In the back corner of the cabin, drawing pads and paints and brushes were scattered next to a giant easel. Sam would stand there for hours painting and talking to me. He'd look at the Delaware flowing not far beyond his window and see something different—the streams and people and adobe huts of the reservation north of Albuquerque where he grew up. His finished paintings hung by adhesive tape all over the walls. They were bad paintings, even Sam knew that. His people were always too big to fit in his houses, and his rivers looked like wandering snakes. Sam told me once that he used to paint better out West, that he had lost his mind's eye for his past. I said he should go back to the pueblo to remind himself of how his past looked. But he said I didn't understand what it meant to leave a reservation. You didn't just show up later to pick up a few memories you had left behind.

Five years ago Sam settled in New Hope and built himself a cabin because he didn't want to feel the hands of strangers around him. The ceiling was 20 feet high with shining pine boards running up to the peak. The beams were 4 by 6—"strong enough to keep the sky from falling in," as Sam said. From the top of the ceiling, a long rope hung down from a pulley. Sam used it to get furniture up to the loft. The only other way up was a steep staircase leading to a 2-by-2-foot hole you had to squeeze through. Sam thought about widening the entrance, but he said the ladies liked the challenge of getting into bed with him. He didn't want to disappoint them.

•

Sam Redstone was a writer, at least he used to be. He came to New Hope some years after his book, *Born Red*, made the bestseller list for two weeks during 1979, the last year, he said, that Indians were "in." He wrote about being raised on the pueblo by his grandmother and scamming white tourists who came to the reservation to feel sorry for how the poor Indians lived. When he grew up he said he figured out how to use white people by fronting for businesses trying to get government loans. He was the token Indian executive for about a half-dozen small companies where whites really did the work. He said it was about time Indians took advantage of white people.

After Sam got out of jail the second time, he started wondering why he was who he was, why he lived like he did, and how his life was going to turn out. Prison didn't really cure Sam's fondness for cheating, but it did slow down his actual pursuit of it. When he was twenty-five, he paid $10 to a fortune teller in Albuquerque to tell him what was in the cards for him. In the course of revealing that he would be dead by unnatural causes before age fifty, she said that he should reconcile as soon as possible with his mother. Sam laughed at her, since he was sure his mother was dead. Oona, the fortune teller, rechecked her cards and then apologized for being the bearer of shocking news, but his mother was definitely alive. Sam eventually believed her because she kept insisting even after he had gone upstairs to her room with her and wasn't paying money.

It took Sam two years to hunt down his mother through tribal records, the Bureau of Indian Affairs, and other government and Indian agencies to whom he lied and bribed until they admitted that she was as Oona had said, alive. It took him a couple of more months to get her address, and when he finally showed up at her door in Las Vegas, she really was dead, just a week in her grave.

•

"Miller heavy," Sam said, handing me a beer. He always let me drink with him, even when I was only fourteen. I swigged down half the bottle as he pulled out the little tin he kept in his shirt pocket and popped a pill in his mouth. He washed down his "psychic pain medication," as he called it, with a swig of Miller. "Just get back?" he asked.

"A couple of weeks ago—but I haven't gotten out much," I added, in case he thought I should have come by sooner. "Jenny thinks there might be trouble again because of the *Gazette* article. She thinks people will start remembering stuff about me." Sam nodded, but I could tell he wasn't listening. Jenny bored him. "How come you're not out front working today?" I said to change the subject. "The town's crawling with people."

He brushed his long black hair away from his face, and when he took his hands away, the hair fell back. "I hired a pretty young lady to work the store," he said. "I was getting too insulting for my own good. So I kicked myself out back here where I can paint and write."

"So, what are you writing?" I asked him, which was always a dangerous question because Sam had a serious case of writer's block. After his first book, he discovered he didn't have enough inside him to make into a second. All he could come up with were random thoughts, with no story to hang them on. His publisher told him that often happened to writers who wrote only about themselves, and a lot of them ended up making friends with whiskey. Sam said he didn't need to worry about that, having made the acquaintance long before.

"I write every day," he said, setting down his bottle and dragging a shoebox from under the chair where I was sitting. He picked out a slip of paper from the box and showed me the date—March 9th, about three months ago: "It's far easier to freeze your ass off than cry your eyes out." He shrugged. "Sometimes I don't remember exactly why I write something. I guess I could have written, 'It's far easier to cry your eyes out than freeze your ass off.'" I nodded that either way made sense to me. "I think I was riding my cycle that day," he said as he picked up another piece of paper and read: "He should have rolled out of his mother's belly and into his grave. That would have been the decent thing to do."

"Who's that about?" I asked him.

"A violent, stupid bastard, a man swimming in the low end of the gene pool."

"What did he do to you?"

Sam shook his head. "Not to me, to this woman I was seeing. He beat her up, left her unconscious."

"Your girlfriend?"

"Yeah, and his wife." Sam threw the paper back in the box and pulled out another one, a paper napkin: "Why do people have to touch each other on the outside in order to feel it on the inside?"

"I don't know," I said.

He crumpled the paper and tossed it over his head onto the floor. "Me either. That's why everything I write goes into this shoebox. Some time later I pick out a paper and see if it still makes any sense. If it does, maybe I'll use it in a story."

Sam finished his beer as I finished mine, and we stared at each other for awhile. He had taught me years ago not to say anything if I didn't have something interesting to say, so we often went long spells saying nothing.

•

It got late. Every few seconds light filled the room from cars going down Main Street. Sometimes I hitched out of town with them just to be going somewhere, too. It was always a long walk back into New Hope, because not even the gay guys would pick up a kid after dark if they couldn't get a good look at him first.

"This is the worst part of the day," Sam said, "when the natural light goes out and manmade light comes on."

That was a new thought for him. He used to just turn on the lights at night like everyone else. I pointed at the candle sitting on the woodstove. "Fire is natural. You could light the candle."

"Sure I could," Sam said but didn't.

I looked around the room for matches, running my hands over the usual places. My head brushed into the string for the overhead light and I yanked it. Nothing happened. I reached up and didn't feel a bulb. I should have pulled my hand away from the socket, but I stuck two fingers in it. The shock kicked me backwards, slamming me through the side window like I had been shot out of a cannon.

"Jake!" Sam yelled and leaped out of the darkness toward me. "You okay? What happened?" I rubbed a glass chip from my face so that I could open my eyes. "Don't move," he said, "you might cut yourself worse." My hip was jack-knifed over the sill, caught on the glass still stuck in the window frame. Sam grabbed a towel from his easel and pressed it to my stomach. "Hold it tight," he said, "I'll call an ambulance."

"No ambulance, Sam."

"You just took 120 volts and you're squirting blood. You have to go to the hospital."

"I'm okay," I told him. "The electricity's gone, and it's just some little cuts. You can stop the bleeding."

"Lay quiet then," he said in his disgusted voice, which he didn't often use with me. It reminded me of the time I told him I'd poured molasses on the seat of Sgt. Decker's squad car—I thought he'd laugh, but instead he took me by my arms and shook me until my brains rattled in my head. Now he began picking the big pieces of glass off my arms and legs and head. Then he got his hands under me and lifted. I felt too heavy for him, but Sam managed to get me off the sill and carry me to his rope chair, which he had made himself.

"You don't want me bleeding into this," I said, sucking in my stomach.

"Fuck the chair. I can't get you up to the loft, so just sit there." The words came out fast, the way Sam talked when he was angry. He went for water, cotton, and bandages. He also came back with a light bulb, which he screwed into the overhead socket. Then he closed the drapes and switched on the light. He was good at cleaning me up, just doing it and not asking me if it hurt every second. Of course it hurt. When he was done, he wrung out the towel in the sink and came back with an old sheet to wrap me in. Then he pulled up a stool and sat in front of me. "You know," he said, "you should have learned by now not to stick your fingers in a socket."

"I guess I wanted to feel electricity."

He nodded. "Everyone gets the urge to turn the current on themselves sometimes, but most people never do."

I did, and maybe I would again. I couldn't be sure.

"It's a risky thing to do," he said.

Just a risky thing? Not a crazy thing to do? I fed him the words to use about me: "You have to be real crazy to shock yourself like that."

"Maybe you are," he said.

If I could have watched myself like he was watching me right then, I figured I could tell. Dad said you could know anybody by watching them for awhile—see what they smile at and what they don't. See what makes them laugh and what doesn't. See what they can look at and what they can't.

"Sometimes being crazy is the only correct response to the world," Sam said. "But other times it can get you killed. You have to know the difference."

"Or get someone else killed," I added.

"Thing is," he said, starting to like the subject he had fallen into, "nobody lets you be crazy nowadays. You're supposed to make sense, do the right thing, act normal." He pulled up one edge of the sheet to see if my arm was still bleeding. "It didn't used to be like that," he said as he let the sheet drop. "Crazy people used to wander around the town or reservation. Nobody tried to change them. They just gave them a meal and let them go on their way."

The shock was still rattling through my nerves. I was sitting cross-legged on Sam's favorite chair, wrapped in a white sheet, with cuts clotting up all over my chest and arms. And Sam was ranting on. "The crazy people are the saviors," he said. "Like Jesus, he acted crazy and look what came of it—a religion that runs millions of people's lives and ruins millions of lives. All religions start with a crazy man who scares people into believing. It's better to believe and be wrong than not believe and be wrong."

Sam took a breather, and I pulled the sheet down a little to check myself. The bandages on my hip were seeping around the edges. I felt hot and itchy all of a sudden but otherwise not so bad considering the big kick from the current. In front of me, Sam was running down religion as usual, as if no good ever came from it. I already knew that. I'd seen what it did to Kenny, the youngest of us at the shelter in Concord, and the only one to swear at all times that he really had a family at home worrying about him. We all knew different.

For days he couldn't keep food down. He was a very religious kid from Manchester, not far away, and he couldn't stand being thrown out on the street having to live with guys like us, which meant he was as bad as us. He spent two weeks in the director's personal house having baby food spooned into him. When that didn't work, they hooked up an intravenous line in a hospital, but he tore out the needle. He came back to the bunks looking thin and dead.

They asked me to help him. First I tried making him feel tough, but that didn't work. When I wasn't around for a minute, some other kid would throw water in his face or stuff him into a closet. So I tried making Kenny feel better about what he did—killing his stepmother when he was 13. It was sort of an accident, he whispered to me one night before going to sleep. He didn't really point the gun, he said. And he was sorry he killed someone, although not his stepmother specifically. Everyone called it a tragic accident, except for Kenny's father. He said Kenny did it on purpose and swung a coal shovel at his head. Kenny decided to run.

One night I came across an old Bible in a bureau. The leather cover was ripped off and pages were missing, but I found the only parts I remembered from church—where God leads the tribes to massacre their enemies. I read to Kenny from the Old Testament where God says, "Don't spare anyone, not even a child." If God did so much killing, I asked him, how could it be so bad?

Those nights I read to him he fell asleep in the cot next to mine with the Bible under his pillow. He said he felt better that he was in a place where the Bible was read every night like his mother used to at home. One night in December he told me he was starting to feel pretty good about himself. He thanked me for being his friend with a handshake, very formal but nice, and the next day he jumped from the barn loft. It was a forty-foot swandive, the prettiest you ever saw. We were gathering kindling behind the sheds when he called something to us we couldn't hear. The director shielded his eyes from the sun and said, "What's he doing up there?" Kenny waved and dove headfirst into the hard snow. It was an awful sound, a body hitting like that, someone you knew real well.

"Nowadays we deal with craziness," Sam said, driving Kenny from my mind. "We don't let it get dangerous or creative. Before technology we didn't pretend to know how rationality worked. Now we say rationality is a machine, and if you don't function like the normal drawing of the human machine, one of your parts must not be working right. That's when they go in with their greasy fingers trying to fix you."

"They tried to fix me," I said, but Sam already knew the story. The school started me in counseling in eighth grade with a woman named Mrs. D'Angelo, who shook her head every time I told her about fighting or hunting. She said violence of any kind was never the answer, and I said violence seemed like the answer to me most of the time. I didn't progress too far with Mrs. D. If there was a fight going on, I usually found myself in the middle of it swinging at anyone near me. Weaker kids paid me to stand up to bullies for them. Sometimes I couldn't remember what I was fighting about or even who I was fighting, but it still felt good getting my kicks in.

I never figured out why I liked fighting so much, or why I was so good at it. I sure didn't learn it from Dad. He wouldn't raise his voice, let alone his fist, at anyone. When he realized he couldn't talk me out of fighting, he sent me to Rocky's self-defense school to learn self-control. Lucky for me, Rocky's idea of control was focusing all of your energy on hurting the other guy before he hurt you. So I just learned how to fight better. I also learned how to punch out car windows without cutting the skin. Rocky didn't actually teach this skill. In class, we broke boards mostly. But glass always sounded better to me—that pop when your fist crashed through, and then the crash of the pieces to the pavement. I punched out dozens of panes in the abandoned warehouses along the Delaware. But more fun was popping the windows of the slick cars parked at the train station in town. I got caught once with my hand sticking through a Mercedes window, which is a hard place to explain how you got there. The judge put me on juvenile probation and assigned Sergeant Decker as my watchdog. After awhile he said he'd developed a sixth sense when a burglar or fire alarm went off—he knew if I did it. I told him that even if caught me, I'd get off soon enough. Judges always believed me when I said I didn't mean any harm—which was true—and that I'd try hard not to do it again—which wasn't true at all. They'd put me on more probation or give me some warning that didn't mean anything to me, and I was still walking around like before. That part killed Decker, knowing that whatever I did, I'd be back on the street right away.

But after the canal attack, the school, town, and police got together "to do something about me," as Jenny liked to say. It didn't matter that I didn't do much of anything this time and that Frankie told them I'd spent the night at his house watching videos. They said that I'd gone too far. I wasn't just attacking cars anymore, but actual people. They wanted to send me to a head hospital in Norristown for tests. They told Dad and Jenny that I was out of control, everybody's control, even my own, which for one thing, was true.

Everybody knew about Norristown. It had places for violent kids, and violent adults, and crazy kids, and crazy adults, and violent crazy kids and so on. It was in the last category they said I fit. I heard Jenny's side of the conversation over the phone as I hid listening in the upstairs hallway. She kept saying, "If you think it will help, I'll talk to his father. Maybe Norristown would straighten him out." It was the kind of solution she'd been looking for all along, someone else to handle me. But I ran. I learned that very early—you can always outrun them.

"I didn't let them fix me," I told Sam.

He was staring at his silver timepiece. It never kept time just right. He was always studying it and trying to figure how far off from real time it was. "Shit!" He flicked the cover closed and put the watch back in his pocket, "I forgot Janice." Then he pulled out the watch again and looked, trying to squeeze more time in where there wasn't enough. "I was supposed to bring her over for food and a fuck."

I stood up and let the bloody sheet fall around my sneakers. "I'm all right now, I can get myself home."

"Hell you will," he said, taking my arm to hold me steady. "I can fuck Janice anytime—or I can bring her back for you, too, if you're up to it. She likes them young."

He was serious. Janice was mine for the taking. But I wouldn't have known how to fuck her right even if I wasn't all juiced out from the electricity. "No thanks, Sam."

"She's white," he said, "if that makes a difference."

"I don't think it does. I just wouldn't know what to do with her, you know?"

Sam didn't know. "You mean you never fucked?"

"Not really," I said, "but I've wanted to," I added fast, in case that was what he was wondering about. "And I bet Janice would be great. But I don't have the experience in how to do it, you know?" I could just imagine her lying there expecting me to fuck her like Sam could.

He shook his head, contradicting me as always. On this subject I figured he definitely knew a lot more than me. "Experience isn't what satisfies women," he said. "They want your feelings more than your body."

That made my prospects with women even worse because if Jenny was right, I didn't have much in the way of feelings to give anybody either.

Twelve

I WOKE UP THURSDAY MORNING FEELING WATCHED. I BURIED MY face in my pillow, but I couldn't smother my curiosity, which was something Jenny always said I had too much of. I rolled over on my back and stared up into the face of my little sister. She was dressed in jeans overalls with a white shirt underneath saying "Hanson Forever." My little sister's musical taste had definitely suffered while I was gone.

"Hi," she said.

"What are you doing in here?" She looked scared all of a sudden, like I was yelling at her rather than just asking a question, so I tried again, "What are you up to, Kiddo?"

"They're fighting downstairs," she said. "Mom threw a banana at Daddy." That didn't seem so bad to me. When Jenny threw the iron frying pan, then you knew she was really ripping mad. "I should be going to school," Krissy said, "it's almost the last day. But I don't have a lunch."

"And you can't get into the kitchen?"

"I don't want to get hit by a banana."

"Okay," I said, sitting up to think about the situation. "Why don't you just do what I used to?"

"What's that?"

"Go in their bedroom, open the drawer in the nightstand next to Dad's side of the bed, and there should be some loose change. He always drops it in there before he goes to bed."

"Isn't that stealing?" Krissy asked.

"Sort of," I said, "but not really, since it's the whole family's money to begin with."

There was a crash downstairs, and Krissy jumped closer to the bed. I reached out and took her hand. "It's okay," I said, even though I didn't believe that. One of these days Jenny was going to land with the frying pan on Dad's head, and it would be lights out forever. "They probably just knocked over a chair," I said. "Don't worry, parents fight all the time."

"I wish they wouldn't fight so loud," Krissy said and waved to me as she left the room. "See ya, wouldn't want to be ya."

·

Things quieted down below, and I tried going back to sleep. But each time I closed my eyes, Larkin filled my mind. I imagined her sitting close to me on the sofa with her leg leaning on mine, listening to me as if I were a really interesting person. I could see her reaching over to play with my hair and brushing her hand against my cheek— then in no time we'd be up in my room throwing off our clothes and rolling around in my bed!

That's how the scene always ended in my mind, and by that time I was so hard that I couldn't get back to sleep. I tried to think of anything else but Larkin. I stared at the white walls of my bedroom, trying to let my mind go blurry. But it was like in that old movie, *The Village of the Damned*, where the teacher is trying to blow up a schoolroom full of weird alien kids who can read minds. He walks into the class talking to them as if everything is fine, but the kids sense he's nervous. They radar in on his brain and see a blank wall. That starts them wandering—why would anybody be thinking of a wall? They zoom deeper into his thoughts, and finally the guy can't stop himself from thinking of the bomb inside his briefcase. But it's too late for them—the bomb explodes.

I was close to exploding myself, so I got up and decided to run like I used to years ago when Dad made me go out for school track. He'd been on the freshman team in college as a distance man, and he told me a person could run a lot of problems right out of their system. He said that the pain you felt during running had a way of relaxing the body and the mind. I guess I never ran fast enough or long enough to feel that relaxation, and like most things somebody thought would be good for me back then, I quit after a few weeks.

I laced on my sneakers and grabbed some shorts and headed downstairs. Jenny passed me on the steps and asked where I was going. She always thought that if she asked, I might not go somewhere I shouldn't.

"I'm running," I said proudly, "down to Metzgar's."

Exercise—that was something Jenny approved of, at least for other people. But she scratched her head to show me she didn't really believe it. "Your father tried running again a couple of months ago—for two days."

"I don't think I'll last that long," I said. "I'll probably just run today."

Outside, I stepped off the porch into the cool morning rain and began thinking about Miles Metzgar, which naturally made me think of horses. When I was eight years old, he bought two mares in Vermont and trucked them down for breeding with his favorite stud, Morocco. Everybody said Metzgar had a way with horses. He raced them in Florida when he was young. He bet on them sometimes, but only when he had a hot tip from one of his friends in the stables. Only a fool risked long odds, he said.

Miles never let me touch his mares. He said a good horse and a wild boy mixed like a lady and a tramp. He told me that every time I went over there. I kind of agreed with Miles that he shouldn't let me near them. But when he was off one Saturday in Atlantic City chasing some other sure thing, I sneaked a ride on Chelsea, the finest horse you could ever put between your legs. I wrapped my hands in her thick brown mane, and she sprinted across the meadow. When she jumped a rock, I lost my hold and bounced off. I hit the ground headfirst but walked away without a scratch. Not many things felt as good as riding bareback on a fast horse.

That was all years ago, before the stroke, before Miles Metzgar became what Dad described as an invalid. Jenny just called him "certifiable."

•

The rain and sweat dripped off my forehead and stung my eyes. When I reached the top of the riverbank, I could see Bantry's burned-out barn still standing about a hundred yards up in the mist. The weathervane on top was an elephant with its trunk as the pointer. I couldn't actually see the elephant, but I knew it was there, and knowing that made me feel at home again as much as anything.

In a couple of minutes I was jogging in eyeshot of Metzgar's Florida Ranch. Outside the main house, near the old white well, there was Miles sitting in his wheelchair. A gray horseblanket covered his knees. His head darted forward every few seconds, like a turtle's. I slowed up so as not to surprise him. He looked shrunken, like a voodoo head. The rain was soaking into him. His hair was wetted down, and his white shirt was stuck to his body. I climbed over the fence rail about twenty feet away from him, and already I could hear Miles muttering. After the stroke, his tongue never stopped.

I walked over almost close enough to touch him and still he didn't see me. "I built everything from doghouses to mansions," he was saying, "and never used an engineer on one of them. I had my 20-inch level with a penny on the tip of it, and I told my youngest boy to go down to the end and line it up. The first board, that's got to be letter perfect or the rest of the place won't hold together. I wasn't off more than 1/64th of an inch my whole life."

Suddenly something clicked in his head and he looked up at me like I was some kind of animal he'd come across in an open field and he was trying to figure if I was trouble or not. The rain sounded between us.

"You're that boy," he said, "what's his name that boy who ran off?" His words took up pointing toward our house since his hands couldn't.

"Jake."

"That's it, Jake, I ain't seen you around here."

Miles knew me right away. That meant that he probably knew me then, too, when he saw me coming from Bantry's the afternoon the fire broke out. Later, when they pushed his wheelchair into juvenile court, he got to coughing so hard it sounded like he was going to bust a lung. Judge Rowe said to seat him in front of the bench, but Miles Metzgar demanded to be lifted into the witness chair. America was his adopted country, he said, and he was bound to follow the rules. That sure made the judge trust what he had to say about me. A couple of court officers locked arms under Miles and put him in the box. His head barely reached over the front rail.

He answered the first question okay—his name. But then the lawyer asked his occupation. "*Invalid*," Metzgar said, and the few people in the hearing laughed. It wasn't the last time with Miles in the chair.

The prosecutor asked all sorts of useless questions before getting to the point: Did Miles see anyone coming or going about the time the Bantry place caught on fire? He'd seen me all right. I waved to him and he waved back. We were always on waving and smiling terms even after he found out I rode Chelsea. He said he liked a boy with spunk. "I see everything," he told the judge, "but I can't say I saw that boy." Miles covered for me.

"Where'd you run off to?" he asked me now as the rain grew heavier. He didn't seem to notice the low thunder rumbling a few miles away.

"North—sometimes the cities, but mostly in the country, like New Hampshire." His head rolled around on his neck. "Aren't you getting awfully wet, Mr. Metzgar?"

"I was born wet—in Newfoundland, you know the place?"

"Never been there."

"You run off there next time. I'd give my right arm to see that land again." We both looked down at his right arm, which was hanging dead over the side of the wheelchair. "I worked on a cod boat when I was about your age," he said, "didn't see the light of day sometimes for two weeks. They only did let me up to spit blood over the side so's I wouldn't foul up the bunks. That's what you get from living in the hold of a cod boat breathing fish oil and sucking fish bones."

"Doesn't sound too good."

"That was another time, boy, another life. I can tell you some things about fish that you only learn by sleeping with them. That fool woman inside, Hattie, I sent her for scallops a month ago or maybe it was more 'cause I can't tell time no more, ain't got much use for it, to tell you the truth, and what she came back with was nothing but cod. That's what scallops are when they package them that big, they aren't scallops at all, they're cod cheeks. You got people today they'd steal a nickel off a dead man's nose."

"You're right there."

"Doctoring is the same way. I got two sons I don't call

my own no more since they carted me off to a hospital. Imagine waking up one day and they got you strapped to a bed with needles in you and tubes down your throat. I waited my time. I knew what they was up to. I wasn't going to give them the chance to get me on the cutting table and bleed me to death. I went to my own doctor for forty-one years and every year I went in there he said, 'My God, Miles, you're as healthy inside as any twenty-year-old and don't let them tell you different.' He's dead now, I don't go to him no more." Metzgar coughed a few times, and his lungs sounded like a muffler with holes in it. "One day I pulled the tubes out of me," he said, gasping for air to finish his story, "and I told the nurses to bring me my clothes or I was walking out of there in my johnnycoat. That's what I finally had to do."

The blanket had come loose under his knees, so I tucked it around him again. The wool was soaked. Raindrops were dripping down his face. "How long have you been sitting out here, Mr. Metzgar?"

"I don't know exactly, about three years, I guess."

"I mean today how long?"

"Since sun up—except it never did come up today."

I took the back handle of his wheelchair and turned him toward the house. I pushed him up the little hill to the patio where he used to sit and watch his horses through binoculars. It was pretty dry there under the eaves. Inside the back door, Hattie was peeling something in her hands. Some people said she came from Haiti, because of her name, but nobody knew for sure. She spoke French, never English, even though Metzgar said she knew how. She didn't wave at me or come out for him. She just kept peeling whatever was in her hands.

"Can I ask you a question, Mr. Metzgar?"

"Can't stop you, can I?"

"You remember the hearing they had about me in town?"

"Course I do," he said. "My day in court."

"You said you didn't see me at Bantry's."

"That's what I told them."

"How come?"

125

He licked a raindrop off his lips. "I done plenty of wild things in my life, like you, and I learned that the sweetest thing is getting away with something, ain't it?"

"I agree with you there."

"Besides," he said, "I never liked Bantry. He shot at Milo, my dog."

That made me feel good, that Metzgar had lied for himself as well as for me. "I'll take you inside now," I told him.

"Don't do that," he said quickly, stopping me with his voice. "I can't stand it inside. If you see me out here dead some day, then you can wheel me inside or anywhere you want. A dead old man in a wheelchair ain't much of a sight for the good outdoors. You can wheel me into the Delaware for all I care, except I don't think the fish would appreciate me fouling up their water. But whatever you do, don't ever take me inside before it's time."

I nodded to Miles and ran off home.

•

The phone was ringing as I came in the door. Jenny had told me to stop answering it and maybe the cranks would stop calling. But I didn't like the idea that I shouldn't pick up the phone in my own house. The curses and threats weren't very creative anyway—mostly about how I was "going to get mine." One guy said he was going to do to me what I did to Kelly, which wouldn't have been much. What he meant was that he was going to do what he *thought* I'd done to Kelly. That didn't sound too good. But I figured that people who threatened me weren't the type to do anything. It was the guys who didn't call that I had to worry about.

So I stood there in the hall, rain and sweat dripping from my face onto Jenny's favorite rug, and picked up the phone. Nobody said anything for a few moments, then a woman's voice said, "Hello, anybody there?"

It was Larkin. "Yeah, it's me," I said, "Jake."

"I didn't hear you say hello," she said.

"I didn't, because I was expecting another crank call, and Jenny says I shouldn't let them know it's me."

"What kind of crank calls?"

"The usual, I guess," I said, wondering how many kinds there were. "People curse or yell. It's no big deal."

"Jake," Larkin said sharply, "you should do something about this—get your number changed, or tell the police."

As usual, she was trying to get me to act like a normal citizen, which wasn't how anybody in town thought of me, or how I thought of myself either. The New Hope police weren't going to investigate threatening phone calls to my house—I could even imagine Sergeant Decker making some of them himself. As for changing our phone number, it would be over Dad's dead body. "We'll never give in to the barbarians," he told me and Jenny at the dinner table a few nights ago.

"Are you still there?" Larkin said.

"Yep."

"I was going to drive over today, but I got stuck in New York. I did listen to the tapes last night, though, and it's going well. I wanted to tell you that."

"Thanks," I said. "So when are you coming again?"

"In a couple of days, I'll let you know. You'll be alright, won't you?"

What did she think, a few stupid phone calls were going to drive me over the edge, that I might hurl myself in front of a train out of fear? And if she was so concerned, why didn't she fuck New York and come back to interview me right now? "I'm fine," I told her right before I hung up.

Thirteen

KRIS PUSHED UP HER SLEEVES AND LOWERED HER HEAD. "OKAY," she said, "when I say 'Go,' you count to ten." I crouched next to her in the gravel of our front driveway, like a runner ready for the starting gun. She yelled "Go" and took off for the backyard. I counted to ten as she passed the porch and ran after her. I caught her by the cellar bulkhead and eased up so that we would reach the patio at the same time. "Did I win?" she said as we fell to the grass, both breathing hard.

"Sorry," I said, "it was a tie."

"Why are you sorry? That means we both won."

She rolled over on her back in the tall grass and pulled her shirt halfway up. She rubbed her belly in circles, then leaned up on one arm and looked at me. "I could take my shirt off," she said. I didn't see any reason why she shouldn't. Nobody could see us in the backyard, and she didn't have anything to see yet anyway. "Do what you want," I told her.

She reached under her shirt and pinched about where her nipple was. "I'm not getting old fast enough."

"What do you want to get old for?"

Her hand bulged out against her red shirt. "I want to be old enough for a new bike. They should get me one for my birthday."

"Yeah, they should, when is it?"

"Don't you remember? December 18."

"Oh yeah, I forgot," I said, although it seemed like something I never really knew. Birthdays had never been big events in our house, not since Mom died.

"December is awful far away, isn't it?"

"Yeah," I said, "awful far." Then an idea occurred to me. "You know, if your birthday is in December, you're coming up to your half-birthday."

"What's that?"

"It's the day halfway between your real birthdays—that's why it's called a half-birthday."

"I never heard anyone having half a birthday."

"That's because not everybody gets one, and not every year. You have to be pretty special, and pretty good."

"I've been pretty good."

"So there you are. You should have a half-birthday."

"Like when?" she said. She didn't know whether to believe me or not, but she wanted to.

"Next week, of course" I said, sucking on a blade of grass. "Your half-birthday is Wednesday, the 18th."

"I bet Mom doesn't know," she said.

"I'll tell her, just in case. You need a bike so you can ride anywhere you want this summer."

Kris nodded seriously. "I want a red one with thin tires. It can be green or blue but not yellow 'cause I throw up looking at yellow. It has to have thin tires 'cause you go faster. I'm not riding in the dirt so I don't need a dirt bike. They have thick tires. I like thin tires."

"Anything else?"

"That's all, just the bike."

"Okay, I'll talk to Jenny, but I can't promise anything."

"I don't want a promise," she said, pulling her T-shirt over her face and flinging it as far into the yard as she could, "I want a bike."

•

Jenny liked the idea of celebrating Krissy's half-birthday, which surprised me. But she said there wasn't enough money to buy her a bike, which didn't surprise me. So I said I'd get one for her, and she didn't ask how.

The best place to hunt bikes around New Hope was at Washington Crossing. That's where lots of happy-looking families came each weekend to picnic and ride around the park. They'd drive out from the suburbs of Philadelphia in vans loaded with bikes. They would never have worried about stealing in such a nice park if the state hadn't put up a warning: "Stop Thieves! Don't Leave Bicycles Unattended or Unlocked." It was the first thing you saw pulling in from River Road, and it kind of discouraged the bike-stealing business. So as fast as that sign went up in the parking lot, some kid like me pulled it out of the ground at night and threw it in the Delaware.

Being Sunday, there were lots of choices of bikes. I sat on the big rock that marked the entrance to the park and watched the vans turn in. After I saw a few possibilities go by, I walked down to the parking lot to take a closer look. I acted like a kid enjoying the outdoors, as kids were supposed to do. I even whistled.

Some of the cars had bumper stickers saying "Ask Me About My Grandchildren," "I Break Antiques," and "Easy Does It," which seemed about the stupidest saying I ever heard because Easy Never Did Anything that I ever saw. One fat Pontiac had a tie sticking halfway out the back under a sticker saying "Ex-Husband in Trunk." I yanked on the tie and it came out—just half a tie. On another car, an old red TransAm, the bumper sticker read, "Guarded by Smith & Wesson." I figured the guy probably didn't even own a gun but wanted to sound tough. I ducked down to rip off the sticker, but my fingers couldn't get under the edge. So I got out my old penknife, which was actually Uncle Toby's until he ran out of things to cut and sent it to me. I opened the little blade and scraped at the sticker until it just read "Smith."

When I stood up, there were no other people in the parking lot. The knife blade was still open and ready to cut. I felt like time was waiting for me to fill it up with something interesting. I crouched down again and held the knife as if I were going to stab someone in the back. I stabbed the tire. The blade bounced off, which I didn't expect, but then again, I'd never tried slashing a tire before. I stabbed harder and the blade nicked the rubber a little. I stabbed a third time real hard and the blade went in about an inch, making a nice popping sound.

That's when I heard voices. I pulled on the knife, but the blade wouldn't come out. The voices got louder, a little kid yelling and a father telling him to watch for cars. I worked the blade sideways, which loosened it a little, but the voices were coming close. I pulled back as hard as I could and my hand slipped off the blade, which spilled me backwards into the side of the opposite car. When I looked up, a man about Dad's age, dressed in white pants and a white shirt, was staring down at me. He looked like an ice cream salesman.

"You okay?" he asked, but he was really wondering what the hell I was doing crouched between two cars in the same parking lot where he'd left his precious car.

"Sure," I said, and that's all because I couldn't think of anything to explain myself. Then I figured that he didn't own either car I was messing around with or he would have landed on me with both feet, so he didn't have any right to hassle me at all. But before I could tell him to fuck off, the little kid threw a stone at the TransAm, making a pinging sound as it skipped over the front hood. That changed things. I jumped to my feet. "What's he doing?" I yelled. "Your little kid is trying to ruin my car."

The father looked from me to the TransAm and to his kid who was bending down to get another stone from the parking lot. "No, Joshua," the man said, "drop it."

"He ruined my paint job," I said, running my hand over the front hood, looking for a scratch, any scratch. "There," I said, finding a mark about an inch long.

The guy leaned over to where I was pointing. "I don't think Josh did that," he said.

"You see anyone else throwing stones?" I asked him, waving around the parking lot. "And that mark wasn't there five minutes ago."

I figured this guy was the kind who wanted to do the right thing, especially in front of his son. "That'll cost me $50 to get out, maybe more," I said.

He seemed to know right away that I was scamming him. "I'm not giving you $50," he said.

"You're paying me something or I'm calling the police. My brother's a cop," I added, "right in New Hope."

That little bit of imagination settled the matter. The man reached inside his shirt and fished out his wallet. It was fat with credit cards. "This is all the cash I have," he said, holding out one twenty-dollar bill.

I took the money and stuffed it in my backpocket as the guy left, dragging scrawny little Joshua behind him.

•

I still didn't have enough money to buy a bike, and finding a good one to steal was harder than I had remembered. I used to be able to just show up on a Sunday morning and be riding away in an hour with a hot bike to sell to a guy in Lambertville who told me to call him Donuts. I didn't really think that was his name. He gave me ten dollars a bike and never asked where I got them. That meant I couldn't ask him any questions either. One time he left his garage door open a little and I could see dozens of bikes hanging by hooks from the ceiling. Some of them were dripping new paint.

I wandered around the park grounds for awhile, from the sheep pen to the Soldiers' Graves to the pavilion. I passed all sorts of bikes, but not the right one for Kris. She really needed a three-speed with thin tires, maybe red, and with streamers on the handlebars and a basket on the front. She told me she'd like to take Buster, her Teddy Bear, on long trips with her. I sat down under the tall maples for awhile, flicking away the mosquitoes diving for my legs, and watched for the perfect bike. I jogged after one or two that had potential, but the owners never left them. I didn't like the idea of yanking a bike out from under someone, particularly a little girl. That was excessive force, which I had never used before, except on guys who deserved it. I thought about trying to scam up more money, since the first twenty had come so easily, but it was getting awfully hot out there, and I felt more like dunking in the Delaware right then than trying to think up a plan. So by the time I got back to the parking lot, I decided to go after the next bike I saw that was close to okay, and I would fix it up myself. The right one came along so quickly that it proved to me again that once you open yourself up to chance, things begin to happen.

A blue Saab pulled into the lot with two bikes strapped to the trunk. A short man got out, then his daughter, who looked about Kris' age. He hugged her like he hadn't seen her in awhile, probably a divorced father who had custody only on weekends. There were a lot of them around New Hope. The man untied the bikes and they climbed on, but then the girl whispered in his ear. A few seconds later, he walked over to me. "Do you know where the restrooms are?"

"Sure I do, mister, I work this lot every Sunday, so I have to know stuff like that." I pointed across the rutted road to the Boy Scout pavilion. "Beyond there," I said.

He bent down to talk to his daughter eye to eye. "The bathroom's over there," he said. "We can't ride there, because it's too rough on the stones."

"But I have to go," she said.

"I know, so you go and I'll stay with the bikes."

"What if I can't find it," the brat whined, "what if I get lost?"

The man looked at me and I shrugged that his little angel might get lost going that far. He tried to see the restroom where I was pointing beyond the pavilion, as if seeing it would make it closer.

"I suppose I could watch your bikes for a minute," I said. "But you have to hurry before my boss gets back." I looked nervously over my shoulder. "I'm not supposed to take responsibility for people's property, you know."

"That would be great," the man said, standing the bikes near the rear of his car. "I'd appreciate it."

He left hand in hand with his little girl, and when they got out of sight, I took off. It was awkward riding a bike that small, but I stood up and pumped hard to the entrance of the park without seeing any of the stupid-looking guards dressed up as Colonials. I crossed River Road onto Aquetong and ditched the bike in the brush. It seemed like an expensive one, a Peugeot, with five gears and metallic red paint. Behind the seat hung a little license plate with the name "Nicole" on it. I used the scissors from my penknife to cut the plate free and hurled "Nicole" into the tall grass. Then I took the meadow route home, twenty yards in from River Road, safe from anyone looking for a bicycle thief.

Fourteen

"WOODSTOCK," DAD SAID TO ME, AS IF HE HAD SAID IT ALL.

He was lying in the hammock on the porch, his hands under his head, an old *Life* magazine covering his bare chest. The late afternoon sun slanted in from the side of the porch, flooding Dad in light.

"Yeah, Woodstock," I said. "What about it?"

"I was there."

The wind was whipping up the dirt into swirls like miniature tornadoes sweeping across the driveway. I sat down on the front steps, stretching out, feeling hot and bored. I was just back from town where I'd picked up a gold chain from "The Artful Hand," a place where the salesgirls never watched the jewelry closely enough. The rush from stealing the bike and the chain in one day made me want something different now. But Dad wanted to talk. He said we never talked enough before, which wasn't how I remembered it.

"Look at this," he said, sitting up in his hammock. He spread *Life* out over his lap. In the giant picture, thousands of kids were sitting on the ground at Woodstock. He pointed at the only words on the two pages: "It was scary. God, I had never seen so many people." He traced his finger along one of the back lines of kids, counting off heads until he reached twelve. "That's me," he said and lifted his hand so I could see. The guy had his shirt off. He was scratching his head. His arms were thin, and the left one had some kind of mark on the muscle, like Dad's peace sign. He was sitting between rows, kind of alone, as much as anyone could be in the middle of 500,000 people. He looked like he'd gone to Woodstock by himself and not made any friends. It could have been Dad.

"You can't imagine that many people all in one place," he said. "There weren't any fights, no stealing, no hate. But still, it was scary. Country Joe MacDonald was right."

"Sounds like some stupid Country Western singer."

"It was Country Joe and the Fish," he said. Dad clicked

his fingers and began to sing, "One, two, three, what are we fighting for? You know I don't give a damn, next stop is Vietnam—"

He stopped, and his eyes went vague, like Mars' eyes. You could see there was nothing going on behind them. Maybe he was thinking about Vietnam again, maybe he was remembering Mom again. Something had stalled out Dad's brain.

"One, two, three," I sang, trying to snap him back to attention. He lay back in the hammock and stared out at things—a passing cardinal, Mars scratching the porch post, the azalea bushes he planted shaking in the breeze.

"'Fixin' to Die Rag,'" Dad said, as his mind clicked on again, "that's what it was called—'Be the first ones on your block to have your boy come home in a box.' Nobody puts words like that in a song anymore. They're too busy making videos to actually say anything. Don't get caught in that, Jake. Always think something. Always have something to say."

"I don't watch the videos," I said. "They're boring."

"That's good. You know, you would have liked living in the Sixties. You would have fit right in."

"I don't think so, Dad. I'm not a love-in kind of kid."

He dismissed my opinion with a wave of his hand. "You would have done fine. The love-ins were just an excuse to have a party. Country Joe said that the most revolutionary thing you could do in this country was to really have fun. In the middle of the war, we were having fun. That had meaning."

"So in the middle of peace I'm having a shitty time now—is that revolutionary, too?"

"Maybe it is," he said, and for some reason we both found that funny.

•

"Frankie," I said low into the phone so that Jenny wouldn't hear me, "I need your car tonight."

"Just my car?"

"And you, too, since I don't know how to drive."

"It's nice to be needed," he said.

"Come over around eight, okay?"

"What are we doing?"

"I have to pick up something. You'll like it," I said. "It's illegal."

"I'll be there," Frankie said.

•

Dad was still on the front porch reading when I came out and told him I was going to walk into town. I wanted to see if Mr. Karoly still ran the mule barge and might hire me for a few days to run tours. I didn't need a whole lot of money, but I thought a little might take the pressure off stealing. Dad jumped out of the hammock. He'd go to town with me, he said, and with any luck we'd be late for dinner. Dad hated meatloaf as much as me, and he knew Jenny would throw it out if we didn't show up on time. She thought she was punishing us.

We walked single file on River Road, close to the wooden posts that kept cars from pitching off the road into the Delaware. At the condos, the sidewalk started, and Dad caught up to my side. "A monstrosity," he said, pointing to the steel girders and cement foundation stretching about 100 yards along the river. "You'd think there would be a limit, that the earth couldn't take one more building, it would just sink."

"There's a lot of open land, Dad. I've seen it in New Hampshire."

"They'll get to it. They'll pave it over one acre at a time. You'll keep thinking there's lots of open land other places because you saw it a few years before. But you'll go back and find it's gone there, too."

We reached the edge of town where the stores started, and Dad stopped at The Indian Reservation. "I like Sam," he said.

"Me, too."

Dad opened the door and waved. Sam came running over, carrying necklaces in his hands. "William," he said, "nice to see you, old man, and that strange kid of yours."

Dad looked at me. "He is strange, I guess."

"There's no guessing about it," Sam said.

"How's business?" Dad asked.

"Bad, very bad. If I wasn't already rich enough, I'd be poor. I can't even give this stuff away." He held up the handful of jewelry, and an idea came to him. "Maybe I can give it away," he said, pulling out a necklace with beads of turquoise on a thin thread of silver. He slid it around my neck. "Looks beautiful on him, don't you think, William?"

It felt like he had just slipped a noose on me. "I don't wear necklaces, Sam."

"Before you didn't, but from today on, you wear a necklace—or a chain, think of it as a chain. A lot of guys wear them."

"Especially in New Hope," Dad said.

"That's true, men are free here, they wear what looks good. It's a gift," Sam said. "I'll be offended if you don't wear it."

I obviously wasn't getting out of Sam's without the necklace—or chain—so I thanked him and we shook hands all around. "Anybody asks, you got the necklace at The Indian Reservation," Sam yelled after us. "I have plenty more."

Dad and I walked across Playhouse bridge where two girls were sitting on the stone ledge, legs crossed and hanging out for everyone to see. "They're staring at you," he said, as we passed them. "Must be the chain." I looked back, and the girls were grinning at me. "I'm going to walk to the church and turn around," he said. "Why don't you talk to them?"

"Wait a second," I said, but he crossed the street between cars and was gone. So I turned to the girls.

"Who's the old guy," one of them said as I leaned against the stone.

"My father."

"I had a father once," she said, "at least my mother says I did."

The other girl, with very blonde hair, unscrewed some bright purple lipstick and held it up to me. "You like it?" I shook my head no. She pulled three more sticks from her

137

pocketbook and showed me the colors. I picked a light pink one. "You're very conservative," she said as she put the color on her lips. "I would have figured you for Stomach Poison."

"Or Midnight Mosh," the other girl said, "something romantic."

"I'm just not into lipstick," I said.

"But you are into necklaces."

"It's a chain, and somebody gave it to me, so I kind of have to wear it."

"From your girlfriend, right?" the blonde girl said, and I shook my head. "Not your boyfriend?" she said, twisting up her mouth like the idea of it was sick.

"No, just an old friend. He sells this stuff."

We watched the tourists walk by, and the girls talked about Trenton, where they lived, and New Hope, where they wished they lived. "In New Hope you can do anything you want—nobody cares," the blonde said.

"That's why we come here," her girlfriend said, "to do anything."

I was going to ask what they meant by "anything," but I could see Dad already coming up the sidewalk, about a half block away. "I'm going to have to go soon," I said, "my old man's coming back."

They leaned off their ledge to see him. "Maybe we could meet you sometime," the blonde said, "you can bring a friend."

"Yeah, I could do that. I know somebody."

"Is he good looking, too?"

"I guess he's alright," I said, figuring that Frankie would meet their standards if I did.

"Okay, then we'll be waiting for you, at 6 p.m."

"What day?"

"Any day," the blonde girl laughed, as if that was a stupid question.

•

We walked home slowly. At The Logan Dad suddenly turned into the street, and cars honked at him. I followed

138

him across and up the grassy hill in the center of the square, and there we leaned on the great cannon, aimed toward the Delaware. Dad read the names on the memorial plaque: "Case, Hopkins, Miller, Cunningham, Solomon, Walker, Phillips, Workman—how many times have you gone by here?" he asked me.

"Hundreds," I guessed, "maybe even thousands."

"How many times did you read these names?"

"Never."

He nodded. "We bronzed over World War I just like we do all of the wars. The dead end up as names on a plaque that nobody reads. We call it a memorial, but it's really an un-memorial." It seemed to me that people would naturally want to forget wars and the soldiers killed in them, and it was good to do that, but I didn't argue with Dad since he'd been there. "Jake," he said, his hands running over the smooth, black barrel of the cannon, "I never told you this before, but you're old enough now to understand—I didn't have to go."

He didn't seem to realize that he wasn't connecting to a previous sentence. "Go where?"

"Vietnam."

I didn't believe him. "They would have put you in prison, Dad. You did have to go."

"No," he said, "they picked kids out of a lottery. I didn't have to go."

"No, Dad, you're making this up."

"Everyone in the dorm got together in the lounge," he said in a shaky voice, still staring at the list of dead. "The drawing was done on TV—the whole country was watching. We passed around joints to keep calm," he said and then looked up at me as if he shouldn't have mentioned that part. "They did it by birthday. When the first numbers were called, guys started pounding the walls and yelling that they'd run off to Canada or go underground. That happened every few numbers up to one hundred and fifty, because those would definitely be called. They knew if they let themselves be inducted, they'd be shipped to Vietnam and probably die in the jungle. Come home in a box."

"What was your number?"

"Two hundred and fifty. They wouldn't have called me."

"You really didn't have to go?"

"I volunteered."

I couldn't believe it. After all the times he had protested the war, all the sit-ins he had told me about, the marches in Washington, the arrests. "Why did you do that, Pop? What'd you have to go into the fucking Army for?" It surprised me that his confession bothered me so much. It just seemed so wrong—Dad volunteering to go kill people.

He shrugged at me. "I suppose it had to do with the philosopher I was reading at the time—Wittgenstein."

I turned away because I didn't want to hear about another one of his stupid philosophers. "Listen," he said and touched my shoulder. "For years he thought about killing himself because he felt he was a failure, and suicide seemed like the only solution. But then World War I came along~ and he joined. He hoped that the nearness of death would bring meaning into his life. That's what he wrote."

"So you went to Vietnam because some fucking philosopher told you to?"

Dad picked a long blade of grass. "It worked for him, Jake. He needed to change himself, and looking straight at death is a powerful way to do that."

"Why did you need to change yourself?"

"I've never had a very strong grip on reality," he said, "even before your mother died. You might say I don't fit in the real world very well."

"So you went to war? That doesn't make any sense."

A big white Chevy turned the corner slowly, and we both looked over at it. A hand came out of the back seat window and lobbed a can of soda at us. It hit on the brick a few yards from us and splattered over the plaque. I jumped to my feet, but Dad didn't move, didn't even flinch. "I wanted to see war up close," he said, as if nothing had just happened, "not just on the news at night." It occurred to me as he kept talking that if we acted as if nothing happened, it really hadn't, or at least, it didn't matter if it happened or not. I understood then why Jenny wasn't yelling at me about all of the prank calls we'd been getting at home. She was pretending they weren't happening. "Nobody I knew had ever been to war," Dad said as he sucked on his blade of grass. "We were out on the streets being so moral about something we had never experienced or even seen." We both looked around as another car took the corner, but nothing came flying out of the window. "Besides," he said, "I didn't like the idea that it was just the fascist types going over to Vietnam, the guys who liked shooting gooks. I thought the army should have more people like me in it, who really didn't want to kill anybody."

"That sounds totally strange, Dad."

He shook his head as if it wasn't strange at all. "I learned a lot, Jake. I could really see why I hate war so much, and why others love it. War is very interesting. Suddenly the worst thing you can do in life is exactly what you're supposed to do, as much of it as you can. Someone else considers the morality of it, or pretends to, and orders you to kill. And once you make your first hit, the rest are easy. It gets just like knocking down those little cardboard birds at an amusement park—pop, pop, pop."

"How many did you kill?" It wasn't the first time that I'd asked him that, but it was the first time he answered.

"Seven that I know of," he said. "I played God seven times. Turns out I had a good eye for shooting."

•

By the time we reached home, we were too hot to go in the house, so we sat on the porch again, cooling in the breeze blowing up from the river. I wasn't sure I believed Dad that he didn't have to go to Vietnam, but there was no one to ask, no one I knew who knew him back then. So I changed the subject. "Dad," I said, "I want to fix up the house."

He took a quarter from his pocket and began flipping it into the air, announcing each heads or tails. "That's fine," he said, "but you should know something before you start."

"What?"

Jenny raised the porch window to call us in for dinner. "We'll be there in a second," Dad said, like he always did.

"I'd hate to hang for one of your seconds," she said and closed the window again. Most people opened their windows in summer to let air in. She closed them to keep the heat out.

Dad kept flipping the quarter in the air, catching it and turning it over on the back of his hand. It seemed like he might go on doing that all night if no one stopped him. "Entropy," he said, "you probably don't know what that means, but you've seen it all around you every day of your life."

He was right. I hadn't heard of it.

"Entropy is things breaking down, like the way your room gets messy if you don't keep cleaning it, or the line of exhaust from a skywriter spreading out into the air." He stopped to think up another example. Dad always talked in threes. "Or the way a tomato rots if you leave it sitting out too long. Entropy is all you need to know about the world."

It seemed to me that Dad had told me a few other things were all I had to know about the world—like pressure, which he said was the cause of all sex, and time, which he said was the cause of all pain. But I didn't bother reminding him of that. "So what's this entropy got to do with me?"

"Look around," he said. "We build things, nail them together, paint them—what are we doing?"

"Fixing the house up," I said.

"We're trying to create order. But it's useless. As soon as we're done, entropy takes over and the destruction begins." He stretched his long legs from his chair to the railing. "Think of it this way—it's a hell of a lot easier to make an omelette than unmake one, right?"

"I don't think you can unmake an omelette, Dad."

"Of course you can't, and the reason doesn't have anything to do with eggs. It's because time only goes in one direction, which is—"

He left the last word unspoken, waiting for me to complete his thought. He often tried to teach me this way. "Forward," I said.

"Right. Time goes forward, and disorder always follows order. It's never the other way around."

"I'm kind of losing the conversation, Dad."

He took a deep breath, preparing for his final attempt at explaining. "You wanted to fix up the house, and I'm saying you should realize that would be against the grain of things. Wildness is natural, disorder is natural, so why fight it? Order is artificial, it's what man brought to the world because he couldn't live in disorder."

It sounded like Dad had made up a nice philosophy to support his natural laziness. I was going to tell him that entropy was just an excuse for him, but my sister came running out of the house licking a grape Popsicle. She saw we weren't doing anything interesting and hopped down the porch steps on one leg. A wasp buzzed her and then settled on a yellow tulip by the railing. She leaned over the flower and let purple spit drip from her mouth. "Yeah!" she shouted when she hit her target and called me to see. The purple wasp was still hovering over the tulip as if nothing had happened.

"I don't think he knows he's been spit on," I said.

"If he's that dumb," Kris said, straightening up. "I'm not wasting my spit on him." She got Dad's old scooter from under the front steps and walked up the drive, still licking the ice cube.

"She's such a happy girl," Dad said, "who can say why?"

"Kris," Jenny called from deep inside the house, "come back in here this instant for dinner."

My sister kept going until she reached the top of the driveway, then rode the scooter back over the grass. She hit a hole just before the porch, and the front wheel sank into the ground, spilling her over the handlebars. She jumped right up and shook the dirt off her blouse. "Are you okay?" Dad said. She looked at him as if she didn't have the slightest idea why he was asking.

Fifteen

JENNY SERVED HER SPECIAL MEATLOAF FOR SUNDAY DINNER. KRISSY emptied the ketchup bottle on her piece, then sucked it into her mouth and swallowed fast so she wouldn't have to taste it. I dipped each bite of meat into my mashed potatoes. Dad pushed his meatloaf to one side of his plate so it wouldn't contaminate the rest of his food. Jenny closed her eyes with each mouthful and sighed.

Dad brought *Alice in Wonderland* to the table. Jenny told him it was rude to read during dinner, but he said he had only a few more pages to go. He laughed once or twice as he was reading and eating his baked beans. But mostly he grunted or shook his head. Finally he ate his last spoonful of beans and wiped up the remaining juice with a piece of bread. "Imagination gone wild," he said as he flipped the book shut. "I never could understand the fuss . . . "

"I went to the dentist on Friday," Jenny said before he finished his sentence. "I didn't tell you."

"You're allowed to go to the dentist without telling us," Dad said, winking at me. He was suddenly in an up mood.

"I didn't tell you how they tried to soak me for X-rays," Jenny said. "This girl comes out, Dr. Gaul's assistant, and she says, 'It's time for you to have your X-rays done.' I figure she's going to take two or three. Well, she takes three and then four and then five and six and I said, 'What are you doing, X-raying each tooth individually? I mean, when they X-ray my breasts, they get both at the same time, don't they?'"

"Actually," Dad said, "I don't think they do."

Jenny didn't care what he thought. She had a story to tell. "I guess she didn't like me talking to her like that, but I'll be darned if I'm going to sit there getting myself radiated just so they can make more money. I said, 'If it's so safe, why do you throw a lead blanket over me and run out of the room? If you want another X-ray,' I said, 'you're going to have to stay in here with me.' That stopped her. There wasn't any more X-raying this mouth." Jenny tapped her lips and smiled proudly. She liked to get her way and always let everyone know when she did. But when none of us said anything, she got angry and turned on me. "Why haven't we seen that writer around here lately? Did you scare her away?"

"That reminds me," Dad said, "she called this morning from New York. She's coming tonight."

"I can't tonight," I said.

"What's more important?" Jenny snapped at me.

I had to tell her, or she would have thought I was up to something worse and tried to keep me home. I said, "I'm picking up Kris' present tonight with Frankie, that's what."

My sister spit out a mouthful of ketchup-covered meat. "A present for me?"

"Sure, your half-birthday is coming up, isn't it?"

Dad looked confused. "Her what?"

"It's halfway between her birthdays," Jenny said, playing along with me for once. "We're celebrating this week."

"Will there be a cake?" Kris asked.

"Of course," I said, "but it has to be half a cake. What kind do you want?"

"Coconut chocolate," she said quickly, "with vanilla icing and raisins."

"What about that woman, that writer?" Jenny said.

"She wanted to look through the stuff in my room," I said. "You can let her do that."

"I can't imagine what a woman from New York would find interesting in your room," Jenny said.

The phone rang and Kris ran to the hall to answer it. She listened for a minute and then hung up. She came back to the table, picked up her fork and stabbed at her baked beans, which she always ate one at a time. "Well, who was it?" Jenny asked.

"Some man—he said the word like Jake says."

"What word?"

Kris looked at me and giggled. "Fuck." Then she leaned toward me and whispered, "Fuck-fuck."

"That's enough," Jenny ordered, waving her hand in the air across the table. The phone rang again, and she got up to get it. "Whoever this is," she said without waiting to make sure it was the same person, "you're a pitiful excuse for a human being." Then she slammed down the receiver.

The phone rang a third time before Jenny could sit back at the table. We all looked at Dad. "What's this person saying?" he asked her as he poked at the meatloaf like it was some dead thing he was trying to identify.

"Exactly what Kris said, and other words I won't repeat."

The phone kept ringing, and Dad picked up his glass of water to take a sip. "Was he threatening, or just obscene?"

Jenny pounded the table with the fork in her hand. "Why don't you just answer it and hear for yourself?"

Dad wiped his lips with his napkin and went to the hallway. "Hello," he said and listened. He tried to interrupt a few times by saying "Excuse me," but he obviously couldn't break in. Finally he stooped under the hall table and pulled the jack from the wall. Then he came back to dinner.

The phone calls had put Jenny on edge more than usual, and she began to gulp down her wine rather than sip it. After we cleared our own plates, she brought in canned apricots for dessert, muttering that we didn't deserve it since we had barely touched her meatloaf. She spooned out the bowls but took none for herself. "Maybe I'm wrong," she said, handing Krissy her apricots. "Maybe we should let Jake answer the phone, since the calls are for him."

"The calls are for all of us," Dad said, "the whole family."

"The whole family?" Jenny said. "That's an interesting idea. How exactly are we a whole family?"

"We eat meatloaf together," Kris said, "and apricots, even though we don't like them." I could have bet Dad loved Kris' definition of a family, but he kept his head down so as not to upset Jenny any more.

•

Frankie arrived ten minutes before eight, as night was falling fast. I met him outside so he wouldn't have to talk to Jenny or Dad. They made him nervous.

"So what's the deal?" he asked from inside his Mustang.

"We have to pick up a bike for Kris."

"Pick it up where?"

"On Aquetong Road, about fifty yards in from River Road."

"Outside Washington Crossing," he said. "Must be hot."

"Yep."

"So that's the big adventure for the night—stealing a little girl's bike? You used to do that all the time."

"If you want more excitement we could trash the new condos on the way back," I suggested.

He treated my idea seriously. "They keep guards posted outside all night. And there's only one bridge to the buildings, so you could get trapped on the other side."

"We could go in and out by the river," I said.

"Who cares about the condos? You can't stop them now, unless you blow them up—and we're not blowing them up," he added quickly.

"Then let's get the bike," I said, "and see what happens."

•

Retrieving Kris' present should have been simple, since I knew exactly where I'd left it and Aquetong didn't get much traffic after the park closed. Frankie pulled off the road where I told him to and left his beams on low so that nobody would plow into him from behind. I climbed up the embankment and found my sister's new bike just as a car turned in off River Road. I dropped to the ground as the big headlights swept over the field. The car came slowly, moving out into the center of the road to get around Frankie's Mustang. But then the lights froze, and a door opened. A larger beam suddenly flooded the road. I figured it was either some Jersey kids looking for trouble or the police. Lifting my head a little, I could see someone stepping up to the window of Frankie's car, about thirty feet away from me. "Having a problem?" a voice asked in a dumb sarcastic tone. It had to belong to a cop.

"No problem," Frankie said.

"This isn't a parking lot," the cop said.

"I wasn't really parking," Frankie answered him. "My car stalled out 'cause it's kind of an old car, you know, a real wreck, and I just got it running again. So I was letting it idle for a minute before driving."

A second cop came walking over from the squad car, and I could tell from the way he rocked side to side that it was fat-ass Decker. "What have we got?" he said and looked in the Mustang. "If it isn't Frank Collins, Jr." he said loudly, as if he were greeting an old friend. "You turn up in the strangest places. I thought all the cruising was done inside the park."

"My car stalled," Frankie said, "I was just leaving."

"That's a good idea," Decker said. "We wouldn't want a nice boy like you caught in some trouble his daddy can't get him out of, would we?"

That wasn't a question Frankie could easily answer, the way it was phrased, so he said, "I'm going."

The cops went back to their car as Frankie pulled away. They followed right after him, but not before swinging their light beam across the field, just over my head.

A few cars passed by in the next few minutes, but not Frankie's Mustang. I left the bike in the bushes and stood behind a tree where I could duck one way or another, depending on the direction a car came from. Finally I sat down on the ground, figuring that Decker had spooked Frankie into taking the long way around instead of just coming back down Aquetong. I lay back in the tall grass, listening to the locusts and grasshoppers and even some frogs croaking from a pond not far behind me. The sound was like a roar of a waterfall, filling up the whole night. Then a short sharp horn cut through the darkness, and I sat up to see the Mustang coasting slowly past me. I slid down the bank and whistled, and the car backed up fast, the rear of it fishtailing across the road.

Frankie jumped out. "Hurry up. Decker followed me all the way back to New Hope. I'm not sure I lost him."

I picked up the bike as Frankie unlocked the trunk. We got the front wheel in and the handlebars, but the back wheel stuck out. "Any rope?" I asked him.

"There's no time to tie it," he said. "Just get in."

He shoved down the trunk as far as it would go and we sped off down Aquetong. The hot, moist air whipped through the car as Frankie turned on the radio to find some music to drive fast by.

•

We dropped the bike at my house, going in through the cellar door and hiding it in Grandpa's old workroom. Then we sneaked back outside without anyone hearing us, not even Jenny who usually heard everything. We could see her in the kitchen drinking coffee with the writer. It made me nervous knowing I was the only thing they had to talk about.

I walked Frankie back to his car. "So, you got your excitement," I said, but he didn't seem too thrilled by it. He was pulling the car door lock up and pushing it down, just wasting time. "Decker seems to have it in for you, too."

"He's a fucking moron. Guys like him should be drowned for general stupidity."

Frankie didn't normally talk like this, and I figured something must have happened between him and Decker while I was gone. "I'm going to give the bike to Kris Wednesday night," I said. "You could come to her party, if you want."

"Maybe," he said.

Thinking of Kris' present reminded me of the one I'd gotten for Frankie earlier that day. "Here," I said, pulling the gold chain from my pocket, "for helping me tonight."

Frankie fingered the chain. "You bought this for me?" he asked, then laughed at himself for thinking that.

"Try it on," I said.

He reached behind his neck to unhook his silver chain and gave it to me to hold while he put on mine. "Looks good," I said, "real good." He smiled and laughed a little because it was the first thing I had ever given him. Frankie used to give me lots of presents for Christmas and my birthday, like T-shirts and knives and radios and tapes, whatever his allowance could buy.

He put his hand out for me to give him his chain back,

but I shook my head. "Gold and silver don't mix," I said and hurled his chain far into the darkness.

"A friend gave me that," Frankie said, starting toward the bushes to look for it.

"Not an old friend," I said, taking him by the arm. "Forget him and his fucking chain." Frankie turned around and shrugged. "I should go in now," I said, figuring that maybe I could get Larkin away from Jenny for awhile.

But Frankie didn't want to leave. "Maybe we could do something else," he said quickly.

"Don't you have school tomorrow?"

"Fuck school. Nobody goes the last week anyway."

"So why don't you go home and play with one of your Dad's toys?"

"The mansion's empty tonight."

"You still afraid of staying alone?" He didn't like my question and shoved me out of the way to open the car door. "Wait," I said, "don't get mad." He sat in the Mustang, one leg in and one out. "You could stay here," I said, but I knew he wouldn't. The one time Frankie slept over, he stayed awake all night listening to Dad wandering around the house talking to himself or reading out loud.

"There's a new bar downtown," Frankie said, "maybe I'll hang out back and listen to the music."

"We could sleep out by the river," I said, "like in the meadow near Sam's."

"Oh right, remember last time? That huge rabbit kept biting my ears."

"It was a hare."

"Whatever it was, it tried to eat me."

He was ruling out all of the possibilities, steering us toward the one thing he always wanted to do, as long as I was the one who suggested it. And I always did. "I guess we could go house-breaking, if you want."

"Yeah, I suppose we could," he said, trying not to seem too eager, "I even know a place. The owners just happened to fly off today—to Italy."

•

"Looks dead enough," Frankie whispered to me as we ducked along the outside hedge of 12 Brevin Circle. The big house flooded in white garden lights showed no sign of life, human or otherwise. The house was Spanish style, Frankie said, with a clay tiled roof and large archways on the back patio—an odd design for New Hope. We walked around the grounds, debating the best way to break in. He wanted to scale the rainspout and push up a second-floor window that was already two inches open. I liked the quicker approach, kicking in the basement window. There was nobody living in a hundred yards of the place to hear the glass breaking, but Frankie wouldn't go along with that. "We decided against forcing our way in a long time ago," he said, "remember?"

"We're breaking in whether we break some glass or not."

"Yeah, but nobody can tell for sure that we were here if we're careful," Frankie said, "so the cops won't investigate. Besides, there can't be any alarm on that window if it's already open." He tested the downspout to see if it was strong enough to take his weight. "This will hold me. Boost me up."

I put my hands together to give him a foothold, and when he told me to lift, I raised him as high as I could. He caught hold of the rainspout about halfway up the first floor, like a bear hanging on to a small tree trunk. He pulled himself up a few inches at a time until he could grab the gutter with both hands and chin himself to the roof. The gutter creaked under his weight, but held.

A minute later, he was opening the sliding door onto the patio and swaggering outside like he owned the place. In his right hand he held a bottle of liquor by its neck. "Let's give it ten minutes," he said as we found a dry spot to lie down under a big white pine tree. It was our usual routine, even for houses that had nothing inside anybody would bother stealing. We always waited to see if a silent alarm would bring the cops.

"Who are our victims?" I said as I rolled over on my back to look up at the huge sky above our heads, and the billions of flickering stars Dad said were there even if I couldn't see them. I always wondered, how come the night wasn't lit up like daytime, with all those stars shining on us?

"The Littletons," Frankie said. "He's a banker who commutes to New York. She's a whore, from what my father says, sleeps with anybody who comes around during the day. She doesn't even charge." He drank some from the bottle, then handed it to me. Vodka was Frankie's favorite drink since it left no smell on our breath.

"Your father knows that for sure, huh?"

"He wouldn't fool around," Frankie said. "The only women he gets are knocked out cold on the operating table."

"Sounds exciting."

"That's my dad. It's kind of strange—I'd find him a lot more interesting if he was sneaking off screwing some whore."

After exactly ten minutes passed on Frankie's Russian Army watch, which his father had brought back from one of his trips, we went inside. Frankie guided our way with his pocket flashlight. The patio doors opened into a family room with a giant TV screen in the corner. We went on through the dining room into the hallway, where a huge staircase curled up to the second floor. "Not a bad little house," I said. "Maybe I'll be a banker when I grow up."

"More like a bank robber," Frankie said, swigging from the bottle. He held the vodka in front of my face. "This stuff is smooth, very fucking smooth."

We walked up the thick carpeted stairs side by side, and Frankie threw his arm over my shoulder. "So, dear," he said in a deep banker-like voice, "isn't it wonderful to be rich and not worry about any little thing?" He pulled away far enough to take another gulp. He did it fast and easily, not like a year ago when the vodka burned his throat on the way down and he needed a root beer chaser. "The poor are so pitiful," he said. "They just don't know how to control themselves—no fucking self-control, dear."

At the top of the stairs, he flashed his light down each side of the long hallway. "So tell me," he said, speaking like himself again, "which way to the master bedroom?" I pointed left. "No way. Must be over here," he said, turning right. "The master bedroom always goes over the living room, never the kitchen. The help sleep over the kitchen."

We looked in a couple of bedrooms, but Frankie shook his head until we got to one as large as a classroom. "The master suite," he said, "with his and her bathrooms placed at opposite ends so they can't hear each other making disgusting noises. I'll take hers," Frankie said, pointing with his light to the farthest bathroom, "it'll be bigger. You get his."

I reached inside to turn on the light, but Frankie grabbed my hand. "No lights, remember? They're too easy to spot from the road."

"Then we should have brought a second flashlight."

He opened the drawer of the nighttable, fished around for a few seconds, and pulled out a mini-flashlight.

"You sure you haven't been here before?"

"Rich people all live alike," he said. "It's part of their charm."

"Speaking of whores," I said, thinking of the woman who lived here, "we need some girls." I fell back on the big bed, throwing my hands out wide, feeling like the man of the house waiting for his wife to come in and jump on him.

Frankie took a running leap and landed next to me on the bed, and the mattress barely bent under his weight. "Girls aren't going to break into houses with us," he said.

"They might. I found these two in New Hope on the bridge. They want to go out with us some night, like a double date."

"Must be class girls, hanging around the bridge asking every guy out."

"Maybe they just asked me."

"Yeah, right," he said.

"Okay, so don't come with me."

"You shouldn't be out like that anyway, after the *Gazette* article and the phone calls."

"I'm not staying in my crazy house all day. I'm either going out doing what I want around town, or I might as well run away again."

A motor started up close by, and we both rolled out of the bed to the floor. I crept to the window, but I couldn't see anything going on in front of the house. "It's coming from there," Frankie whispered, pointing to a closed door next to a giant chest of drawers. We crawled over and listened as a switch clicked on and off, and then there was a sound of water sloshing around. Frankie stood up. "Figures," he said, kicking open the door, "a jacuzzi."

I followed him into an exercise room filled with weights, a massage table, a wall of mirrors, and a boxing bag. Frankie pulled back the leather cover on the jacuzzi as I took a few punches at the bag and a roundhouse kick. "What's the thing doing on," I said, "if they're gone for so long?"

"There's a timer," Frankie said. "It turns on automatically every few hours to keep the water circulating. Otherwise you'd die from bacteria—a dead Legionnaire." He dipped his elbow in the water. "Perfect, let's go swimming," he said, kicking off his sneakers. He pulled off his T-shirt and dropped his orange shorts, which looked a weird lime color in the blue light from the jacuzzi. He climbed over the side and sank into the water up to his neck. I did the same, and we just sat like that, across from each other, the hum of the motor the only noise between us. Jets of hot water shot from nozzles into my back, stinging my skin but feeling good. Frankie flapped his hands every once in awhile, and the water lapped at the edges and spilled over onto the tile floor.

"She probably lures guys up here to show them the jacuzzi," he said, "then fucks them right here."

"Maybe we should stop by some day when she's home," I said, "if she's that hot."

"She's old," Frankie said, "very old—maybe even forty."

That's how old Jenny was, which made the idea of fucking this woman kind of revolting. The water was so hot that I was getting dizzy fast, so I climbed out and stood dripping on the blue tile, looking for a towel. Frankie got out and grabbed two terrycloth robes hanging on wall hooks. We wrapped ourselves in them and headed back to the bedroom.

"That whirlpool knocked me out," I said, collapsing on the bed.

"Have another drink. That will keep you alive."

"I don't want to be alive. I want to be dead to the world."

He lifted my arm up, but I let it go limp and fall back to the mattress. "Drink," he said, "to the rich people who have inherited the earth. They won't leave anything for anyone else, you know. What they can't own, they kill."

"Frankie," I said, raising my head up on one hand, "you are rich, and drunk."

"Exactly," he said, "so I know what I'm talking about."

"Maybe you talk too much. Maybe you should just enjoy the money you have like anybody else would instead of turning it into some curse on you."

He offered me the vodka again, but I shook him off. "Then I'll drink for both of us," he said and downed another capful. "It is a curse to be rich, if you don't want to be, just like it's a curse to be poor, if you don't want to be."

"Why don't you want to be rich?"

"I don't want to be anything. That's kind of the problem—as diagnosed by the famous surgeon, Dr. Frank Collins, Sr."

I swiped the bottle from his hand. "Stop drinking," I said, "you're twisting yourself up."

He stared at me, the vodka burning his face. "I am twisted," he said.

"I know. But just lie down. It'll go away."

He lay down, then bolted right up again. "It's too fucking hot in here," he yelled. "How do these people live like this?" He flung off his robe and crawled naked under the sheet.

I sank back on a giant feather pillow, and my head felt like it was floating away. I closed my eyes and thought of living my whole life in this house, a place where the paint wasn't peeling and the ceiling wasn't caving in and the mother was a whore.

"You asleep?" Frankie said loud enough to wake me if I was.

"No."

"Take one more swig with me, okay?"

I rolled over and Frankie grabbed the bottle from the

table behind our heads. I took a fast swallow and the vodka slid down my throat. "You're right," I said, "very smooth."

"Do you remember breaking into that junky house in Carversville across from the inn?"

"Yeah, the people came back while we were sleeping, and the little girl saw us running bare ass out the back door."

"She'll probably always remember that, somewhere in the back of her mind, that she saw two naked guys in her house, and nobody would believe her. Years later it will come out in therapy, only she'll get things mixed up and say her father used to strip and run around in front of her."

"The same thing could happen tomorrow morning," I said, "someone could burst in on us if we sleep here."

"I told you, the Littletons flew off to Rome. They won't be back until next week. We could live here for days."

"But maybe they have somebody checking the house, like a neighbor, or even the cops."

Frankie swigged down some more vodka. "Let them catch us—who cares?" He lifted the bottle to his mouth again but I took it away and set it on my side of the bed.

"You've had enough."

"If I want to drink myself into a coma," he said. "I should be allowed to."

"Do it at home, not with me. I don't want to have to carry you out of here."

We both settled back for awhile, and I felt warm and clean lying in this bed that was big enough for four people. Even the darkness felt richer in this room, with just a faint arc of moonlight hanging outside the window.

"Jake, you falling asleep?"

"No."

"Tell me something."

"What?"

"When you left," he said, and it took him awhile to finish his sentence—"you know, you just left."

His voice was shaky, but I knew what he was trying to ask. "They were thinking of sending me to Norristown, I told you that."

"Yeah, but you didn't tell me you were going to run away," he said, speaking through his pillow, as if these were things he couldn't say to me any other way. "One day you were here, and we were house-breaking and smoking and feeling good. Then I call up, and Jenny says you're gone and doesn't know where. Doesn't sound like she cares, either. And I'm still here."

"What do you want me to say, Frankie?"

He pulled the pillow off his face and took in a deep gulp of air as if he had been suffocating himself. "Say anything, you know, just say something."

He wanted me to say that I missed him and should have said goodbye to him, things I didn't usually say to people. "That woman you saw, the writer, she thinks something's wrong with me," I said, "because I only have one friend."

He understood what I meant, even through the vodka that was drowning his brain. "I guess there's something wrong with both of us," he said. "That's why we like each other."

Sixteen

FRANKIE DROPPED ME OFF VERY EARLY MONDAY MORNING AT THE top of our driveway on River Road so that his Mustang wouldn't wake up Jenny and get me in trouble for being out all night. I figured she knew I'd been out, but she wouldn't know exactly how late if I could get into bed without her hearing me. The stars were already fading out of the sky in the first light. It was the time I used to hate most when I slept out by the river, when the nighttime of bats and raccoons and strange sounds of the darkness gave way to cars and people's voices. It always seemed to me that night was where I belonged.

I made it up to my room the usual way—the giant beech tree whose thick branches reached up to my window like scaffolding. It was still an easy way in, but I found myself being careful this time, which surprised me. I crawled through my window and jumped into bed just as I heard footsteps in the hallway. I pulled the covers over me as my door burst in. "Jake," Jenny shouted, "come out here!"

"Leave me alone," I groaned, "I'm sleeping."

She came into my room and threw the covers off me before I could hold onto them. "I suppose you always sleep with your clothes on, and your dirty sneakers?"

"Sure, in case some crazy person busts in on me."

Jenny wasn't in the mood to be fooled with. She marched me down the stairs and through the hall and out into the kitchen. Then she opened the screen door, and I saw what was bugging her—a rock-size hole in the glass. "I suppose you slept through this last night?"

Actually, I had slept through it—in a different house, but I didn't say that. "This is terrible," I said, trying to react like she wanted me to. "What happened?"

"A carload of maniacs woke us up in the middle of the night throwing rocks—that's what happened. They were calling for you, Jake. Your sister was scared half to death. I'll tell you, I'm not risking her getting hurt by some drunken bums coming after you."

"It's not my fault they attacked the house," I said. "What do you want me to do—sleep outside so they can just stone me if they come again?"

Jenny didn't answer. She bent down to pick up a long sliver of glass that she had missed brushing up before and then held the piece up in the air between us. "I told you when you came home—behave or you'll have to leave again."

It seemed to me I was behaving well enough, at least as far as she knew. But there wasn't any arguing with Jenny when she was as mad as this. "You better stay out of my sight today," she said, "do you understand?"

I nodded, and she stomped out of the kitchen.

•

I walked into town to Sam's, which is where I'd spent plenty of days getting out of Jenny's way. There was no sign of life at his Indian Reservation, which made sense since it wasn't even six o'clock yet. Life for Sam didn't start until noon. He told me never to come around until the church bells rang proving that the morning was done with. He said he guarded his sleep like his whiskey, and besides that, he might be shacked up with some lady and not want to be disturbed.

Those all seemed like good reasons to me for staying away, but this was almost an emergency—I didn't have any other place to go, and it was starting to rain. So I walked down the alley by his store and knocked on his back door. After a few minutes of my rapping, he appeared, dressed in a long white nightshirt that looked like something an old cowboy would sleep in. "Nice pajamas," I said as he opened the sliding window. Sam closed one eye, then the other, as if trying to get his focus right. "It's not even daylight yet."

"Sure it is," I said.

He waved me in and shut the door behind us. Then he sank his big body into the rope chair and closed his eyes. After awhile he said, "Let me guess—Jenny threw you out."

"Not exactly, I mean, not all the way. She just told me to get lost for awhile."

"So you came down to wake up good old Sam."

"Yeah, I didn't know where else to hang out. The stores aren't open yet. And Frankie lives too far away."

"So I'm convenient for you, is that it?"

"I guess you are."

He nodded and scratched his chest. His eyes closed, and I thought he might fall asleep on me. "I don't enjoy mornings," he said after awhile, "have I told you that before?"

"Yeah, lots of times."

"The day seems too long when it starts so early. There's too much time for bad things to happen." His eyes popped open and he got up from his chair, groaning a little at the effort to raise himself. He found his tobacco pouch among the paints and brushes on his drawing table. Then he circled the room, looking behind and over everything until he found his pipe in the middle of a book, used as a marker.

"That stuff will kill you faster than cigarettes," I said.

"It's no use telling an Indian to stop smoking. In fact, it's no use telling an Indian anything." He lit the pipe and took in a few long breaths. The smoke smelled familiar and good to me. "Besides," he said, "with this body I don't have to worry about smoking killing me. My genes will do me in soon enough, which is fine with me."

"Most people want to live a long time, don't they, Sam?"

He nodded. "They're very confused. They think life's important, so they don't want to give it up."

"Life isn't important?" I said, to keep him talking so he wouldn't kick me out. Being out with Frankie all night had left me wicked tired. I closed my eyes and listened.

"Life is just an accident of evolution," Sam said. "The only thing that makes it important is that people say it is. If people said living wasn't important, then they wouldn't worry so much about death." He seemed to have struck on a subject of interest to him, something that could wake him up. I opened one eye a little and watched him blow smoke in rings over his head. They floated up, broke apart, and finally blended in with the air—entropy, just like Dad said.

"What about that book you used to read to me all the time, *The Importance of Living*?"

He shrugged. "I threw it out. I couldn't fool myself into believing it anymore." He took a big yawn and shook his head to clear out the lingering sleep. "I made a list one time of what was important. Food, clothing, shelter—that's it."

It seemed to me there had to be other things, but I couldn't come up with any.

Sam sucked on his pipe. "But people are never satisfied," he said as he exhaled, "they always want more of everything. They want to win at everything—jobs, sports, wars. But when has winning ever made any difference in the world?"

I agreed with him about jobs and sports, but didn't some wars make the world better? "You think wars never do any good, Sam?"

He looked at me as if I should know better. "Of course they don't. It doesn't matter who runs things. Go into any society you want and squeeze out all the hatred and fear and sadness—it will fill back up every time, no matter if there's war or peace. It will overflow and drown you, if you let it."

"You're pretty depressing about things, Sam. I came here to get cheered up."

"Then you came to the wrong place," he said, "and you came too early. I didn't make life like this. I'm just trying to get through it like everybody else."

"Isn't peace better than war?"

He shook his head hard. "There isn't any better or worse, Jake, you know that. Nothing improves. Nothing changes. For every gain in one place, somebody else is losing somewhere else. It's zero-sum, no way around it."

"What's that?"

"For one person to gain happiness, somebody else has to lose it. There's only so much in the world to go around."

"So war and peace don't matter?"

"Not to me," he said. "But at least in wars people are honest. You know they hate you and want to kill you."

Sam set down his pipe and stood up. He told me to eat whatever I could find and stay as long as I wanted but be quiet about it. Then he climbed up to his loft. In a minute I could hear his heavy breathing. I found myself a bag of corn muffins on top of the refrigerator and a carton of orange juice inside, which were enough for me for breakfast. By the time I finished eating and looking through Sam's paintings, it was nine o'clock. I tried sleeping a little, but his breathing turned into snoring that sounded like some giant slug was inching along the floor getting ready to swallow me whole.

I decided to head down to The Logan to see if Larkin had stayed overnight. That's where she said she would stay, if she was staying over. It was only a few blocks from Sam's to the hotel, which surprised me because I had always thought of going from one to the other as a trip. Lots of times I'd be hanging around Sam's trying to figure if it was worth walking all the way to The Logan to bum money off Jenny. Sometimes if I asked her with the other waitresses around, she'd give me a couple of dollars so she would look like a good stepmother.

As I cut across Main Street in front of The Logan, a cop car stopped in my way. When the driver looked up, I was staring into the stupid-ass face of Sergeant Decker.

"You're jaywalking," he said, pointing his fat finger at my feet, "that's a serious offense in this town." I started to walk around his car, but he pulled forward to block me. "What's your hurry? Don't you have anything to say to an old buddy?" I had decided on the bus ride back to New Hope that I wouldn't let Decker get to me. I figured he'd try to bait me into doing something illegal so he could arrest me. Now I just smiled at him and waited until somebody in the cars behind him got impatient enough to hit their horn. "We'll be seeing each other again," Decker said as he started to pull away. Then he leaned his head out of the window. "I've seen that woman around town asking about you. Can't wait till she comes in my office," he said, emphasizing *comes* like some stupid kid. "Nice ass, don't you think?"

I could have reached out and torn some of his ugly face away. But I kept my hands in my pocket and repeated one of Dad's favorite phrases, "By letting go, all gets done; the world is won by those who let it go!" I didn't know if this wisdom was written for situations like this, but it kept my mind occupied long enough that the moment passed without me doing something stupid. Jenny would have been proud.

•

It was a hot, sunny day in New Hope, and already the tourists were sipping fancy drinks on the front terrace of The Logan, along with their eggs and muffins. I tried to get Decker out of my mind, but the question kept coming back to me—who would create a world and let him in it? Not any sort of God that I could think of. Whenever anyone brought up God, which they often did at the shelters, I thought of Decker and said there was no way I believed in any divine creator stuff. Human life had to be a mistake. Somewhere evolution took a wrong turn, and Neanderthals like Decker were the result.

I looked down Main Street one last time to make sure The Big Ape hadn't doubled back to tail me, then I went inside The Logan to find Larkin. A few of the breakfast waitresses remembered me and waved, and my favorite, Donna, kissed me on the cheek and said that the girls had better watch out now that I was back in town. She meant it like I was a heartbreaking kind of guy, but then I could see in her face that she remembered the canal attack. "Well," Donna said, "what can I do you for?"

"I'm here to see a woman from New York. I think she's staying upstairs. Her name is Daily."

Donna reached over the main desk and pulled out the guest book. "Daily," she said, reading the names upside down, "Larkin Daily—room 402."

I thanked her and headed for the stairs, taking them by twos to the fourth floor. The long hallway was damp and dark and very quiet. The yellow carpet looked like it had been trampled on by thousands of dirty shoes. The wallpaper was worn away so you couldn't tell what the pattern was anymore. I walked down the hall quickly, checking the room numbers and watching my back. This was a hallway where you could get hacked to death and nobody would find your body for weeks. Of course, nobody ever got hacked to death in New Hope, but if they did, it would be here.

I found No. 402 at the far end of the hall and reached up to knock just as the door opened. Larkin was fastening her pocketbook, and when she looked up and saw me, she screamed a little and shoved me away. I figured that was a typical New York reaction to being surprised. "Oh, Jake," she said, "you scared me. I didn't mean to hit you, are you alright?" She reached out to touch my shoulder where she had pushed me. Did she really think she could hurt me with that little tap?

Before I could tell her I was fine, the door opened wide behind her, and a huge guy filled the doorway. He was holding a brown towel around his waist. Shaving cream covered half of his face. "Are you okay, Lark?" he said as he pulled her back into the room a little.

She unhooked herself from his grip. "Oh sure, Doug. Look, this is the boy I've been telling you about—Jake. He was at the door when I opened it, and I guess I hit him."

She smiled and Doug smiled, but I didn't feel like smiling. He looked like one of those guys in the lineup of evolution, just one step ahead of Decker. His head hung forward. His arms were busting with muscles. His chest was covered with thick, dark hair. I couldn't imagine Larkin wanting this guy to touch her, let alone do stuff with her that I didn't want to think about. But inside the room, there was only one bed, and the sheets were all tossed around like they had just gone at it.

I turned to go, but Larkin grabbed my arm. "I want to introduce you." I looked up at the guy. "Jake, this is Doug Maslow, a friend of mine from New York."

He wiped his hand on his towel and stuck it toward me. I kneeled down pretending I had to tie my sneaker laces. When I stood up again, he still had his hand out. He couldn't take a hint. "I have to go," I said.

"Wait," Larkin said again. "I was coming over to talk to you today. Didn't you get my message?"

"Not today," I said, "I'm busy."

"Then why were you coming to see me?"

"To tell you that—I'm busy."

I knew it didn't make sense. There was no way for me to look good in this situation, so I just left them standing there thinking I was weird and ran down the hallway.

164

Seventeen

KRISSY CAME RUNNING IN THE HOUSE AFTER SCHOOL WEDNESDAY
yelling "I'm home." From the basement, I could hear her
going from room to room. I started hammering again at the
old mahogany chair, and soon my sister came rushing down
the stairs and over to me. "What are you doing?" she asked,
breathless and happy. It was her half-birthday.

"Fixing this chair," I said.

"What was wrong with it?"

"It wasn't a chair anymore. It was a pile of broken
wood."

"I liked it better that way. It hurt to sit on."

"It's not a kid's chair," I explained to her. "It's for adults
who don't mind being uncomfortable when they sit."

She put her hand over the top of the next nail as I was
about to hammer it. "It's my half-birthday, you know. I'm
getting a new bike tonight."

"You think so, huh?"

"You promised."

"Promises get broken sometimes."

"Maybe sometimes," she said, "but not today, 'cause I
already saw my bike back there." She pointed behind
Grandma's old mattress, which Dad kept in the back of the
cellar. He said we might need a spare one someday. But who
would want to sleep in a bed where a person had thrown up
for a year before dying? And this was a mattress perma-
nently sunken in the middle because Grandma was a very
large woman.

I moved Krissy's hand and hammered the last nail
through the back support to attach it to the seat. "Done," I
said as I lifted it off the workbench to the floor.

My sister climbed on. The chair creaked even under her
little weight and she hopped off right away. "You're as bad
as Daddy at fixing things," she said.

I tried the chair myself. The legs bowed out and the
back columns were sticking into my spine. It felt like a tor-
ture seat. "You're right," I said, "this wood doesn't deserve
to be a chair."

I picked up Grandpa's big hammer and whacked at the front legs, splitting the wood. Krissy cheered and grabbed the hammer from my hands. She swung dead center into the seat, which didn't do anything, so I pointed to the joints, and she aimed again. After a few chops, the back rungs splintered away from the seat. I took the hammer and finished off the job in one swing. The chair collapsed back into a pile of wood.

•

Krissy's half-birthday dinner went off just about as I had expected. Jenny came home from the bake shop with a day-old birthday cake smeared with chocolate icing instead of vanilla, and no raisins or coconut inside. She said it was the best she could do—her usual way of explaining herself—when she set it on the table after dinner. She stacked the paper plates full of the crusts from the pepperoni-mushroom pizza, Kris' special request meal, and handed them to Dad to throw in the trash.

"What about candles?" I whispered in Jenny's ear.

"We're out of them," she said and gave Krissy the knife. She cut out a big piece of the cake and handed it across the table to Dad. "You get the special first slice," she said.

He seemed overwhelmed by that, as if my sister had just declared him the greatest father who ever lived. He got up and walked around behind Kris and hugged her. She sat frozen in his arms, her face looking out over his bare arms at me. It made me sad that my sister didn't know how to act when her father gave her a hug. Jenny took the knife from Kris' hand and cut herself a piece. After a quick bite she declared it "the perfect birthday cake."

Krissy stuffed her cake in her mouth as fast as she could and then whipped open the two presents from Dad and Jenny. They seemed like pretty good gifts to me—a headset radio and a book about large cats. Krissy smiled and said "thank you" and kissed them both just enough to be polite. Then she dragged me by the hand downstairs. I pulled the bike from behind the mattress, and suddenly the shiny metallic red racer didn't look very special. "The light's kind of dull down here," I said, "it'll look better outside."

She insisted on helping me carry "her bike" upstairs, through the kitchen where Dad and Jenny were arguing over something in the refrigerator, down the hallway and out to the front yard. "It's beautiful," she said to me as soon as she saw the chrome glinting in the evening light. She motioned for me to bend over and then gave me a big wet kiss on my cheek. "I love it more than anything," she said into my ear. "I'm glad you're my brother again."

I held her to my neck, feeling the warmth and excitement of her little body. Now I was sure that it was right to steal from one little girl, if it could make another so happy.

•

Frankie couldn't make it for Krissy's birthday. He had to stay home for dinner and pretend to be a good son in front of his father's doctor friends. He said he would escape after dessert and meet me at Gerenser's to hang out.

I left Krissy riding her bike up and down the strip of grass next to our driveway, singing to herself. Night was falling fast as I walked on the road toward town. Cars kept swerving around me, with the drivers riding their horns for me to get out of their way. I figured nobody wanted a dead kid on their driving record, so they'd make sure to miss me.

At the edge of town, the long line of antique streetlights were just coming on. Frankie and I used to sit in the shadows of the alleys, firing stones from our slingshots at the fake candles. We weren't actually trying to break the bulbs, just hit the casing. The stone would make a sharp sound against the metal that made people jump if they were walking underneath it. The first one to make somebody jump won, which meant they got to take whatever the other had in his pockets. Frankie was a better shot than me, but I think he lost sometimes just so he could give me money without really giving it to me. That way we could go buy tapes or see a movie and I could pay for myself.

When I reached Gerenser's, Frankie was already there, sitting on the outside railing. He was wearing a tight red muscle shirt that actually made you notice that his arms didn't have much muscle on him. He jumped to his feet as soon as he saw me. "So," he said, "what's up?"

"Nothing much." I said.

We started walking down Main, checking out the stores along the way, and quickly things got interesting. A blue Camaro drove by more slowly than the other cars. The back windows were wide open. "It's Siever," Frankie whispered, "and his moron friends." He grabbed my arm and tried to pull me down Canal Alley, but I wouldn't let him. "Just keep walking," I said. "They'll get tired of making themselves look stupid."

By the time we reached the corner, the car was gone. "Let's head to Jersey," Frankie said, steering me right, toward the bridge, away from the direction the Camaro was heading. "We can get some subs at The Dog. It's a new place."

On the other side of the river, about 100 yards away, Lambertville Station was lit up in white lights. Underneath the bridge, a boat sped by, bouncing high in the chop. The moon was crescent shape, silvery, glowing. I could remember many nights like this on the bridge. When the wind whipped up a little, it always stirred my skin and made me think about jumping. It seemed to me that would be the way to go out of this world—jumping from a bridge into a dark river far below.

"Here's where we talked the first time," Frankie said as we reached the center. "You were swinging from the supports."

I leaned over the railing next to him. "We used to think about jumping."

"You thought about it, not me."

"You did, too—Butch and Sundance, remember?"

"You're crazy. That's about a 100-foot drop. We'd die hitting the water."

"Not if we landed feet first."

He shook his head. "You couldn't count on that."

"We'll get pounded first," I said, "so even if we land wrong, we won't feel a thing."

"Oh great, we'll jump off the bridge stoned out of our minds and then try to swim to shore?"

A car skidded to a stop behind us at the rail, and five guys jumped out. We were suddenly surrounded, and it amazed me how quickly life could change. They didn't say a word, but I knew what they had come for. They tackled me off my feet and shoved my face into the pavement. Then the biggest guy pulled me up by my arm pinned behind me and stood me face to face with Patrick Siever. I looked around, but Frankie was gone, just as if he had dissolved into the air or jumped in the river.

"Nice buddy you have there," one guy said, pointing back to New Hope. "Took off like a scared little rabbit." This guy was wearing an Eagles cap with the brim turned up. He didn't look like the kind I could reason with.

The muscleman behind me jammed my arm higher up my back, stretching it as tight as it would go without breaking. "How do you like these odds?" the Eagles guy said. He was carrying a baseball bat. "It's kind of like when you jumped Kelly, isn't it?"

He handed the weapon to Kelly's brother, who was wearing a "Sunny's Sunoco" T-shirt. There was a little yellow smiley face sewn over his pocket.

"What's up, Pat?" I said. We weren't really on speaking terms, since he was two years older than me and lived north of town, but I figured it wouldn't hurt to be friendly.

"Smash the shit out of him," the muscleman said.

Pat didn't look to me like he had murder in him. He held the bat loose, as if he was stepping up to the plate for hitting practice, not like he was ready to knock my head out of the ballpark. "Why'd you have to come back?" he said. "Why couldn't you have just stayed out of town?"

"It's my home, Pat." These words sounded strange coming from me, but I meant them. The longer I'd been on the road, the more New Hope did seem like home.

A few horns sounded through the darkness as the traffic started to back up. "Stop talking and slam him," the Eagles guy said. "We don't have all night."

Siever dropped the bat and made a fist. But then he just stared at me, and I could see his heart wasn't in this. He'd probably been pushed into coming after me by his drunken buddies.

"Go ahead," I said to him, "you won't kill me, if that's what you're worried about."

Cars were slowing on both lanes of the bridge as the drivers tried to see what was going on. The muscleman was wrenching my arm off, which I figured hurt worse than anything Pat could throw at me. So I leaned back and kicked my legs into his stomach.

That got the fight rolling. He came back at me with a roundhouse to my jaw. I stomped on the foot of the guy holding me and freed myself with an elbow to his ribs. The five of them circled me, and one guy dove at my legs to get me off my feet again. That was the end of my chance to get away. I covered my head and curled into a ball, just as Rocky taught me years ago in karate class. He always said there would be times when you were going to get beat up, but you still had a choice of where to take the damage. Siever and his friends kicked me around the pavement for a while, and I squirmed like a snake so I'd take only a few direct hits. Still, when they got tired and raced off in their car toward New Hope, my body felt like it had been hung up on a hook for kicking practice.

Someone shined a flashlight in my face. "Are you alright?" a woman asked from her car.

"Not really," I tried to say, and that scared me, because either I couldn't hear what I was saying or I wasn't saying anything. My chest felt like a car was parked on it. The woman leaned back in her window and drove away. I pulled myself up by the railing. I tried breathing deeply, but something was choking off my lungs. I was used to getting the wind knocked out of me from karate, and this wasn't the same thing.

A cop car came speeding into the center of the bridge with its lights flashing. For once I was happy to see the police. They stopped diagonally across both lanes, blocking all the traffic, and two cops came hurrying over to get me. "You okay?" the first one asked as he held me up.

I shook my head that I wasn't. "Can't breathe," I said.

They helped me to the car, laid me in the backseat, and did a U-turn back into town. They radioed ahead to New Hope Memorial that they were bringing in a kid with trouble breathing from being in a fight. The passenger-side cop looked over his seat at me every once in awhile. "Guess you lost, huh?" he said, trying to be cheery, and I nodded. "How many were there?" I held up five fingers and he shook his head. "You might want to even the odds a little next time, find a few friends of your own."

The driver tapped his partner's shoulder. "You know who that is?" he said, thumbing back at me.

"No, who?"

"The Paine kid, the one who ran away last summer after they molested that girl at the canal."

I tried to say I never molested anybody, but the cop just shook his head and said, "Save your breath, kid."

•

They took me to the emergency room of New Hope Memorial, which I had never been inside before. The cops dragged me in by the arms and stood me up at the front desk where a nurse asked my name.

"Jake," I said in a whisper.

"What did he say?" the nurse asked the cops.

"Jake Paine," the younger cop said.

"Cause of injuries?"

"Some kind of fight. He lost."

"Do you know his age?" she asked.

The cops shook their heads and she guessed seventeen. They all looked at me, and I pointed lower with my thumb. She said "sixteen" and I nodded yes.

"Insurance?"

I shrugged that I didn't know, and she told me to sign her paper and take a seat. I never made it back to the waiting room. I collapsed on the hard floor and woke up in a hospital bed, feeling the stick of a needle in my chest.

"How you doing?" a young doctor asked me. He was watching himself pull a syringe from my skin.

I tried to take the mask off my mouth to answer him, but a nurse stopped my hand. "Relax," she said, "breathe the oxygen." The doctor told her to go ahead and shave me. She spread some cold cream on the right side of my chest and took a razor to the area. That seemed strange to me since I only had a little fuzz on my chest to begin with.

171

"You might be wondering what we're up to," the doctor said, which I definitely was. When someone's poking around your body, you get curious. "You have a broken rib," he said, "right about here." He touched my chest below the nipple, but not hard enough that I could feel anything broken. "That's one problem we're not too concerned about. It will heal itself in a few weeks. The main thing we have to worry about is that the broken rib punctured your right lung, and it collapsed a bit. That's why you can't breathe normally. In a few minutes I'm going to fix that, too. When the anesthesia numbs the area, I'll put a little hole through your chest and insert this tube." He held the device up so I could see it. "Through the tube we'll suck out air from your chest and allow your lung to reinflate. Understand?"

All I understood was that trying to breathe on one lung didn't feel too great. I gave him the thumbs up sign for him to do what he had to do. Then I closed my eyes to block out whatever pain was coming my way.

•

That night Jenny came to see me. I acted like I was in a coma, dead to the world. I didn't want to answer any of her questions or see that look on her face that said that I had gotten what I deserved. She still talked at me—I couldn't stop that. She told me that she had always been afraid this kind of thing would happen, that trouble seemed to follow me around like a stupid old dog. She said that she couldn't take much more of this—the phone calls, the attack on the house, having to rush to the hospital. She said Dad was getting stirred up again, almost beyond her strength to deal with. She went on like this for about half an hour. At the end she said she knew I was listening and I better start taking responsibility for myself. She said we would have to have a serious talk and decide a few things. Then she straightened the covers over me and said she hoped I wasn't hurt too badly. After a minute, I heard her leave.

Dad showed up the next afternoon. He sat next to me on the bed as I flipped through the channels on the TV hanging over me. But there was nothing much on except weird soap operas and even weirder talk shows, so I turned it off again. Then Dad pulled a book from his back pocket and waved it in front of me. "Albert Schweitzer," he said.

I had heard the name before, but I couldn't remember why. "Who's he?"

"He was a doctor who went to Africa in the first half of this century. Devoted his life to healing people."

"Good for Albert."

"That's not all," Dad said. "He was more remarkable because of his reverence for all life, not just human. You know the expression, 'He wouldn't hurt a fly'?"

"Sure. Did he make that up?"

"No, but you could say that about him, and it would be true. He'd coax snakes out of his tent rather than kill them. He wouldn't pull a wildflower out of the ground." Behind the curtain next to me Mr. Ricci coughed or spit up or sneezed—I couldn't tell. Dad didn't seem to notice.

"Why'd you bring me this book, Dad? What's Albert got to do with me?"

He reached under my pajama top and lifted the tube stuck in my chest. "When I see what people will do to each other," he said, "I get embarrassed being human. Albert Schweitzer makes me feel a little better."

•

Larkin came at dinner time. She was wearing a shiny black raincoat still dripping rain. Her nails were painted a light shade of red. She looked like she was going out, probably with Doug, and had just stopped to see me on the way.

"Jake," she said, as she rushed through the door, "are you alright?" She sounded like I was on my death bed.

"Checking up on your investment?" I said. She cocked her head, wondering how she deserved that question, and I felt rotten for asking it. "That for me?" I said to change the subject and nodded at the bag marked "Chang the Younger's Better Food." Young Chang had opened his own restaurant across Main Street from his father after they fought over what to serve at Sunday brunch.

"Of course it's for you," she said, pulling out a half dozen small white boxes, "if you can eat."

"I can always eat," I said. "I just can't breathe right."

Larkin cleared away the table and opened the boxes. "Beef with pea pods," she said, "moo shi pork, boiled rice, extra pancakes, egg rolls, dumplings." She pulled the tray part of the table over the bed between us and we dug in with the plastic forks, eating from the same boxes, not saying anything. She seemed as hungry as me, and she laughed a couple of times at the sauce dripping from her fingers. After about fifteen minutes, we were pretty much done. Larkin dried the duck sauce from her hands with a napkin and pushed the food tray out of the way. "Let's see what they've done to you," she said, pointing at my chest. I opened my hospital shirt to show her the tube, and she fingered the strings on the hospital top. "You're supposed to put this on backwards, you know."

"Yeah, but I get nurses coming in here every hour checking this thing. This way it's easy to show them."

"Maybe it's you they're coming to see." She laughed when she said this, as if making a big joke. Actually, it was a joke. So far the only females coming around were a few old nurses and some candy-stripers who brought stupid magazines like *Field & Stream* and *Sports Illustrated.* None of them ever stayed to talk. They just looked under my shirt, said anything like, "Does it hurt?" and then left before I could think of something funny to answer. It was kind of hard to come off cool wearing hospital pajamas.

"So," Larkin said, "how does the tube work?"

"It's sucking air out of my chest so that my lung can expand again. The doctor said it's a mechanical problem, like fixing a car."

"Does it hurt?"

"Not really. I guess it's supposed to because the nurses keep offering me pain pills, and they're surprised I don't want them."

"I hate pain," she said as her fingers felt my ribs below the tube. "I can stand anything but physical pain."

My stomach tensed at her touch. "It does hurt a little when I laugh," I said, "but I don't do much of that in here. And it hurts when I try to lift up on my right side, like this." I lifted my back off the bed and the pain stabbed through my chest until I eased myself back again.

"I guess you'll have to stay away from fighting for awhile," she said.

"Sure," I said, but how can a kid pick his fights? Mostly they just came on me when I was minding my own business.

"You know, you really shouldn't fight at all," she said.

"Why shouldn't I? Countries do, either fight or threaten like they're going to kick the shit out of some other little country."

"You're not a country. You're just a boy."

I didn't like the "just a boy" part. It made me sound too young to know anything. I knew I wanted her to keep rubbing my chest. "I'd do better as president than some of them. They just lie, like Dad says, and tell you what you want to hear."

She smiled at me. "I didn't know you were so political."

"I read things, I know what's happening. Just because I ran away doesn't mean I'm stupid."

"No," she said, "I'd say in your case running away definitely shows you aren't stupid."

•

She sat back in the visitor's chair and put her feet up on my bed, as if she was planning on staying after all. Maybe Doug had trotted on back to New York, like a good dog. "So, tell me exactly what happened," she said, but she didn't pull out her tape recorder or pad like usual.

"Don't you have a date tonight?" I asked, just to make sure she wouldn't run out on me.

"No, as a matter of fact, should I?" I shrugged that it was up to her. "You're acting very strange," she said. "Is something wrong?"

What was wrong was this image in my brain of that mongrel, Doug, laying his paws on her. "Must be the operation," I said.

"Well tell me how the fight happened."

"Okay, Frankie and I were walking to Lambertville—across the bridge," I added, in case she didn't know that was the only way to get there. "We were hacking around, throwing stuff into the water, not paying much attention, which was pretty dumb. Then this car pulls up and these guys jump out in front of us. There was nowhere to run. I got some good kicks in but there were like five of them, so I just covered up and let them hit me till they got tired."

Her face twisted up as I described the scene. "That's awful," she said. "How bad is Frankie?"

"Okay, I guess. He got away."

"How did he manage that?"

"He's pretty fast running. Besides, they weren't interested in smashing him, just me."

"Your father said the police came."

"Oh yeah, late as usual. They didn't catch anybody— they didn't even look."

"You know who these boys are, don't you?"

"One of them."

"Then you could have him arrested," she said, which made me laugh. She didn't understand how it would look to people if I had somebody arrested for attacking me. "You need a good lawyer," she said. "Doug's a lawyer. He usually handles divorces, but I'm sure he could get someone to do it from his firm. It wouldn't cost you anything."

I shook my head. "Dad says we're not pressing charges."

"Why not?"

"When you get into trouble a lot, and get away with it most of the time, it's not really right to try to nail somebody else for hassling you. You know what I mean?"

She lifted up my chest tube. "You call this hassling you? I'd say they were trying to kill you."

"They were just getting their licks in," I said. "You can't really blame them."

●

Larkin left for a few minutes to have a cigarette outside, then came back with her recorder in hand. "I could do some interviewing," she said, "if you're up to it."

"I can talk some," I said.

She nodded over at the curtain. "Can we go out in the lobby or somewhere private?"

"He's barely breathing," I said, "and he only speaks Italian anyway. The nurses come to check whether he's alive every half hour or so."

"Okay," she said, clicking on the recorder and then finding a place for it on the tray, "talk."

That surprised me. She'd always had a question before, lots of them. "You're the writer," I said, "what do you want to know?"

"You be the writer tonight. Tell me whatever you want."

I couldn't figure out if she was trying to trick me somehow or not. Before I could stop myself from saying anything, I said, "I had a snake once," which seemed like a strange thing to jump out of my mind, but she nodded for me to keep going. "I called him 'Miami' because he was this big Florida Indigo. Uncle Toby sent him to me."

"Your parents—I mean your father and Jenny—they didn't object?"

"She wanted to throw him in the Delaware, but Dad said that would be making the snake pay for being a snake. So he got this eight-foot long glass box for Miami to live in. He'd pull his chair up close and stare at the thing sleeping. Jenny actually got to like the snake because it kept Dad busy. The only thing nobody liked was feeding him. I had to trap rats along the river and kind of deaden them in a bucket of water before dropping them in with Miami. Otherwise they'd get really wild in the box trying to get out. He took a nice long time swallowing them. It was kind of amazing to watch. You ever see that?" I asked her. Larkin shook her head. "He needed two a week to keep him alive and happy."

"It's odd, isn't it," she said, "that all some living things need to be happy are two rats a week?"

"Actually, I think he would have liked three a week, but rats aren't that easy to trap. And he probably would have liked moving around more, too, because he escaped from the glass a few times, which got Jenny really crazy. We usually found him right away in some warm spot, like near a radiator. But one time he crawled into the wall through one of the floor registers and hung around there for a few days. We banged on the wall for hours, but he wouldn't move. So we had to wait until he got hungry for his rats. He came out one night and wrapped around Jenny's leg while she was talking on the phone at the top of the stairs. She jumped and kicked and that scared Miami and he started tightening around her leg, and it was a mess trying to calm both of them down and peel him off her. So then we did have to throw him out on the riverbank. He probably scared a few animals before freezing to death. I kind of missed having him around, and I know Dad did."

Larkin didn't say anything for a minute, and I listened to the whirring of the recorder, thinking of how strange it was to have your life being listened to by a machine. "Tell me about your father," she said as she kicked off her shoes and propped up her long legs on my bed, "how was he while you were growing up?"

"He's always been sort of crazy, at least as long as I can remember. I can't say how he was before Mom died."

"Crazy in what way?"

"Like one time I came home from school, he was sitting on top of the refrigerator. I remember that seemed odd to me, but for Dad, not so odd I even asked him what he was doing."

"You came to expect such things?"

"Yep. I knew he wasn't like most dads."

"Did that bother you?"

"No, 'cause I wasn't like most kids, so why should he have to be like other fathers?"

Larkin took out a cigarette and tapped it on the tray as if she were going to light it, but didn't. "But was he just different," she asked, "or actually crazy?"

I shrugged that I didn't know, but I did have a theory. "Maybe he was just always different, and then when Mom died, that knocked him over the edge into crazy."

"That was a very shocking thing to happen to him."

To him? "It happened to me, too, remember? I was in the car. I saw everything, too."

"Yes," she said, "that accident happened to your whole family."

•

"It's freezing in here," she said, rubbing her bare arms. I lifted myself off the bed and pulled the blanket free from under me. I handed it to her and sank back into the pillows as the pain twisted into my chest. She wrapped the blanket around her shoulders. "I've talked to some people about you," she said, "both in town and at your school. You've made quite an impression—everyone remembers you."

"Yeah?"

"But not many people are glad you're back."

"Guess not."

"They say you tried to rape a girl, you and some other boys."

"That's what they say," I said quickly, hoping to get off this subject fast. I didn't want Larkin to think I was some terrible kid, and just talking about the canal incident would make her think that, like everyone did.

"What do you say about it?"

"It doesn't matter. People believe what they want no matter what somebody like me tells them."

"What did you tell them?" she asked.

"I told them I didn't try to rape her."

"There must have been some reason they thought you did."

There were lots of reasons, since I was with the guys who grabbed Kelly under the Mechanic Street Bridge, and I tried to kiss her like they did, but I wasn't going to hurt her, no matter how full of beer I was.

"Why did they accuse you?" she asked again.

"The girl recognized me. She said there were other guys from Jersey she didn't know, but she described someone like me who used to go in Gerenser's where she scooped ice cream. Decker figured it was me."

"Decker?"

"What kind of reporter are you? You can't be writing about me without running into Sergeant Decker. He's my personal fascist cop just watching for me to get in trouble."

"He's a New Hope policeman?"

"Yep, a smalltown lifer cop."

"And he arrested you for the rape?"

"Not arrested really. He just took me in."

"Were you brought to trial?"

"Nope, the girl couldn't make an absolute ID since it was dark, and she wasn't really raped, so there wasn't any of that kind of evidence. The guys got her dress off but then some old queer with a German shepherd chased them away."

"You mean some old *man* with a German shepherd . . . "

"Some gay sort of gentleman," I said, "with a nice, friendly dog chased them away." It seemed stupid to me that I couldn't call the guy queer when lots of them called themselves that.

"But people still believed you were involved, even though it wasn't proven?"

She seemed to be having trouble understanding how that could happen. She obviously hadn't learned much about New Hope. "That's what got them mad," I said, "that they believed something but couldn't prove it or do anything to me."

"You had a reputation for doing some wild things."

"Yep."

"How did you get that?"

The answer seemed obvious to me: "By doing wild things."

"Such as breaking into houses and getting into fights?"

"Nobody knew about the house-breaking, and maybe only a few ever saw me fight. But when I climbed to the top of the bridge as the Fourth of July parade came across—a lot of people saw that. They thought I was going to jump." I remembered waking up that morning at six o'clock so I could plan my adventure. I sneaked out of the house before either Dad or Jenny were downstairs, and I headed for town. Only a few cops were there, blocking off the bridge to traffic. I walked on the pedestrian path out to the middle, along with some families setting up early for the best view. Then I ducked over the rail on the Lambertville side of the big steel rafters and started my climb. It took me a half hour to pull my way up the bridge supports, and the wind was whipping into my face, getting stronger every foot I climbed. From the top it seemed like I could see the whole world— at least as far as I had ever gone in it.

"That sounds pretty dangerous," she said, "climbing to the top of the bridge."

"Yeah, especially when I hung by two hands as the band passed underneath. I guess the cops thought I might drop down and flatten people. They stopped the parade and yelled at me, but I couldn't hear them. It was like the words didn't reach that high. Then they called off the rest of the parade and stationed a cop on the bridge to wait for me. I stayed there until about noon, then it got so hot the steel was burning my skin off."

"What did they do to you when you got down?"

"Nothing. They tried to find a law I broke, like being a public nuisance, but things got kind of mixed up because actually it's a state bridge, and I was just over on the New Jersey side anyway, so the New Hope police didn't really have jurisdiction and they were the ones who took me in. That made them pretty mad that they couldn't do anything to me."

"The police and you never got along, did you?

"I'm just a punk kid to them, somebody who gives them trouble."

"What other trouble did you give them?"

There was a lot to choose from, I had to admit. "One summer I got in the habit of messing up their cars every few nights," I said. "I put shaving cream on the seats, or soaked them with water, stuff like that. It was a pretty cool game trying not to get caught."

"You did these things for fun?"

That seemed like enough reason to me, but obviously not for her. So I said, "Dad's been beaten up in town, you know, he's had cars try to run him over, he had a brick thrown at him, and the police never did anything. People laugh at him all the time, nobody will give him a real job . . . "

"Why? I mean, who did those things to him?"

"Just people around town. They see Dad being crazy, and that's reason enough, you know, because he's different. Like, he can't stand fur coats, you know, because he thinks they look better on the animals."

"A lot of people agree with him."

"Yeah, except some people think he was the one who kept pouring molasses and peanut butter in the door locks at Lowery's, which is the only place that sells furs in town."

"Peanut butter?" Larkin asked.

"Yeah, he boiled it till it was runny and then squirted it in somehow."

"Did they catch him?"

"Not red-handed or anything. He stood outside the store with a sign that said Fur Stinks and watched old man Lowery trying to get his door open. So it was kind of obvious he did it, but they couldn't arrest him. Then a couple of years ago he chained himself to the fence at the pump site for weeks after everybody gave up."

"What dump site?"

"The *pump* site, for the water to the nuclear plant. It was a big deal around here before I left. They wanted to take water from the Delaware to cool this nuke site miles from here. Lots of people protested for awhile and then gave up. But Dad didn't. One time he laid down in the road to block the construction trucks. The traffic backed up for a mile until the cops got there and dragged him away.'

"Your father sounds committed to his causes."

"Yeah, he still thinks it's the Sixties when you could do stuff like that and people would think you had a conscience. Now they just say you're mental. They don't understand how Mom's death hit him. They just see what he is now, which is crazy, and they don't want him in New Hope."

"So you're saying that through the things you did, you were just getting back at New Hope?"

I nodded that I was saying that, but I'm not sure I even believed it myself.

•

Larkin left for another smoke, promising that it would be her last one for the night. She even gave me her pack of cigarettes to crush, but I saved them under my pillow for myself. She came back in a few minutes saying that it might be easier for her to give up sex than cigarettes. That made me sit up in bed, and I blurted out, "You don't want to do that."

Larkin laughed and put her hand on my leg. "I was just kidding." Then she acted like a reporter again asking her stupid questions. "Are your grandparents alive?"

"They live out West somewhere—my mother's parents, I mean—we never see them. Grandmom on Dad's side died upstairs in our house—I think she puked to death, or at least that's how it sounded. Grandpa died about seven or eight years ago. He lived with us for awhile at the end, which was pretty strange 'cause he had Alzheimer's."

"A bad case?"

"Not like where you become a baby again or anything. He'd lapse into it, like his brain was hooked up to a socket and the cord would come loose sometimes."

"So Alzheimer's killed him?"

"No, the *Inquirer* did."

That made Larkin sit up. "*The Philadelphia Inquirer?*"

"Yeah, he went out front one Sunday morning in his bathrobe to get the paper. It was right before Christmas, very cold, and he bent over to pick it up, but it must have been too heavy and he fell into a snow bank. We didn't know he was out there for a couple of hours because he used to hide in the cellar sometimes. He just keeled over and froze."

Larkin opened two sticks of gum and stuffed them in her mouth. "That must have been a hard time for the family," she said, chewing on the wad. Her breath suddenly smelled like strawberries.

"Not really. Jenny hated him living with us because it was tough enough for her looking after Dad without having to watch Grandpa, too. She said he didn't accomplish one thing in life except staying out of debt. That's all he talked about—dying a free man. He did, too, which is kind of an achievement for a Paine, from what Dad says. Jenny couldn't imagine that being your only goal in life."

"What's your goal, Jake?"

I shrugged. The last person to ask me this was Kinnert, and he put it in his newspaper story to make me look stupid. "Do I have to have one?"

Larkin nodded. "Most people do." I started to say that I wasn't most people, but she said, "I know you're not like most people, but still, you should have something you want to do with your life."

I wanted to fuck her—that was my goal, but not one I could really tell her. So I faked an answer, something I knew she'd like. "I want to feel like I'm okay," I said, remembering what a counselor told me once during a therapy session. "I don't want to be great," I said, "just okay."

She tossed aside the blanket and shut off the recorder, meaning I'd said enough for one night.

•

A hand on my shoulder shook me awake. I kept my eyes closed, hoping the nurse would go away, but the hand kept shaking me. I rolled over and there was Frankie grinning at me. "How you doing, Paine?" he said cheerfully.

I sat up and rubbed my eyes clear. "What time is it?"

"Late, very late," he said. "Let's just say that visiting hours are over." He kept grinning at me as if he were flying on the best weed of the year. Frankie loved good marijuana and always had the money to buy it.

"How did you get past the nurses?"

"Diversion," he said, sitting on the bed next to my legs. "I dropped a match in the wastebasket."

It was our favorite trick because it gave us plenty of time to get away from the scene, and everybody would think it was some sneaky smoker who started the fire. "So what's going on?" I asked him.

"You," he said, "I came to check you out."

I opened my shirt so he could see the chest tube. He felt along the bandages and then lifted the tube for a closer look. "Pretty simple rig," he said. "My dad could have put this in with his teeth."

"Think so?"

"Nothing's too tough for my old man, the best chest-cutter in the East. He'll tell you that himself. People beg him to cut them open." I turned my face into my pillow to show I wasn't interested in hearing his super-father routine. "So, it's working okay?" he said.

"Yeah, I'm breathing better."

"That's good. Breathing is good." I nodded to that, and Frankie reached over my bed to grab the plastic cup of water from my tray. He drank a swallow. "I'm glad I didn't stick around on the bridge. I would have ended up looking like you."

"I don't care that you ran," I said. "You saved your skin. I would have done the same thing."

He shook his head. "No you wouldn't. You would have stayed there and gotten beaten up, if they were after me."

We heard footsteps coming down the hall, and Frankie rolled off the bed into the corner of the room. The door opened on him, hiding him. Nurse Harris burst in as always, already talking. "Time for your checkup," she said as she reached over my bed to turn on the bright light. She peeled back the plastic around the thermometer and stuffed it in my mouth. She picked up my wrist and counted beats as she looked at her watch. Then she pulled my shirt aside and made sure the bandages were still holding the tube in place. "It's working loose," she said as she pulled some tape from her jacket pocket. She cut a few strips and layered them over the tube. Then she took out the thermometer. "Normal. Everything's normal with you," she said. "You'll be gone in no time."

"You mean going home in no time."

She poked her head through the curtain to Mr. Ricci's bed to check he was still breathing, then shut off the light and left.

Frankie kicked the door shut after her. "So how's the service in this joint?" he asked, talking loud enough for someone to hear in the hallway.

"You take something tonight besides weed, Frankie?"

His face changed, trying to get serious, but then in a second the silliness took over again. "I took everything—some weed, a little beer, some coke . . . "

I sat up and flicked my bed light on again. Frankie put his arm up over his eyes. "What are you doing?" I said.

"The light . . . "

I reached up and pulled his arm away from his face. "I mean mixing all that stuff. We never mixed."

"That was then, this is now."

"What's the matter with you?"

"Nothing's the matter right now. I feel good," he said, and then he sang it, "*I feel good, like I knew I would, if I just ran away. So good,*" he drummed his hands on the back of the hospital bed, "*so good, so good.*" He twirled on his heels for the finale and almost fell over.

"Frankie, what the fuck's wrong?"

"Wrong?" he said, steadying himself on the bed rail, "with me? I'm fine, you know. I finished the year with an A-minus average, but I can work on the minus part. And anyway, my father's going to buy me into some Ivy League school by endowing a chair or something. And I'm living in a great house with plenty of room because nobody ever comes home."

"I'm not going to feel sorry for you being rich, Frankie."

"See, that's the problem. The rich have feelings, too, you know. But nobody cares about them."

"You've got two normal parents, a fucking huge house—"

"Oh yeah, the house is great. Solid stone, that's the way they built them in the eighteenth century. Built to last. Built for solid people." He stopped and stared at me for a long time. Then he bit his lip, closed his eyes and said, "You know who lives in that house now?"

"Yeah, you do."

"No," he waved his hand in front of my face, "you don't know who lives there."

"So who lives there?"

"A fag." He let the word sink in, staring at my eyes now for a reaction. "You hear what I said, Paine?"

"A fag lives in your house."

"Yeah, but not just any fag." He tapped himself on the chest. "This fag. This fucking coward of a screaming fag."

His voice was shaking, his eyes were looking into me to see what I was thinking of him now. "Frankie," I said, "I already knew that."

He collapsed into the chair next to my bed, and the cushion let out a disgusting burst of air. His eyes closed, then popped open. "You didn't know, you're just saying that."

"I knew, Frankie."

"You couldn't have." He jumped out of the chair and grabbed my chest tube. "I pull this out and you die, right?"

"In a matter of minutes," I said.

"So tell me the truth—you didn't know?"

"What difference does it make if I knew or not?"

He tugged a little on the tube, enough to send a dull pain to my right lung. "Tell me!"

"Frankie, you're a little fag, and I knew it years ago."

He let the tube go. "How could you? I wasn't old enough then to be queer."

"I knew you'd grow up queer," I said.

"And it didn't bother you?"

"You never tried anything with me."

"What if I thought about it?"

"I don't care what you think about. Just keep your hands off me."

He pulled back from me as if I meant he shouldn't be touching me now. Then he took a button from his pocket and held it out for me to see—"Possibly Queer" it read in pink letters. "That's the name of a group," he said. "They threw the buttons into the crowd at City Garden last week. I caught one." He stuck the pin on his T-shirt, right above "CCCP" and a giant red hammer and cycle. It was another souvenir his father brought back from the old Soviet Union. "Seems to fit," Frankie said, polishing the button with his shirttail, "don't you think?" I shrugged that it was up to him whether he wanted to advertise that about himself. "My father will kill me when he sees it," he said, smiling again, and he put his hand up for me to give him a high five. I did and smiled with him, because it hurt too much to laugh. "Serves my old man right," Frankie said, "to have a queer for a son."

Eighteen

BY THE NEXT DAY I WAS SO SICK OF MR. RICCI WHEEZING IN THE bed next to me and nurses sticking needles and thermometers into me that I was ready to bust out of the hospital, just like old man Metzgar had done. Then a doctor came by with a breathing tube for me to blow into and I moved the marker almost to the top, which he said was amazing. My lung was inflating just fine and I could walk around a bit, if I wanted to.

So I started wandering around the hospital, even to the maternity ward on the fifth floor. I liked going up there to look at the crying kids lying in their baskets behind the display window. A guy sweeping the floors asked if one of them was mine, which was a pretty stupid thing to ask a kid dressed in hospital pajamas. But it made me realize that I was old enough to make one of those babies, if I wanted to. Of course, I'd need a girlfriend for that.

Sometimes I talked to my favorite kids behind the glass, the scrawny or blotchy ones. I told them that they might think life was pretty tough right then, but it was going to get a lot worse, so they had to become strong enough to take it. Whether they were starting out rich like Frankie or poor like me, chances were they'd run into a lot of trouble along the way.

•

Late in the afternoon Larkin came to take me home. I was dressed and ready to go. She walked into my room just after the guy delivered my food tray, so I had to rush through the turkey, cranberry sauce, peas, mashed potatoes, and biscuits. I offered her some, but she said no, that I needed my strength, and anyway, she was on a diet. I looked her over when she said that, and I couldn't see any extra pounds I'd take off her. She looked good in a baggy purple sweater and black pants, and a beaded white necklace. "Jenny goes on diets all the time," I said. "You don't look like Jenny."

"Maybe that's because I don't stuff myself with terrible food like this."

"It isn't so bad," I said, as I dunked the last bite of the turkey in the gravy and chomped it down. "Okay, let's go."

"We have to call an orderly," she said. "Hospital rules—everybody leaves in a wheelchair."

"Not me," I said and picked up my jacket. We walked down the hallway, past the nurse's station, and no one even looked up at us let alone tried to jump in our way.

We got in the elevator and when the doors closed, I felt totally alone with her for the first time. She was standing just a few inches away from me. I leaned closer to smell her perfume, and she caught me. I smiled like I wasn't doing anything wrong, and the elevator doors opened to let us off at the ground floor.

She drove slowly through New Hope to avoid bumps. When we pulled in our driveway, the Buick was gone and the door to the house was closed. Nobody was home. "I told your father and Jenny that I would bring you at six," Larkin said as we climbed the front steps. "We're only a few minutes early."

"She probably had to go to work," I said, "and maybe Dad's out selling books."

The front door was unlocked, as usual. Jenny used to say that God hadn't made the man stupid enough to rob us. Larkin and I went into the living room. I flopped down on the sofa and she sat next to me, close enough that I could feel the heat from her body. "Can you stand some interviewing, or are you too tired?" she asked.

I was tired, but I didn't want her to leave either. "I'm okay."

She pulled out her recorder and turned it on. Then she picked through her large black pocketbook until she found what she was looking for—a white sheet with lines drawn across it. She unfolded the paper and held it up for me to see. "Do you recognize this?"

I shrugged that maybe I did, maybe I didn't.

"'Dear Harassers of Mankind . . . '" she read from the top of the paper, and then paused—"You know what this is?"

"Looks like a letter."

"A letter you wrote."

"Doesn't say that on there," I said, pointing to the bottom of the handwritten page. "It's unsigned."

"People put their signatures on things in a lot of ways. Everyone that received this said it came from you."

"So if they know who sent it, why are you asking me?"

She didn't answer my question. "The words really scared them," she said.

"Then I guess it was worth writing, to whoever did it."

"Read the words, Jake, outloud."

Sure, why not? I took the letter from her. "'Dear Harassers of Mankind: You call people crazy and try to put them away where you don't have to see them. But some people you can't catch. And when they come back, you'll be sorry.'"

Larkin waited for me to say something, which I wasn't planning to do, so she said, "The people you sent this letter to—Sergeant Decker, Mr. Schneider at the record store, your counselor at school—they took it as a threat."

"That's how I would have taken it, too."

"So that's how you meant it?"

"I didn't exactly say I wrote this."

Larkin snapped the paper out of my hands. "Stop playing games, Jake. You wrote it to scare these people. Don't you understand, they felt that you were harassing *them*?"

"So you believe them?"

She wasn't expecting that question. Sure she believed them. I could see that in her eyes. If she didn't believe them, she would have just told me that. "What should I believe?" she finally said. I shrugged that it was up to her and left the room for her to think about it.

•

She followed me upstairs to my room. She opened my door and saw me stretched out on my bed. I knew she'd come, so I'd pushed my shirt up a little from my waist. She stood in the doorway, looking around my room. "Can I come in?"

"Sure you aren't scared to, if I rape people, and harass them, like everybody says?"

She didn't answer, but she did come in. She wandered around my room picking up things on my bookshelf—rocks, coins, shells—all stuff from Uncle Toby. "You know, Jake," she said, shaking a giant conch at me, "this book isn't turning out anything like I expected." I thought she was going to say that I wasn't telling her enough good stories, so she was going to cancel the deal and go back to New York. But she didn't say that. She said, "You can be very surprising." I nodded, even though I didn't seem all that surprising to myself. Larkin walked over to my desk, past a pile of my dirty underwear and socks. While she was turned away from me, I pushed my shirt up a little more and pulled my shorts higher so she could see I was getting hard. She opened my desk drawer and got out my journal. "When I was here last week," she said, turning around to face me now, "I found your diary."

I watched her eyes, trying to see if she was looking where I wanted her to.

"You said I could look at anything in your room, so I assumed you wouldn't mind."

"I don't mind," I managed to say, as she sat on the bottom of my bed. My throat was clenching up. I was almost choking on the smell of her perfume.

I spread my legs a little, but Larkin looked away from me and began to read: "'July 5—Jenny grounded me for a week for climbing on the bridge during the parade yesterday. She said I made a fool of myself. I said if what I did was so stupid, how come people cheered when I hung from one arm? She said that they were probably hoping I would fall.'"

Larkin looked over at me. "Was Jenny right? Did people in town really hope you would get hurt?"

"She was just exaggerating. She likes to believe that everybody thinks the way she does."

Larkin considered that for a moment. "You mean *she* was hoping you'd fall from that bridge?"

That's what I seemed to be saying, but I didn't really believe Jenny would go that far. "She probably figured I deserved to fall, but I don't think she actually wished it."

"But you're not sure?"

"You can't ever be sure," I said. "She just wanted to get

rid of me, to Norristown or wherever. Even running away—I think that was fine with her."

Larkin turned to a different page in my journal and read: "'August 2—I dug up the possum again. The worms had eaten away his stomach. But his eyes were still open. He looked like he was alive and feeling himself being eaten. His guts were all brown and crawling with ants, and when I stuck my hand . . .'" Larkin stopped reading and screwed up her face in that kind of expression that women have for things that boys like to do. "What do you mean, 'I dug up the possum *again*'?"

I made it sound like a science experiment. "I used to catch animals on the riverbank in the summer, and sometimes I buried them in the yard out back. Then every month I'd dig them up and write what they looked like, kind of like research into what happens after things are dead." That was the lie part—writing down what I saw.

"Was this something you learned about in school?"

"Yeah," I said, lying again, "in biology."

Larkin flipped through the pages, and I wondered what else she had found in this journal that she thought was strange about me. I'd written so much stuff that I couldn't remember it all. "How did you come to write in a diary in the first place?" she asked.

"It's a journal, not a diary."

"What's the difference?"

"Girls have diaries, boys have journals."

"Oh, I see," she said, in a way that meant she really didn't. "So how did you come to write in a *journal*?" She hung on the last word, so I'd catch her sarcasm.

I took the book from her and turned to the front page where the explanation was: "'May 13—I started scribbling stuff in here today and Dad saw me. He said that once you start a journal, you can't stop. He should have told me that sooner so I wouldn't have started it.'" I looked up, and Larkin motioned for me to continue. "'This is boring,'" I read. "'Nothing happens to me. Maybe if I start a new line for every sentence, it will seem like more is happening than really is. I got up this morning, went to school, beat up this kid named Jason during recess because he ripped my shirt playing tag. It was the Jason with red hair, the one whose father drives him to school in the Mercedes . . .'"

Larkin laughed a little, and I didn't know what was funny. "So your father tricked you into writing?" she said.

"I believed him that you couldn't stop once you started, especially since Uncle Toby gave me the journal."

"He was a special uncle?"

"Oh yeah," I said, "he was the best."

"What was he like?"

"Well, I never actually met him because he lived in Wyoming and traveled a lot, but not here because he doesn't like people very much. He's into animals."

"But he must have liked you."

"I guess so, he sent me all sorts of neat stuff."

"So that's why you liked him—he sent you gifts."

"No," I said quickly. "I liked Uncle Toby because he was—" The phone rang, which was good, since I didn't really know how to explain my uncle. There weren't five or ten things I could say that I liked about him, since I had never even met him. He was just my great Uncle Toby. I jumped up to get the phone at the top of the stairs. I said hello, forgetting that Jenny said I shouldn't speak first. The caller didn't try to scare me with breathing or bust my eardrums with some high-pitched noise. This time he spoke very calmly. "I heard you were in the hospital," he said. "I'm sorry about the beating. I didn't want to hurt you that bad."

It was Pat Siever. I waited for him to say more, but he didn't. I figured he was waiting for me to forgive him. "It wasn't your fault," I said. "People get crazy sometimes." He grunted that he agreed, "I get crazy," I added, "sometimes."

"Yeah," he said, and that's all. I didn't know what else to say. It wasn't like I could invite old Pat out for a beer or anything. I mean, he wasn't calling to be friends. He cleared his throat to let me know he was still there, so I cleared my throat to let him know I was, too. "I thought we killed you," he said, "when I saw the ambulance."

"I couldn't breathe right for awhile," I said, "but I'm getting better at it."

"We weren't trying to kill you," he said, "just scare you."

It sort of felt like they had been trying to kill me, with all of the kicks to my chest. As for scaring me, I couldn't say they had done that. Now that they had beaten me up, I

193

figured I wouldn't have to worry about them doing it again. Revenge usually only happened once.

"So," Pat said, "you going to tell the police?"

Suddenly I understood why he was calling. He wasn't really feeling sorry for me, he was scared for himself.

"No, Pat," I said, "me and the police don't get along too well. Anyway, I've been beat up worse. It's no big deal."

"Well," he said in a stronger voice, now that I had told him what he wanted to hear, "like I said, I'm sorry, but I still wish you hadn't come back." He hung up before I could say that sometimes I wish I hadn't either.

When I got back to my bedroom, Larkin had turned on my boombox and was swaying to some old song I had never heard. She laughed and snapped her fingers when she saw me. "Come on," she said, as I sat on the bed to watch her bounce around. She grabbed for my hand and pulled me standing. "Let's dance."

"I can't," I said.

She stopped quickly. "Sorry, I forgot about your rib."

"It's not that," I said, "I just never learned how to."

Larkin took my hands again. "We'll change that right now." She started bouncing again, side to side, and pulled me along with her. "Feel the beat," she said, "and stop looking at your feet." She touched my chin with her hand, and when I raised my eyes I was looking into the most beautiful face I'd ever seen. And she was dancing with me—in my bedroom!

The music got louder, and she brushed past me, twirling herself under my arm. I tried to close my eyes and feel the beat like she wanted me to, but my legs wouldn't move. She suddenly dropped my hands and got behind me. I could feel her breasts grazing my back through my T-shirt as she reached around me and took my arms. Her knees pressed into the back of my legs to get me to bend, and we moved like that together. If this was dancing, I sure didn't want to stop.

When the song ended, we turned toward the radio at the same time, and there was Jenny filling up the doorway.

Nineteen

A FEW DAYS WENT BY, AND I BARELY GOT OUTSIDE, EXCEPT TO SIT on the porch and watch the afternoon storms sweep across the sky. My rib gradually stopped hurting, except when I tried to reach for something or rolled over on my right side. My lung was staying inflated. Jenny said I was healed and should stop lying around the house like Mars and contribute something. She didn't say what, and I didn't ask.

The prank calls let up to just about one a day, usually in the afternoon. But then the *Gazette* put me at the top of the police blotter: "A 16-year-old New Hope boy, Jake Paine, was attacked by five youths while walking across the bridge to Lambertville," the paper said. "Police have no motive for the unprovoked attack and no suspects." It sure didn't do much for my image in town to be written about as an innocent victim. After the article, more calls started coming in— a few hangups each morning, some blaring noises by the afternoon, and threats in the evening. Jenny told me about one call where the guy said he was going to drag me out of the house some night, stuff me in the trunk of a car, and run it into the Delaware. She waited for me to say how scared I was, but I didn't feel scared, so I just shrugged, which really bugged her. "If this family is going to have to suffer through this," she said, "at least you can show some feeling about it."

"I really *am* scared," I said. "It's just I don't want to show it and make the rest of you more scared." I know she didn't believe me, but at least she left me alone.

Dad drifted into his weird world again where things always seemed very strange. He lay around the house all day reading, listening to his Spanish tapes, or just staring up at the ceiling. Each night after Jenny went up to bed he'd hurry into the living room to watch the videotape of Mom working in the garden. It was the only image left of her, except for a few pictures from when she broke her leg and couldn't move out of the way of Dad's camera. He said that she was so camera-shy she wouldn't even have a photographer at their wedding. Pictures lie, she said. Pictures always show you from the front or back or side, never all around at the same time, the way people really were. Video was better, she said, but even that she allowed only once.

So there she was now every night, a series of moving pictures, on her knees digging in the garden. Sometimes Dad saw something new about her and called me to come take a look. He'd replay the moment, pointing out the way she sat back on her heels or wiped the sweat from her forehead. He loved every little movement she made.

After watching the tape a few times, he'd tiptoe up to bed and fall asleep next to Jenny in whatever clothes he was wearing. The next day he'd get up and start the routine all over again. He liked having me home, and everyday about noon when I came downstairs for breakfast, he was waiting for me in the kitchen.

"Hey, Dad," I said.

"I think I'm missing something," he said as I opened the refrigerator. "My Spanish isn't as good as it used to be."

I found a piece of pizza wrapped in tin foil, which looked only a few days old. "What's the problem, Dad?"

"A professor named Galan goes walking near a river," he said, recounting the story from the book in his hands. "He spots something strange lying in the water, and looking closer, he sees it's a watermelon. Then some boys appear, American boys, playing war. They talk to the professor and notice his Spanish accent, so they ask where he is from. He says Argentina. They say that Mexico is very pretty." Dad paused a minute so that I would appreciate the mounting number of strange events. "Then one boy, who is pretending to be Kit Carson," Dad said, as he found the particular passage, "'vinó de atras, despacito, con una gran piedra entre las manos alzadas, y la descarga con todas sus fuerzas sobre la cabeza de Galan. La cabeza, abierta y sangrando, cayó al rio, junto a la sandia.'" Dad looked at me as if to ask what I made of it. I took another bite of the cold pizza. Finally he realized that I couldn't make anything of it. "The boy came up from behind," he translated, "very slowly, with a big stone in his hands, and threw it with all his might at Galan. His head, cracked open and bleeding, fell into the river, next to the watermelon." Dad closed the book and laid it on his lap. "That's the end of the story."

"Pretty weird," I said, stuffing the pizza crust into my mouth and washing it down with a few handfuls of cold water from the spigot.

"One could say Galan was imagining the attack on himself—he seems to be given to fears earlier in the story."

"That's probably it," I said. "The guy just imagined that this little kid whacked off his head and sent it rolling into the river next to the watermelon."

"Fear of death," Dad said, "can be a powerful opiate to the imagination for some people. For me, the opposite happens—it's like thorazine."

"What's that?"

He shook his head in fear at the thought of it. "Another drug doctors use on you when they can't figure out what's really wrong. If anyone tries to give it to you, run."

"You can count on that, Dad. They're not putting any drugs in me."

He stared at me. He kept staring until I pointed out of the window as if something was out there. He turned back to me, and I saw that his eyes were watery. "I'm going into town today," he said. "A new store opened not far from Sam's. They sell animals."

"A pet store?"

"They can call it what they want," he said. "The animals get mistreated all the same."

Knowing Dad, he was on a mission of liberation.

•

He left for town with his hands in his pockets, looking casual, like someone who would blend into a crowd—until your eyes happened to latch onto him. Then you'd think, that guy looks *too* casual, and you wouldn't look away until he was out of eyeshot.

"Be careful," I said to him, and he glanced over his shoulder with a little grin. This was strange—me worrying about him.

From the front porch, the afternoon seemed to stretch

out ahead of me like one of Sam's big white canvasses with only faint marks of a picture emerging on them. The heat was sticking to my body like hot glue. I needed to move. I headed inside the house, pulled my shirt off over my head, and threw it up in the air. Before it landed, Jenny had swept out of the kitchen yelling at me to pick up after myself. She had been yelling all day, about the way I shook the house when I came down the stairs, about the way I slouched over the sofa, about the crank calls that had woken her up in the middle of the night. What she meant was, Dad was acting crazier than usual, including all of these stories about death he was reading to us. And I was to blame.

I picked up my shirt and started upstairs. "Where are you going?" she demanded. She hated it when I moved out of her sight.

"I'm taking a cold shower," I said. "You want to watch?"

Even that didn't shut her up. "Keep it to five minutes," she said. "We're conserving water."

I grabbed a towel from the hall linen closet and turned on the water in the tub. It was the only time a shower felt good in this house—when the heat outside was so unbearable that the Arctic water felt good. I stayed under the ragged stream of water as long as I could, knowing that Jenny was just below in the kitchen, counting off the minutes. After awhile she banged the pipes to let me know my time was up. If I didn't get out, she'd go downstairs and turn the master water lever off, which would really put her in a bad mood. So I turned off the shower.

I toweled myself dry, and as usual lately when I didn't have clothes on, I began thinking of Larkin. But this time something else came to mind, too—the hairy body of Doug the Lawyer. That sure killed my interest in jerking off. But I was so worked up I needed to get out of the house and do something. An idea came to my mind like it always does—stomping its way in, shaking me awake and saying, Let's Do It! But this idea needed a second player—Frankie. I pulled on shorts and a T-shirt and called him. He picked up on the first ring. "It's me," I said.

"Jake?" He sounded surprised, which surprised me until

I remembered his confession at the hospital. Maybe he thought I'd never call again, especially since he had deserted me on the bridge. Being a queer and a coward were tough qualities to show a friend. Most guys wouldn't have called again, but I was in no position to be choosey about who I hung out with. Besides, I figured that Frankie was just over-dramatizing this queer stuff like he did all of his problems.

"Come pick me up," I said. "I need to get out of the house."

"I don't have any wheels," Frankie said.

"What happened to your Mustang?"

"My father took away the keys after he finally saw my report card. I got a B- in advanced biology."

"I thought you had an A average?"

"All A's except for the B-. He says I won't get into Princeton with any more Bs, and then I won't be a doctor."

"He took your car away over one B?"

"Maybe it was because I told him I'd rather suck gas than be a doctor like him. He's kind of sensitive that way."

"So, can you get into town some other way?"

"I still have legs, I can hitch."

"Okay, meet me at the train station at 7:30, and we'll find some trouble to get into."

"Legal or illegal?"

"Very illegal," I said.

•

Dad met me in the hallway as I was heading toward the front door. He was balancing a sandwich and a carton of milk on top of a book he was carrying in one hand.

"How was your trip to the pet store?" I asked him.

"I saw what I expected to see," he said. "A robin red-breast in a cage/Puts all Heaven in a rage."

"They had robins in cages?"

Dad looked at me to see if I was kidding him, which I wasn't. "No," he said patiently, "they don't put robins in cages yet. I was being metaphorical. It's a poem by Blake."

"I'm not too quick on metaphors, Pop. I'm pretty literal."

199

"Yes, I know," he said. "Where are you going?" he asked as I turned to leave.

"Maybe to steal a car, something fun like that." He laughed a little, like he thought I was kidding but wasn't sure. "See you at the police station," I said and ran outside.

When I got downtown, I found Frankie lying on the bench outside the railroad ticket office, his arms crossed, eyes closed. He jumped up when he heard me coming. He was dressed as usual for Frankie: jeans with holes in the knees and a "Corona" T-shirt—"La Cerveza Mas Fina." He collected beer T-shirts. "So," he said, "what's up?"

I tried to be offhand, so as not to scare him away. There *was* something to be scared about this time. We had always done misdemeanors in the past, if you overlooked the house-breaking. Any trouble we got into before, the courts treated us as kids just being kids. Now when we got caught, the judge could treat us as adults if he wanted to, which would make it a lot more difficult to squirm free. So I had to be careful not to frighten Frankie away. "I met this kid once," I said, "he was from Indiana, and he told me about a game they used to play in the stone quarries."

"What kind of game?"

"A car-flying contest."

Frankie rolled his eyes. "Car flying," he repeated, trying out the words. "How exactly do you do that?"

I waved him to follow me, and we walked along the train tracks toward Route 202, him balancing on one rail, me on the other, just as we had so many times before. "The game is this," I said as I concentrated on the rail, trying to stay on longer than he could. "We each steal a car and drive out to the Christiani Pits. Then we put a brick on the accelerators and see how far they'll fly off the cliff. The one whose car goes farthest, wins."

Frankie nodded at the beauty of the game. There was only one thing he wanted to know. "Wins what?"

"I don't know, just wins. It doesn't have to be something specific."

"It's more fun if it is," Frankie said as he turned to me and lost his balance. I reached out my hand, palm open, and Frankie remembered what he had to pay for falling off first.

He pulled out a quarter from his pocket and flipped it to me. "Okay," I said, "you name the prize."

He sat down on the rail to think, and in a minute he was smiling. "Anything the winner wants," he said. "He just names it, and the other has to do it, if it's within his power."

I sat down, too, and leaned my ear to the rail to see if I could hear the vibrations of a train coming. There was no sound at all, just the cold steel pressing against my cheek. "You thinking of something perverted, Frankie?"

"Whatever it is," he said again, as he leaned down to listen to his rail, "you have to do it, or me. I'm taking the same chance as you."

I nodded okay, and we shook on it, like blood brothers, as the 7:45 pm train to Trenton came into sight, far down the tracks in front of us.

•

The sun was still up, making stealing cars more dangerous than necessary, so we decided to waste time eating dinner at Salvi's. Frankie was treating, as usual, which gave him the right to order: One large pizza—half cheese, half everything. He ordered two beers, too, and the waiter, Crazy Paul, wrote this down. Sometimes he was so weirded out on pills that he didn't think about how old we were. But tonight he brought us back two root beers.

While we waited for the food, I made up the rules to the game: we had one hour to steal a car and get to the sand pits. If one of us didn't show up by then, the other automatically won. "And," Frankie repeated, "the loser has to do whatever the winner wants." He definitely was making me wonder what he had in mind, but since I wasn't planning on losing the bet, I didn't worry. The kid from Indiana had told me the secret to winning at car-flying: picking a lightweight foreign car, automatic transmission, with six cylinders. Avoid Buicks, Pontiacs and even Cadillacs, despite the natural desire to wreck them. None of them have wings, the kid said. They fall like a block of cement in water.

When the pizza came, Frankie dug in. He was obviously eager to hit the road. "I got one question," he said, ripping another slice off his half of cheese. "What if we don't find cars with the keys in them?"

"Then you have to hot wire it."

"How do you do that?"

"Look, I'm not giving lessons. We have a bet—you go your way and I'll go mine—and we meet in an hour. One more thing," I said, pulling a pair of rubber gloves out of my back pocket, ones Jenny used to wash dishes. "You better stop in Fleck's Hardware and get yourself a pair of these," I told him, "unless you want to leave your fingerprints all over."

Frankie paid the bill and we left Salvi's together. He turned left, toward Fleck's, and I went right. I hopped up on the hood of the nearest car—a newly polished BMW—and thought about how to make stealing easy. I didn't really know how to hot wire an engine, even though I'd made out like I did to Frankie. I figured that maybe only one person in a thousand was stupid enough to leave the keys in the ignition, which meant that I might have to check out a thousand cars before I'd get lucky. That was too much effort just to win a bet, so I decided to put some intelligence to the problem—"use my brain for more than a hat rack," as Grandpa always told me. He lived when people would leave their houses unlocked all day, not to mention their cars. They'd come back and everything would be sitting right where they left it, he said. Stealing must have been a lot easier in those days. Then it occurred to me that I was going at this the wrong way. Instead of looking for an unlocked car in places where everybody locked them, I needed to find a place where people might leave their keys inside on purpose—like outside a convenience store.

So I walked down Route 202, away from town, toward a Store 24 not too far out of New Hope. Cars whizzed by me a few inches from my body, and I could feel the rush of air in their wake. I reached Store 24 in about ten minutes. I sat on the curbside that ringed the parking lot, watching the cars pull in and the people running inside to buy things. Most of them didn't lock up, but they did take their keys, which I saw by looking in their windows. I figured that sooner or later some guy would drive in, flip his car into park, and leave the engine running in order to make a fast getaway—maybe a guy stocking up for a hot date. So I waited for ten more minutes, then fifteen, then gave up. There wasn't enough time in the game for me to sit outside a Store 24.

I walked out on Route 202 again and started thumbing. Right away a guy stopped in some Japanese car that looked like all of the other Japanese cars, and he asked me where I was going. "That way," I said, pointing ahead, and got in. After a minute he offered me some potato chips and some advice—don't ever get in a car with someone like him. I started to laugh when he said it, because this guy looked straight and harmless in his Dockers pants and Members Only jacket. "What were you thinking of doing to me?" I asked him just for fun.

"I don't know," he said in a kind of dead voice that made me a little nervous. He offered me another potato chip, but I passed this time. "And since I don't know," he said, in that same strange voice, "you can't possibly know, right?"

"Yeah," I said, "I guess I did make a mistake. Why don't you just let me out right here?"

He swerved off the road and we bounced along the soft shoulder, which always seemed like the wrong name to me for something so hard. I got out and the guy pulled away without looking back at me. It made me wonder whether the world was full of weirdo people like this, or if they just all happened to be traveling on the same road as me.

Anyway, at least this guy had gotten me about another mile down 202, far enough for me to see up ahead the sign for "Smiley's Used Cars Sales and Service." Dad had taken the Buick in there lots of times for work, and as I walked closer I remembered Smiley's advertisement: you could drop off your car after hours. All you had to do was leave the key in the wooden lock box outside of the garage doors. That sounded like easy pickings to me.

Smiley's was lit up like all used car lots—with lights strung around the edge. Old man Smiley used to keep a guard dog on the grounds, but he had to get rid of him after one of his back legs got run over. A three-legged dog wasn't much of a deterrent to intruders even if he was a German Shepherd. I looked around and made a little noise but didn't see any replacement dog. Outside the garages there was a lineup of cars that people had dropped off for next morning's repair. That meant the wooden box would be stuffed with keys. It also had a big lock on the front, the kind that you can't bust open even if you shoot a bullet through it. So instead of bothering with the lock, I decided to attack the box. I needed a crowbar, which I found inside the third trunk that I tried. I pried open the wooden box just enough to reach in. The first envelope I pulled out had "Saab, 1989, AE4-379." I tossed it back in and kept fishing. Next was a "Red Camaro, 1987, LP2-41," which was tempting, but I figured it was too heavy to fly very far. Then I pulled out the keys to a "Silver Toyota Camry, 1992," which I figured was probably pretty peppy. So with the license number in my hand, I found the Toyota toward the end of the line, hopped in and was gone.

I pulled out on Route 202 without smashing anyone and was cruising along at 40 mph as if I did this all the time. I sat up straight and rested my elbow out on the window, trying not to look like a kid without a license who had just stolen a car. I had only driven once before in my life— around a parking lot in New Hampshire—but how hard could it be if almost everybody did it? Going straight was easy, and I could even take one hand off the wheel to put on the radio. But then I had to make a right turn and for some reason I swerved left getting ready for it. The driver next to me hit her horn and shook her fist at me. A few more scary turns like that and I made it to Maplewood, the road to Christiani's.

I pulled into the driveway that led to the cliff, and there was no sign of Frankie. I figured the hour was about up, so he'd have to do whatever I told him. I didn't have anything in mind yet, but I knew I could think up something great— maybe jumping off the bridge with me. I strolled around the pits for awhile, looking for the best approach, the firmest ground, to the 100-foot drop. Then I lay down next to the Toyota, listening to some strange Cajun music on the radio. The sky was big, and I counted hundreds of stars. But I knew there were billions out there, and knowing that made me feel awfully small. I was thinking about how meaningless I was in the universe when I heard a car come spinning off Maplewood into the pits. I scrambled to my feet and ducked behind the Toyota. The car skidded to a stop in the sand, its headlights fixed on me. I figured it had to be Frankie, but when I stepped out of the beams, I saw the strip of lights on top—it was a police cruiser. The driver's door opened, and I thought about running, but I didn't want give some trigger-happy cop like Decker a reason to shoot.

"Hands up!" a weird voice ordered me.

"Frankie?"

"Sure, who'd you think?" he said coming around the car, swinging the keys in his hand.

This didn't figure. "You stole a cop car?"

"Yeah, I guess I did," he said. He threw his hand over my shoulder. "It seemed like a good idea at the time."

I opened the passenger side and got in. I'd been in cop cars lots of times before but never in the front seat. Frankie got in, too, and started fumbling with the dials. The radio crackled with so much static that we could make out only a few words—nothing about us.

"I think we crossed the line with this one, Frankie. Cops don't like it when you take one of their toys away."

"Fuck the cops," he said. "Fuck everyone."

This was a serious new attitude of Frankie's, and even though I couldn't argue with his opinion, I was worried about what I was getting him into. For me, it didn't much matter if I got caught for stealing a cop car, because if I didn't get arrested today, it would just be tomorrow or next week. It didn't take a psychic to see where I was headed. But Frankie—he had a family with money, and he was supposed to graduate from high school next year and go to Princeton. I didn't know much about college, but I didn't think grand theft auto would look too good on his application.

"Let's see how this thing flies," Frankie said and gunned the engine.

I took his hand off the parking release lever. "Wait a second. Maybe this is a bad idea. We're not twelve years old anymore. They could really screw us for this."

Frankie looked at me wide-eyed. "You scared? Jake Paine is scared of getting caught?"

"I'm not scared for me, Frankie. But this could end up wrecking things for you."

He laughed at me. "That's really funny, you know. My life *could* be ruined? Didn't you hear me in the hospital? I'm queer, Jake. My father won't even talk to me."

"You're exaggerating like you always do. Maybe he's a little shocked, but he'll get over it."

"I won't get over it," Frankie said. "He looked at me like I was a serial killer or something—I'm not going to forget that." He gunned the engine. "Now let's fly these fuckers and see who wins."

I got out of the car and ran around to Frankie's side to make sure he did, too. I didn't want him sailing into the pits just to get even with his father. We found some bricks near the quarry shack and brought them back to the cars. I put the Toyota in position, about fifty feet from the cliff. I started the car forward slowly, put the brick on the accelerator and jumped out into the sand. The Toyota picked up speed and then swerved left a little before sailing over the cliff. I ran up to the edge next to Frankie just in time to see it land nose first in the sand. He jumped when it hit and whistled. "That was great," he said. "It was hanging in the air, then it just dropped like it was shot out of the sky."

We watched the Toyota for a few moments, seeing if it would burst into flames, but it just lay there in a cloud of stone dust. I tapped Frankie's shoulder and pointed at the cruiser. "Your turn."

He hopped up and ran to his car. He started the engine, turned the static on the radio up full blast, then eased the brick onto the accelerator and jumped free. The car built up speed and took a straight line over the cliff. It soared out over the pit, then its front end dipped and down it went. It slammed into the ground behind the Toyota, but then rolled sideways twice and stopped a few feet further out. Frankie looked at me and smiled his devilish look. In the distance, a siren sounded faintly through the summer night, coming nearer.

•

It took an hour for us to make our way to Frankie's house, a mile away. We couldn't hitch a ride for fear of being spotted by the cops. Decker and his pals wouldn't be in too great a mood after finding one of their squad cars busted up in a gravel pit. Every time headlights appeared on the road ahead or behind us, we ditched into the bushes.

When we reached the Collins' long driveway, Frankie slowed his steps. His house looked deserted, with just one light on downstairs and one upstairs, both on timers. He bent down and picked up a few stones. He threw one toward his house, and it made a nice solid crack as it struck the wooden porch. He wound up like a pitcher and threw another. This one sailed wide to the right, over the garage. "Fuck," Frankie said and took aim a third time. He threw the stone higher and harder this time, and it crashed through the upstairs window into his parents' bedroom. "Match that," he said as he handed me a stone the size of a golf ball.

I dropped it to the driveway and found myself a larger one, with a nice sharp edge. I threw it as hard as I could, and it smacked into the house, missing the window. I didn't usually miss. In fact, Frankie almost never did something like this better than me. I figured I lacked his motivation.

He started to aim another stone. "My old man will go ballistic over this," he said. "He'll say some rotten kid must have done it—and he'll be right." Then he dropped the stone and walked toward his front door.

"You're not rotten, Frankie," I said as I followed him.

"What do you call a kid who throws rocks at his own house?"

"Confused."

"I'm not confused. I hate this house and the people in it."

I didn't believe that. "If you really hated it all so much, you'd be throwing rocks somewhere else. You wouldn't be wasting your time here."

"So you're a shrink now?"

I shrugged. "You asked me what I thought, so I told you."

He picked up a rock and threw it straight up in the air over our heads. This was a game of chicken we played—see who would look up first. Frankie always lost this game. This time neither of us looked up, and the rock bounced a few feet away from us. "Your turn," he said, handing me a larger rock, one that would definitely dent your skull. I leaned back and hurled it in the air, then straightened up and faced him, as we always did, staring each other down, waiting for the rock to smash one of us in the head. He didn't look like the same Frankie to me now. There was no fear in his eyes, no tension in his face. He looked as if he wanted the rock to hit him.

It fell next to us, and he kicked it out of the way. "You could stay over tonight," he said, "like old times."

"I have to get home," I said, in case he was thinking of claiming his prize tonight, and I was it. "Jenny will kill me if I stay out all night again."

"You're going to walk six miles home with the cops all over town looking for their squad car?"

"They don't know I had anything to do with it."

"They'll still pick you up, if they see you. Decker always picks you up."

"That's all right, he can't prove anything."

Frankie stooped to get another stone, and he threw it straight and long through another of his parents' windows. The sharp crack of breaking glass was a beautiful sound. "You scared of staying over?" he said.

"No."

"I'd never try anything with you, if that's what you think—I just wouldn't."

"I'm not your type?" I said, pretending to be offended.

"No, you *are* my type, but I wouldn't do anything, you know, because we're friends." I nodded that I believed him, but that didn't seem to be enough for him. He turned away and kept talking. "You're the only one I've told, you know, so if you're scared of being alone with me, then . . . I don't know."

"I've been alone with you all night, remember? I called you up. I didn't have to."

"Yeah," he said, "thanks."

That made me feel bad all of a sudden, that Frankie needed to thank me for being his friend.

Twenty

DAD WAS READING BOOKS NOW BY THE HANDFUL. HE BROUGHT UP cardboard boxes from the cellar stuffed with hundreds of paperbacks he had picked up at yard sales and second-hand bookstores. When he came across a special book, he'd find some comfortable spot in the house, lay back and devour it. Jenny tried to get him on the road selling again, but he'd hang tight wherever he was, saying that nobody bought books in the summer except trashy beach novels, which he didn't sell. The only time Dad moved was when he read an interesting part and needed to tell somebody about it. Then he'd call out for me or Jenny, and when we didn't come, he'd track us down.

After dinner, he found us both in the kitchen cleaning up the dishes. Jenny had ordered me to dry while she washed, so I stood next to her, taking the dripping glasses and dishes as soon as she rinsed them. She kept muttering how bad books can be when used in the wrong way, as Dad did, as a substitute for real life. Just then he came rushing into the kitchen carrying a book. "I almost forgot this," he said, holding up *Akenfield: A Portrait of an English Village.* "It might be my favorite book." Dad often declared whatever he happened to be reading as his favorite book, so neither Jenny or I paid any attention. She kept rinsing and handing me dishes as fast as I could dry them. "I mean it," he said, "my all-time favorite."

"That's something, Dad," I said.

"It's just voices of people living in a small village," he said. "But they're more powerful than any characters a writer could create, and more truthful, too. These people don't lie." Jenny was washing and rinsing so fast that the glasses were piling up on the counter. I shoved some away from the edge, and when I turned back, she was holding a fistful of dripping knives and forks for me to take from her. "When people died in the early part of this century," Dad said as he sat down at the kitchen table behind us, "their relatives would keep possession of the body for awhile."

"That's not so strange," Jenny said, which surprised me because I didn't think she was listening. "Maybe they wanted to hold onto the person as long as they could."

"Must have really stunk up the house," I said.

"The reason they did this," Dad said, "was to make sure the person was really dead. That was a problem back then in England, people being buried alive."

"Shouldn't be hard to tell if someone's dead," I said. "If they aren't breathing, it's kind of a clue, isn't it?"

"Sometimes people go into a state of suspended animation," Dad said. "Their breathing becomes barely noticeable." He reached between us to the cabinet over the counter and stretched to get a hold of the bag of chocolate bits that Jenny hid there from him. He tilted his head back and poured a stream of them into his mouth. "And remember," he said, sitting back down, "there weren't doctors in these villages, so it was just a regular person, like a minister, deciding that somebody was dead." Jenny let the dirty water drain out and ran a fresh sink of soapy water to do the pots. I put away the plates and glasses in the cupboard over the counter. Dad kept skimming through his new favorite book. "People were so scared of being buried alive," he said, "that they put it in their wills to have a vein cut in their arm and let them bleed for a day before being put in the ground."

That seemed really strange to me. "If they were so worried about being buried alive," I said, "why didn't they put it in their will for their relatives to do everything to try to wake them up, instead of definitely killing them?"

"Death isn't logical," Dad said. "Death . . . "

Jenny whirled around, a pot of soapy water in her hands, and dumped it into Dad's lap. He jumped out of his chair faster than I'd ever seen him move. Jenny headed out the backdoor as we looked at each other wondering what had gotten into her.

•

Later that evening, after reading *Mrs. Piggle Wiggle* to Kris in her bed, Dad came downstairs so quietly I didn't hear him. He was barefoot, carrying his beat-up Nikes. Jenny came in the front door holding Mars out in front of her. When she saw Dad lacing up his sneakers, she dropped the cat to the floor. "Where are you going?" she demanded.

He didn't want to say. All he would ever say was, "Out for a walk." He didn't want to admit that his nerves were shaking inside him and he needed to get out of the house to somewhere cool and dark.

"You're going to the canal, aren't you?"

"Maybe," he said.

She hated when he took off like some creature slithering out of the light. She hated worrying that he might lose himself in the darkness. She was scared for him, and I think for herself, too.

"I want you to stay home," she said. "Just sit on the porch for awhile."

He nodded, which meant that he understood what she wanted even if he wasn't going to give it to her. He stood up to face her but then lowered his head. "I need some air," he said. "I'm feeling smothered, like breathing through a pillow."

"The air *is* heavy tonight," Jenny told him. "That's all it is."

"I need a walk," he said.

"I don't want you wandering all over Creation at this hour," she said, her voice rising. "You could get hit on the road, or slip into the canal, or . . . " There was no use saying any more. Unless she tied Dad down, he was going out for a walk. She said, "Go ahead then" and turned away from him.

Dad looked puzzled at her permission to go, but he left quickly. At the door, he gave me a little wave and smile.

•

Jenny spent the next hour trying to sew up some of Kris' shorts. She looked up at me from time to time, muttered and cursed at the sewing or me, I couldn't tell which. I knew she was hoping I would do something wrong so she could yell at me. I decided it was better to get out of her way, so I went to the kitchen to make a snack to take upstairs. She followed me after a minute, as I was pressing together a peanut butter and jelly sandwich. She wiped up the crumbs on the counter with a sponge and said, "Why did you have to come back?"

Jenny was out for blood, I could tell. "It's my house, too," I shot back at her, "since before you lived here. Why shouldn't I come home?"

She threw the sponge in the sink. "Don't you care what happens to him? He can't get himself out to work at all. He had to go on lithium again. Now he's roaming around town."

"That's not my fault—he's been that way since Mom died."

"But he was getting better. You got him going again."

"He likes having me back," I said. "He talks to me."

"Can't you see, Jake, all he talks about is death?" She took a breath and stared at me oddly. She was quiet for a minute, and I couldn't imagine what she was thinking. "Don't you understand?" she said. "You remind him of her. He looks at you and sees her."

That shocked me. Could Jenny be right for once? Was I triggering all of Dad's worst behaviors because I reminded him of Mom? That couldn't be true. "It's you," I said, "you're the one who doesn't want me here." Jenny reached out to touch my arm. She used to do that a lot when she wanted to pretend she was my mother. "You never wanted me," I said as I stepped away from her. I took a bite out of my sandwich.

"You're wrong. I always wanted a son."

"A real one maybe."

"You're real," she said.

"But I didn't grow up like you wanted. That's why you never married him—you didn't want me for a son."

"Jake," she said, shaking her head. She looked out of the back window where geese were honking, but she only looked there for a second, nowhere near as long as Dad would. As soon as he heard them he'd go to the window and call me to see, too. He loved seeing geese flying low overhead. "You were out of control," she said. "I couldn't understand you or handle you."

213

"I didn't hurt anything," I said, and she looked at me like I must know I was wrong about that. "I didn't hurt things that much," I corrected myself.

"There was something every other week, Jake, at school or with the police. You can't just forget that."

She was exaggerating again. I was actually only picked up by the cops six times. "It wasn't that often," I said.

"Let's just say it was a lot more than most boys."

"Most kids don't grow up in this house, do they?"

"So you're blaming us for how you turned out."

"How did I turn out?"

She started to say something but then didn't. Still, I knew what she thought of me. "You think I'm crazy, right . . . Mother?"

She stepped back from me. It was the first time I had ever called her that. I took an apple from the bowl on the refrigerator and quartered it. She watched every cut I made. I jabbed the knife into a slice and stuck it in my mouth.

"You act crazy," she said, as I pulled the apple off the blade with my lips.

"That's different," I said.

"It seems the same to other people."

I looked out of the kitchen window, and then I found myself looking at the window. It was a smokey old pane of glass, foggy in places and streaked with dirt. It shattered easily as my fist punched through it.

Jenny jumped out of the way of the flying window. "Does this make me crazy?" I yelled at her, shaking my bleeding hand. Drops of blood flew off into her face.

She grabbed a dishtowel from the hook over the sink and ran water on it. Then she wrapped my hand in the cold wet towel. "Do you remember what we used to talk about after the fire at Bantry's?" she said. Sure I remembered. She wanted me to change how I did everything. She wanted me to be someone else, a kid who never got into trouble. "I told you that you had to think first. You can't just do everything that flies through your head."

"There's no time to think," I said, pulling my fist from her hands and letting the towel fall to the kitchen floor. "I told you—things just happen." She bent down to wipe the blood from the floor. But the more she wiped, the more blood dripped from my hand to replace it. When she straightened up, I looked her straight in the eyes like she always made me do. "This doesn't mean I'm crazy," I said. "It means something, doesn't it?"

I left by the back door, with Jenny on her knees picking up the glass. My right hand was throbbing, and blood was seeping through the towel. I headed toward town. I didn't know where I was going exactly, but I was walking fast to get there. At Joy Street, just past the condos, I turned right for the river. At Odette's, I lay out on the dock and dunked my hand in the cool flowing water.

It was a pretty stupid thing to do—punching out a window. I knew that. And I figured that since I knew that, I couldn't really be crazy, at least not like the kids who splatter their friends in the school cafeteria. The dock was rising and falling with the flow of the river, and it felt like the waterbed I tried one time at a house I broke into. The longer I lay on the dock thinking about things, the more I could see Jenny's point about me causing problems. Dad was getting crazier, she was getting angrier, Frankie was getting queerer and I was getting beat up. It seemed to me I needed to make a decision, and I knew just where to go.

•

"Sam," I called as I opened the back door to his cabin, "you here?" I knew he would be. Sam was always there.

"Part of me is," his voice floated out from the darkness, "but not the best part."

I felt my way in and found a chair. Sam lit a match, and in the small glow of the fire, I could see him sitting on the floor against the far wall. He flicked the match into the air, and it went out before it hit the slate. He lit another.

"I don't know what I'm doing anymore, Sam."

"Nobody does," he said. "Just some people pretend to better than others."

That didn't sound right to me. Lots of people seemed to know exactly who they were and what they believed in and how to act. He flicked another match into the air, and it sparkled in an arc, then snuffed out.

"I don't think it's just a matter of faking it, Sam. Sometimes I feel like I'm slipping out of control."

"Out of their control? That's not so bad."

"Out of my control."

"That can be bad," he said. "But I don't think I'm the one to give you a lecture on self-control tonight." He lifted a bottle to his lips, swigging the liquor down into his bones.

"You have to, Sam. Nobody else will."

He raised himself off the slate a little. "It's a curse to be needed, especially when you're drunk. People keep coming to me expecting help, and I'm supposed to give it to them."

"You're good at it, Sam. You always know what to say."

"Some people think I say too much, like Jenny."

"What's she have to do with it?"

"She called last week. Told me to stay away from you."

"She can't make you do that."

"No, but maybe I agree with her. I'm not the best of influences. If she had only asked me, then who knows? But she didn't ask. She told me—stay away. I don't take orders well."

"Me either, Sam."

He held out the bottle, but I waved it away. "The boys on the reservation never turn away a free drink," he said.

"I guess Jenny is right—you are a bad influence."

"Everybody you meet is an influence one way or another, and everything you see, everything you do. I'm just one speck in a sea of influences. I'm surprised you haven't drowned by now." He took another swig from his bottle.

"I guess I'm a good swimmer, Sam." He nodded and tried to stand up, but his legs wouldn't stay under him. "How long have you been drinking for?"

He looked at his wrist, but there wasn't a watch there. "What time is it?"

"About nine."

"So I've been drinking for seven hours. That's a long time, but not a record. My record is seven days." He put the bottle to his lips again, but nothing came out. "I suppose this means I have to stop. State stores don't deliver, do they?"

"I don't think so."

"Then it's good luck you came by tonight. You can go get me some." He checked through the pockets of his shirt and pants and came up with a few dollars.

"I'm sixteen, Sam. They won't sell me liquor. I'd have to steal it."

He stuffed the money back in his pocket. "Then I guess I'll have to sober up," he said, straightening himself against the wall. "I can do that, if I have to. I've done it before."

"Sure you can."

"The thing is," he said, "sometimes I feel more sober when I'm stoned drunk. You know what I mean?"

"Yeah, sometimes things make more sense that way."

"That's it—things make more sense." He smiled at me a little, then his eyes closed slowly, like a cat's eyes, as he slid back down to the floor. I watched Sam for a few minutes. He didn't look like he was going to wake up anytime soon and give me advice, so I left him dreaming in his whiskey and let myself out the back door.

•

I walked around New Hope awhile, trying to figure what to do. People were staring at the bloody towel wrapped around my hand, so I threw it into the falls by The Playhouse. Then people started staring at my bloody fist, which I had to admit, looked pretty gruesome. So I stuffed it in my shorts pocket, which made it look like I was playing with myself.

There wasn't much action in town. Sunday nights were always quiet, since the shops closed early. So I decided to go home and see if Dad had come home okay. When I opened the front door, Jenny was standing in the hallway holding the phone out toward me. "It's Frankie," she said, with a hardness to her voice. Usually she liked when he called, because he was a respectable boy from a respectable family, as she put it. "He's been calling every five minutes for the last hour."

I took the phone from her, and she waited next to me to hear what was so important. I held the phone down to my side until she got the hint and disappeared.

"What's up?"

"Jake," he said and took a big breath, "I got busted."

That was a first. Frankie had never done anything worth getting arrested for without me along. "For what?"

He took a minute to answer. "Decker caught me behind Jack's, in the parking lot."

"Caught you doing what?"

"I was with this guy. Decker says we were . . . he says I was with this guy."

"Yeah, doing what?"

"You know."

"No I don't. How would I know?"

"Don't make me say it."

"You mean you can do it but you can't say you fuck around with guys all of the time?"

"I don't fuck around, and not all the time."

"So what, just Saturday night? You only get horny on Saturday night?"

"Jake," he said, "don't do this to me. I really wasn't doing anything with this guy. We were just talking. Decker has it in for me, like he does for you. He's trying to nail me this time. I have to get out of this somehow."

"So why don't you go running to one of your buddies to take care of you?"

"That's what I thought I was doing."

He was right—I was his buddy, so why was I acting like this? Because why was he hanging out at Jack's with the leather crowd? I'd seen enough on the road to know you didn't want to get near that scene. "You told your parents yet?"

"Mom had to come pick me up, so she knows, but Dad's giving a big talk tomorrow at the AMA convention in Houston. She won't tell him until after it's over."

"How's she taking it?"

"Like I told her I had cancer. She thinks I'm going to die from AIDs." Frankie paused for a moment. "Maybe I will."

•

218

Dad wasn't home by midnight. Jenny grabbed her car keys to go looking for him along the canal, but the phone rang as she headed for the door. She looked at the phone and at me. We both knew there were only two choices—either it was another obscene phone call or else an emergency call about Dad, the kind she'd been dreading for years. She picked up the receiver. "Hello?" she said. After awhile she nodded and then hung up. She turned to me and scratched the back of her head, looking puzzled. "He's down at the police station . . . in a cell. It seems he broke into a store in town."

"The pet store?"

Jenny locked on me with her eyes. "You knew about this?"

"No, I mean, I know Dad hates pet stores, and one just opened up, didn't it? So I figured . . . "

"It seems he broke in the back and took out all of the animals. He won't say what he did with them."

"Pretty radical," I said, which was the wrong thing to say.

Jenny came at me like she was going to shove me through the front window. "This is serious!" she yelled in my face.

It didn't sound that bad to me. "They're just trying to scare him," I said. "They won't even keep him in jail all night."

She sighed like it was useless talking to me. "Don't you understand, Jake—people in their right mind don't go breaking into stores. Your father is losing his mind."

I thought he'd already lost it, but I didn't say that. For Jenny, it seemed, things had somehow changed tonight.

•

The police released Dad in Jenny's custody, but he had to appear the next day for a hearing. We got to the tiny courthouse in town at 10 A.M. sharp on Monday. Jenny took us in a side door so people wouldn't see us walk in. We all had a lot of experience with this sort of thing. The lawyer appointed to defend Dad met us at the top of the marble staircase and steered us into a conference room. He pulled a folder from his briefcase and looked at it while Dad sat there reading *Swann's Way* for about the tenth time. Jenny tapped her fingers on the table. I wandered about the room, looking at the pictures of old judges in black robes, wondering why they never smiled. It seemed to me it would be fun spending your whole life deciding who was innocent and who was guilty. Finally the lawyer said that the prosecution had offered a good deal—probation—as long as Dad brought the animals back, paid for the window he broke, and agreed to stay away from the pet store forever.

He looked up from his book. "I'd rather not do that."

The lawyer didn't understand. "What do you mean 'you'd rather not'? Either you accept these conditions or you don't."

Dad shook his head. "I don't wish to accept them."

"Then you're rejecting the offer from the pet store?"

"If you say so."

"It's not if I say so, it's what you say."

"I could never put animals back in their cages. Besides, the fish are swimming in Loker Pond, the rabbits are running around Washington's Crossing . . . "

"They understand some animals won't be found. You can compensate the store for them, just as if you had bought them."

"I don't think I could do that," Dad said.

"You mean you don't have the money?"

"I don't have the inclination."

The lawyer stood up. "Mr. Paine, you're willing to go to trial and risk jail for up to a year?"

Dad wouldn't want to risk that. He hated being caged as much as any animal. He looked up from his book again, keeping his finger at his place. "I don't want to go to jail either."

The lawyer closed the folder and slipped it into his briefcase. "Perhaps you want a new attorney, someone who understands your position better."

"No," Dad said quickly, "you'll do fine."

•

The *Gazette* did a front-page story on "The Pet Store Terrorism," with photos of the busted window, the empty cages, and the owner, Mr. Schuyler from Philadelphia, looking as if someone had just stolen his kids. Dad's picture appeared over the caption: Trial Begins Friday.

The trial began and ended Friday. Dad waived his right to a jury, saying he was sure the judge was fair, for which the judge thanked him. The lawyer entered a "Not Guilty" plea, but Dad said he wouldn't deny what he had obviously done. Besides, they had caught him at the pond with fish in his hand. Jenny suggested half-jokingly that he could probably get off by pleading insanity. Everyone in town would grant him that.

The prosecutor presented the evidence in the morning, and by mid-afternoon, Judge Barton returned a verdict of guilty. Sentencing was delayed for a week, until Dad could be evaluated by a psychiatrist. Apparently the judge had heard a lot about my father's antics over the years.

I told Dad he better make the shrink think he was crazy or else they might toss him in jail. He nodded that he understood. "You know me, Jake," he said. "I can't be locked up, even for a day."

Twenty-One

THE FOLLOWING THURSDAY, THERE WAS NO SOUND IN THE HOUSE AS I got up around noon, pulled on shorts and went downstairs. That was odd, since Dad wasn't supposed to go outside until tomorrow, when he was due back in court for sentencing. The psychiatrist had found him only a little strange—"crazy around the edges" is how Jenny described it. The judge would have no reason to sentence him to psychiatric treatment rather than a jail cell. Dad would have to ask for mercy.

When I went to the kitchen to find something to eat, I couldn't believe my eyes—spread out on the table were a dozen little white boxes of Chinese food, all open. The first one had white rice in it, with a single spoonful carved out of the top. There was vegetable lo mein, fried rice, shrimp with pea pods—all with about a forkful taken out of it. But the dumpling box was empty, a sure sign that this was Dad's doing.

It didn't make sense, though. There was food enough for five people and no one around to eat it. I grabbed a fork from the sink and poked in the boxes. The food was still warm, which meant Dad wasn't far away. I picked up the shrimp with pea pods and walked out of the kitchen. When I rounded the staircase in the front hall, there was Dad in the living room rocking fast. The rocker was squeaking like it was going to split. Mars was asleep on his lap, curled up like a ball of orange and black fur. She could sleep through anything.

"What's up, Dad?"

"More than you know," he said.

Most people would just say "Not much" or "Same as usual," but Dad always came up with a different answer. "Shouldn't you be on the phone selling books today, like your boss suggested? There's probably some poor sucker out there who doesn't know Aesop was a hunchback." I was trying to have fun with him, but Dad didn't seem interested today.

222

"Jake," he said, "I'm not very good at living in this world. Things don't make sense to me."

"Things don't make sense at all, Dad. It's not you. The whole world is fucked up."

"Maybe, but either way, things don't make sense, right? It's not very comfortable living in a world like that."

It didn't take a genius to see where Dad was heading, and it didn't surprise me. In some ways I felt that all of my growing up had been leading me to this scene, the moment when Dad would finally get around to killing himself. He looked calmer than I had ever seen him. It scared me that he didn't have that scared look to him. "You see what I got, Jake?" He picked up a red towel from the floor and unwrapped it.

"Your gun."

His arm was shaking, and the gun was shaking, the short barrel pointing straight up, toward the ceiling.

"Why don't you put that down, Dad, and we'll go to town to see Sam. You like him."

"That's a very nice offer," he said, "but you don't need your old man around anymore. I'm wrong for you, just as I am for Jenny and Kris. You'll all be better off without me."

That made me angry at him all of a sudden. "You think Kris would be better off with a father who puts a bullet through his head?" I said, trying to shock him into realizing what he was going to do. He nodded yes. "Well, you're wrong," I said. "Kris wouldn't be better off, and I wouldn't either."

He stroked Mars with his free hand, and the old cat twisted her face upwards, sinking her head between his legs, deep in sleep. "You got over your mother dying," he said. "You'll handle this, too."

I set the box of Chinese food on the hall table to free my hands. I figured that if I could distract Dad for a second, I could knock the gun from his hand. He picked up a thin paperback that was wedged along his leg. *Man's Search for Meaning*, the title said, and I knew right off it was something he shouldn't be reading. Looking for meaning in books was trouble for Dad. "The man who wrote this was a great psychiatrist," he said. "People paid him to sort out their lives—these were miserable people who didn't know what to do next. They went to him, and do you know the first thing he asked?" I shook my head and wondered how it would be seeing my father raise the gun and kill himself. Would it be loud and bloody like in the movies, or quick and quiet and clean? "The first thing the psychiatrist asked them," Dad said, "was, 'Why don't you commit suicide?'" I had heard him use that word before, but always he seemed scared of saying it, let alone doing it. This time, he just seemed tired. "I asked myself that question today," Dad said, "and I couldn't think of a reason." He turned the gun towards himself. 'He who has a *why* to live'," Dad said, "'can bear with almost any *how*.' That's from Nietzsche. I told you about him, didn't I? You should read him, maybe when you get older."

"What about us, Dad, your family? Isn't that something to live for?"

"They're going to send me to jail, Jake. I can't go, you know that, just like you couldn't let them send you to Norristown. The only difference is, I'm too old to run away."

Decker—he was the cause of this. He'd been waiting for Dad to get into trouble. He couldn't catch me, so he had gone after easier targets—Frankie and Dad. Now he had both of them nailed. Dad laid his book on the floor and I started toward him, but his right arm quickly aimed the gun at his head. "Don't try to stop me, Jake," he said. "It's taken me a long time to get ready to die. Today I am. If you stop me now, I'll just have to get ready some other day."

"You're afraid to die," I said. "You're going to feel yourself dying, remember? You hate even the thought of that."

"I'll go quickly," he said, "and maybe on the other side of this trigger I won't feel so bad all of the time. Maybe I'll even meet your mother again. Did you know there's no marriage in heaven? She told me that when she was dying in the car. We could be best friends there," she said, "but not married." A dreamy look came over him. "I'd just like to hold her hand one more time," he said as he rubbed Mars, "and this time I'd never let her go."

"Dad, please don't do this."

"It's really, okay, Jake. I want to." He pointed the gun barrel at the faded wallpaper with the pattern of purple corsage boxes that Grandma Paine had picked out. "Now I know what Oscar Wilde meant—'Either the wallpaper goes, or I do.'" Dad cocked the trigger. "Give your old man a hug, will you?"

My legs wouldn't move. My father was asking me to hug him and say goodbye so he could shoot himself.

"Come here, Jake."

My eyes suddenly flooded with tears. I couldn't even see him sitting in front of me. "I can't, Dad."

He came to me and put his arms around me. I couldn't ever remember feeling him like this. His voice filled my head. "I'm sorry I have to do this to you. Tell Jenny I'm sorry, too. I left her a note explaining everything. I don't think she'll be surprised. Maybe she'll be relieved. I haven't been a very good husband to her." He patted me on the back. "I feel good about this, I really do." He kissed me on the neck and pulled away. His eyes were wet and red. I could have knocked the gun out of his hand right then, but I knew we would just have to go through this some other time, and this wasn't a day I wanted to repeat.

"Dad?"

"No more words, Jake, go now."

I turned and left the room. I didn't look back. And when I closed the door, the sharp blast of the gun exploded through the house. And then a second one.

•

I ran.

Outside the crows were cawing wildly. I held my hands over my ears, but the sound of the gunshots was already inside my head. I ran through the backyard and over the edge of the hill, hurling myself down the muddy bank. At the bottom, I got to my feet and headed for the river. The water was high, and the rapids were crashing over each other. I walked on the rocks until I was far enough out to dive in.

The cool water shocked my brain. I quickly reached the bottom and dug my hands into the roots there, holding myself under with all of the strength in my arms. I couldn't see through the turbulence. I couldn't hear anything but the swirling water around my head. I couldn't feel anything but the water, and that's where I wanted to die.

But my hands couldn't hold me under. My fingers loosened from the roots, and I floated to the top just as my mouth burst open for air. It was so shallow that I could stand up and walk to shore just a few yards away. I sat on a rock there, looking out over the gray Delaware, remembering how Dad used to sit on the bank and watch me when I was little so I wouldn't go out too far. I hated how everything about Dad would be memories like that, that he only existed now in the past tense.

I walked slowly up the bank and back toward our house. You couldn't tell from the backyard that anything important had happened inside. There should have been ambulances and police and neighbors running around. There should have been screaming and crying. There was nothing. We had always been alone on this land overlooking the river. Nobody was within gunshot range.

The screen door to the kitchen was wide open. I walked in and picked up an apple sitting on the counter. I took one bite, but it was too tart for me—a Mac, the kind Jenny liked—and I spit the piece into the sink. It occurred to me that maybe I had imagined it all, that my mind had simply foreseen what would happen someday but hadn't happened yet. I walked down the hallway saying to myself "Please don't let him be there, please don't let him be there." But from the steps I could see his legs stretched out on the rug. At his feet there was something else bloody—Mars! She was shot through the side, lying stretched out as if it was a hot summer's night, too hot to move. "Dad," I said outloud, "how could you do that to your cat, too?"

He didn't answer. Blood was spreading across the rug, turning it dull red. Near Mars was the gun, where it had fallen from his hand. I backed into the room so that I wouldn't have to see his face and picked it up. The gun felt warm and dangerous.

Twenty-Two

I PUSHED OUT THE SCREEN DOOR TO THE PORCH AND RAN OUTSIDE, with the gun swinging in my hand along my leg. I raised it at arm's length and aimed at a sparrow sitting on the high wire strung from the house to the street. I could have popped it easily, added one more death to the day, but the bird took off before I pulled the trigger.

I stopped in the driveway. My clothes were soaked and I was holding a gun—where could I go looking like that? I went back inside, closed my eyes and passed by the living room. I took the stairs by twos to my room. I set the gun on my desk and stripped off my wet shirt and shorts. I found dry clothes under my bed and pulled them on. I couldn't take my eyes off the gun. It seemed magical to me, just like when I was seven and found it in Dad's closet. Each night while they were doing the dishes I'd sneak in their room, unwrap the towel, take out the gun. It was heavy in my hands. I aimed it out the back window at the fat robins. I flicked it around my finger like a cowboy. I spun it on the table like I was playing a game of Russian roulette. One night Dad came upstairs early and I didn't have time to put the gun back. So I slept with it under my pillow, pressing my face down to feel the hard barrel. It was like sleeping on top of a bomb.

I stuffed the gun now under my shirt and ran downstairs past the living room, past Dad and Mars lying in their own blood, ran outside. The screen door banged behind me and I wondered, why did I always think about that? Why did I always hear Jenny's voice saying "Don't let the door bang after you," and then the door banged?

I took the river path into town, cut through the meadow and then out onto Main Street. I was at The Logan in five minutes. I walked in the back door past the kitchen and nobody saw me. I ran up the stairs and down the fourth-floor hall to Larkin's room, No. 402.

She answered on the first knock. "Who is it?"

"Me," I answered softly.

"Who's there?" she said again.

"Jake," I said a little louder, and this time she opened the door a crack. I could hear the elevator settling onto the floor, getting ready to open, so I pushed myself inside quickly. She was dressed in a black slip, with a towel pulled over her shoulders. Her hair was wet.

"Jake," she said to me, "what's the matter? You're shaking."

I looked out her window onto Main Street, but nothing was happening. It seemed to me something should be happening. When I turned around, she had disappeared into the bathroom. She came out a moment later wearing a yellow T-shirt and tight black shorts. "What's going on?" she asked me.

"My father . . . " I said, but the rest of the words wouldn't come out. He was dead, gone from the world forever, disappeared. He'd blown his brains out—that's how everyone would say it. He didn't shoot himself because that's what he thought was best for him and his family—he blew his brains out because he was crazy! A really mental person does it like that, just about in front of his son, too. You couldn't stop a moving finger as it pulls the trigger. It clicks, the gun fires, the bullet rips through your head, you're dead. Your ears don't even have time to hear the blast.

"What about your father?" Larkin said.

"He's dead." My eyes squeezed shut when I said the words, and the tears came pouring out. For some reason, telling her Dad was dead made it more real to me.

"Oh God," she gasped and put her arm around my shoulders. "What happened?"

"He shot himself . . . in the head . . . at home. He was talking to me about not wanting to go to jail. Then he pulled out his gun and . . . ." I said the words fast, the way I always told people how Mom died. I had a lot of practice describing death.

Larkin squeezed my head, pressing my face against her chest. I could feel her heart beating faster and faster. I held onto her tighter and tighter. She was very warm and moist. She smelled like she had just taken a shower.

She pulled away from me and grabbed her towel from the dresser. She began drying her hair, and that surprised me—that she would do something now that she would have done before I told her that my father had shot himself. Hadn't everything changed? "Jake," she said, "are you sure he's dead? I mean, there's no chance he could still be alive?" Her hair was wild about her face.

I shook my head—there was no mistake about it. Dad made sure he was going to die, and die fast. She sat down next to me, and as I pressed my head to her chest again, I imagined holding her like that some day when she felt more for me than sadness. I turned my head a little, and my lips brushed her breast. I could have bitten her, or licked her, or sucked her—

"Jake!" she said and shook me away from her. I looked into her eyes—she was suddenly scared of me.

"I need to hold you for a minute," I said, pushing her backwards.

"You need to relax," she said, trying to stand up, "we'll work this out." I didn't want to relax. I'd just practically seen my father blow his head off—how was she planning to work that out? My blood was pumping hotter than I had ever felt it. I held her on the bed, and she stiffened against me. She tried to roll off the side but I pulled her back. I swung my leg over her and lay down on top of her warm body.

"Don't do this, Jake, I'll scream," she said.

"Just lie here for a minute," I said into her ears, "I won't do anything, if you just lie here."

She softened under me. I shifted my body a little so she could feel me growing hard between her legs. I wanted to rip off her thin shorts, and rip off mine.

"Please, Jake," she said, "think what you're doing."

Think—that's what Jenny always said, as if thinking was always the answer. "Thinking killed my father," I said. "Thinking left him like a fucking shell. He thought too much!"

Her arms and legs tensed under me, and I let her throw me off the bed. I didn't really want her anymore, anyway, not like that, scared to death of me, not with pictures in my mind of Dad soaking in blood in the living room. What if Krissy had come home? Would he have shot himself in front of her? Or did he just save his best moments for me?

Larkin moved toward the door, but I stepped in front of her. "I'm going to kill Decker," I said, "smoke the bastard." Suddenly the water pitcher was in my hand and I hurled it into the wall. It broke into flowered pieces that fell on the bed.

"Jake!"

I picked up the light from the dresser. "Don't," Larkin yelled. Why shouldn't I throw a lamp against the wall and watch the bulb explode into little pieces? I was going to splatter a cop, why shouldn't I smash a lamp? "We can work something out," she said again. "You don't know Decker caused this. Your father has been crazy for a long time, you told me that yourself."

"But he never killed himself before! Don't you understand that? Decker set him up, just like he did Frankie."

Larkin moved toward the open window. "What do you mean? What happened to Frankie?"

"Decker caught him fucking around with some guy behind Jack's."

She shook her head like this was too much for her to understand all at once. My father dead, Frankie arrested—it seemed simple enough to me. I remembered the gun. I took it out of my jacket pocket and twirled the barrel. It made a quick clicking sound.

"Give me that, Jake."

"I got to do something," I said, rolling my palm over the barrel, loving the smooth feel of it. "I can't watch my father kill himself and do nothing!"

"Yes you can. People die all of the time, even like your father, and their kids don't go out . . . "

"Don't you get it?" I yelled at her. "I'm not like other kids. I'm crazy!"

I think she was starting to believe me. She looked at the door, measuring the distance. Could she get out before I stopped her? "No, you're not like him," she said, edging around the bed. "You're different, Jake. I know that, I've been talking to you for weeks. You're smart, and sensitive. It's everything around you that's been crazy."

"I *am* crazy," I said, "like him. The only thing is, he shot himself."

The phone rang on the nighttable. Larkin looked at me

as if I might stop her from answering it, and that told me that I should stop her. "Let it ring," I said.

The phone rang a second time, and a third. "People know I'm here," she said. "They'll think something's wrong if I don't answer."

Why did people talk to me like that, as if I were stupid? "Yeah, sure, they're going to come running over just because you don't answer your phone. Like maybe Doug will fly in from New York to find out what's wrong."

The ringing stopped, and Larkin sat on her bed. She put her face in her hands for a moment, and when she pulled away, her cheeks were smeared with tears. "What do you want from me, Jake? I'm trying to help you."

"You just wanted my story. And now you can have a great ending—I'll do you a favor by popping off Decker."

She leaned down and found a pair of sandals under the bed. She pushed her feet into them and stood up. "You're going to have to trust me, Jake. I'm going to the police station to tell them what happened. And you're going to stay here."

I didn't say anything this time, so Larkin felt free to reach for the knob, open the door and slowly walk away.

•

When she left, I fell back on her bed and pulled the pillow to my face. I could smell her perfume. I couldn't believe I had just had her there under me a few minutes before. She felt smaller than I'd imagined, and harder.

My father was dead—vanished. It amazed me to think of it. Dad gone, sucked out of the world. But to where?

And what could Larkin do? How could she help Dad now? How could she make Frankie straight? What did she think the police would do—change death into life again? They were experts at doing the opposite, turning life into death. Maybe she was just going to get them to arrest me for attacking her. How could I know what she would do?

I wrapped myself in the bedsheets and listened to the hum and rattle of the air conditioner. It felt nice and cool in this room now, a place where I could close my eyes and think of the Delaware, where ice floated to the top in some very cold winters.

Twenty-Three

MY FATHER—DEAD, SHOT THROUGH THE HEAD. THAT'S WHAT I thought when I woke up, and I wondered, for how many days or years would that be the first thing I thought of every morning? And what about the first time that I thought of something else? Was that when Dad was really dead to me?

I couldn't tell how much time had passed—minutes, hours? It was still bright and sunny outside, still the afternoon. I couldn't wait for Larkin any longer. And why should I trust her? Who the hell was she in my life before a month ago? If I was going to trust anyone, it would be Frankie.

I called him from the room phone. He answered in a dazed voice, like I'd just wakened him. "Yeah?" he mumbled.

"He's dead."

"Who?" Frankie yawned, as if I must be talking about some actor or singer we didn't actually know.

"Dad."

"What?" he shouted into the phone.

"My father, he's dead. Shot himself and . . . "

"And what?"

"And Mars."

"Are you there?" he said, "I mean, looking at him?"

"No." But in my mind I could still see Dad lying on the floor, stretched out as if he'd just fallen asleep. "Frankie," I said, "I got his gun." I held it against my face. The barrel smelled smoky.

"Put it down, Jake, it could go off."

Of course it could go off—that was the point of a gun. In fact, it had to go off, otherwise it might just as well be a doorknob or some other stupid piece of metal.

"You hear me, Jake?"

I laid the gun on the pillow of Larkin's bed, and it suddenly looked right to me there, something hard pressing down on something soft. "I put it down," I said.

"Okay, listen, I'll come get you, okay? Where are you?"

I wanted to see Frankie, but then again, I didn't want to.

He would just make it harder for me to do whatever I was going to.

"Tell me where you are, Jake."

"At The Logan," I said, "in Larkin's room, 402, but . . . "

"I'm coming over," he said and hung up before I could tell him that where I was now wouldn't be where I was when he got here.

•

Time passed. I sat there thinking about it the way Dad always did, as if time were a trap. I couldn't believe it. He had finally done what I never thought possible—sent himself into the forever that scared him so much. I just hoped it was the same forever where Mom was.

I got up and stuffed the gun inside the waist of my shorts, covered by my long T-shirt. I started toward the door, but my hand picked up the remote and flicked on the TV. On the screen a row of girls materialized. They were sitting on stools in tight skirts, their legs crossed. A sentence popped up underneath them—"Girls Who Had Sex Before Age 15." I sat down on the edge of the bed and watched. Why couldn't I meet one of them, like Jade, the girl on the end twirling her long hair around her finger?

The show cut to a commercial, and I ran out of the room, down the back stairs and through the kitchen into the alley. In a few seconds I was out on the sidewalk of Main Street, just like any other kid in town. Except I had a gun pressing against my stomach, and a score to settle.

•

From the far end of the parking lot, I could see the door of the old brick police station sitting high on Memorial Hill. Everything looked quiet, as if it was just another boring day in New Hope. Outside on the front steps two women smoked and talked. A squad car pulled into the parking lot, and a cop got out, tipped his cap to the women and passed between them.

Larkin was probably inside telling them everything—

what happened to Dad and maybe even what she thought I was going to do to her. I wasn't going to do anything. Why did people always think I was going to do something horrible? I just wanted to be close to her for a few minutes, that's all. She felt so soft and smelled so good that just being near her made me forget about Dad for a moment.

I crouched behind the big memorial stone on the grass strip next to the parking lot. There were only two names—Monaghan and Pinazzi—cut into the granite, New Hope cops killed in the line of duty. I ran my fingers into the grooves of the letters and then over the smooth stone below them. There was plenty of room for one more.

"Jake!"

I looked to the street, and there was Frankie calling to me from his Mustang. He pulled quickly into a driveway, reversed direction and sped into the parking lot. He swung his car into the space marked For Police Cruisers Only and jumped out.

"What are you doing here?" he said as he ran over to me.

I pulled up my T-shirt so he could see the gun. He put out his hand. "Give it to me, Jake. You can't be carrying a gun around town."

"Not till I use it."

"Use it how?"

I nodded toward the police station. "Decker caused all of this. He wouldn't leave my father alone. Or you."

The heavy front door of the station banged shut, and Larkin came out, then Decker. They stopped on the front steps. I ducked behind Frankie's Mustang and raised the gun to my eye level, steadying it on the car roof with my two hands. The sun was in their eyes—they wouldn't be able to see me. Decker was only about 100 feet away, but I had no idea if a bullet would reach him.

"Jake," Frankie whispered, "please don't do this."

"Why not? How should Decker be in this world and not my father?"

"He shouldn't. But you can't just go around gunning down all the jerks in the world. Besides, they'd hunt you down and kill you or throw you in jail forever. Decker's not worth that."

My hands were still sticking straight out, like some TV cop who has cornered his suspect. I couldn't see my index finger, but I could feel it touching the trigger. One little squeeze and the bullet would be in the air flying toward Decker's fat belly. One little squeeze and the world would be changed forever. Why hadn't my finger done it already? What was I waiting for?

"Come on, Jake, it's crazy to shoot someone, even him."

Crazy—there was that word again. People were always using it about me or Dad. "Maybe that's why I'm going to do it, Frankie—I am crazy."

"Don't say that."

"It's true. Dad was crazy, and I'm just like him. That's what he always told me."

"You're not like your Dad. If you were you'd be aiming the gun at yourself, Jake, not Decker."

I turned the gun around and pointed it at my face. This was the last thing Dad saw of the world—the small, round barrel of a gun. A bullet came out of it, and all of his fears and all of his philosophies couldn't stop it.

Frankie's hand reached up and moved the barrel away. "You're scaring me, Jake. That thing could go off accidentally."

I turned the gun around toward the station. Larkin was gone. Decker was still standing on the front steps, puffing on a cigarette. He made a nice fat target.

Frankie leaned next to me on the car. "Remember our bet at the quarry?"

"Yeah, so?"

"My car went farther than yours, right? So I can ask you for anything I want and you have to give it to me."

"That was just a stupid game, Frankie."

"You promised, Jake. You wouldn't go back on a promise to me."

He seemed so sure of that, and I wondered why. Why would he think that I would keep my word?

"I'm asking you now, Jake. What I want is for you to put down the gun."

I eased my finger off the trigger. "Then what, Frankie? I just walk home and clean up the bloody mess my father left? What am I supposed to do—pretend it's nobody's fault?"

He took me by the shoulders and turned me toward him. I couldn't ever remember looking at him before like this, from just inches away. "Yeah, Jake, pretend . . . pretend you never came back, if you have to. You can leave New Hope right now."

"You mean run away from everything again?"

"Sure, remember what you used to tell me? You can always run from trouble."

At the edge of my vision, Decker turned back into the police station and suddenly, there was no one to shoot. The gun felt strange in my hand, like something I'd just picked up from the gutter and didn't know what to do with. I stuffed the gun inside the waist of my shorts. Frankie took my arm like I was mental and walked me over to his car. "So, which way should we head?" he said as I sank back in the seat and he pulled out onto Main Street.

"We?"

"Yeah, I'm going with you."

"Frankie—"

"I have as much to run away from as you do, Jake. Besides, I have a car and money. We can get as far away from here as we want."

"Okay then, let's follow the river north," I said, "wherever it goes." He turned right in the center of town, and in a few minutes we were speeding across the New Hope bridge to New Jersey, with the music on the radio blaring so loud I thought my brain would burst from the beat. He slowed in the middle, and I tossed the gun out of the window and over the rail into the rapids of the Delaware far below.

Twenty-Four

Dear Larkin,

You probably know by now that Frankie and me ran away. I hope that doesn't ruin your book or anything. Maybe it's better because now you have an ending— Runaway Kid Comes Home, Messes Up Everything and Runs Away Again. That's what I'd write, if I were you.

I called Jenny last week and she said she's moving back to Maine with Krissy. She was pretty friendly on the phone, which surprised me. I thought she'd blame me for pushing Dad over the edge. But she said that you can't save somebody when they're dead set against being saved, like he was. She even said I could come visit them sometime.

She told me that you got the police to move Dad's body before Krissy got home. I'm glad she didn't have to see him. I should have called somebody right away to do it, but I guess I wasn't thinking straight.

It's strange being on the road again, especially with Frankie. He's jumpy about being caught, so we never use our real names or stay too long anywhere. He gets scared whenever I talk to anyone. We figured his father has the police looking for the Mustang, so we sold it and bought another car off a kid. We have enough money to last for months because Frankie emptied his bank account the day we left. I think he was saving to run away for a long time.

I don't have any idea where we're heading. Frankie wants to drive to San Francisco, but I don't think I'll go that far with him. I'd like to live in the woods somewhere, or maybe in the mountains, someplace where there aren't many people. I seem to get in trouble around people. Anyway, wherever I end up, I know it will be a better place for me than New Hope.

I have lots of time while we're driving to think about things. You asked once about stuff Dad used to tell me. I was remembering that on Sundays he'd cook breakfast for Krissy and me while Jenny slept in. One time he was breaking eggs into the frying pan and he said, "Imagine trying to unmake an omelet." He was stirring this gooey mass of eggs, and as usual I had no idea what he was getting at. He handed me the broken egg shell and told me to glue it while he scraped up the yolk. I tried doing that, and the shell kept breaking even more in my hands. Finally I told him to forget it—there was no way you could unmake an omelet. He said of course there wasn't, and it was because of possibilities. Cracking an egg takes only a single flick of the wrist. But putting the shell back together requires an unbelievable number of fittings. "Going from order to disorder is always easy in this world," he said. "Going from disorder to order is impossible."

It wasn't just eggs he was talking about. He told me to think of a water glass, a mirror, a human heart—any thing that can shatter. "Don't be fooled," he said. "When you break something, it's never the same again." I guess that's what I'll never forget about my dad.

See you around,
Jake.